SELECTED SHORT STORIES FROM BANGLADESH

Selected Short Stories from Bangladesh

Edited by
Niaz Zaman

 The University Press Limited

The University Press Limited
Red Crescent House
61 Motijheel C/A
P.O. Box 2611
Dhaka 1000
Bangladesh

Fax: (8802) 9565443
E-mail: upl@bttb.net.bd, upl@bangla.net
Website: www.uplbooks.com

Second impression 2007
First published 1998

Cover design by Shamarukh Mohiuddin
Inset picture "Gabriel's Wings", oil painting, by Syed Enayet Hossain

ISBN 984 05 1309 5

Published by Mohiuddin Ahmed, The University Press Limited, Dhaka. This book has been set in Galliard BT. Designer: Babul Chandra Dhar and printed at the Elora Art Publicity, 635 North Shahjahanpur, Dhaka, Bangladesh.

Contents

Acknowledgements   vii

Preface   ix

Syed Waliullah
THE TALE OF A TULSI PLANT   1

Shaukat Osman
THE ROOSTER   11

Abu Rushd
THE DRIVER   21

Fazlul Huq
HARAN'S DEATH   28

Shahed Ali
GABRIEL'S WINGS   33

Alauddin Al Azad
THE RAINS   45

Khaleda Salahuddin
RELIEF CAMP   60

Syed Shamsul Haq
THE POET   70

Kayes Ahmed
THE TALE OF THE TWO SINGERS   87

Razia Khan
THE NIGHT OF THE VULTURES   99

Hasan Azizul Huq
THE HOMESTEAD YONDER   103

Makbula Manzoor
FLOTSAM   115

Rizia Rahman
WHAT PRICE HONOUR?   127

Akhtaruzzaman Elias
TARABIBI'S VIRILE SON   136

Selina Hossain
MOTIJAN'S DAUGHTERS   153

Humayun Ahmed
THE MAN WHO WOULD NOT DIE   166

Farida Hossain
THE CUSTOMER   174

Purabi Basu
RADHA WILL NOT COOK TODAY   182

Shamim Hamid
THE MATCHMAKER   188

Nasreen Jahan
ENVY   197

Notes on Writers   205

Acknowledgements

Among the people whom I have to thank are first of all Khaleda Salahuddin to whom I spoke of my project of translating women's stories and who unstintingly and immediately gave me a collection of anthologies which formed the nucleus of this book; Professor Syed Ali Ahsan who suggested that I include men's writings as well; Ameerul Momenin of the Bangla Academy who helped me locate stories in addition to the ones I had—and many of which, I hope, will be included in a later, thematic collection; the writers who gave me permission to include their stories; the translators who kept enquiring when the book would be out; and Penguin Books India (P) Ltd., for giving permission to reproduce "The Rooster." Thanks are also due, as usual, to both Babuls who, despite their demanding duties, unhesitatingly typed some of my stories for me; and to Arun who, despite being bogged down with invoices and business letters, cheerfully typed the rest, struggling through my scrawling marginalia.

Preface

When I planned this anthology I had thought it would be confined to women only. My reason was that though Bangladeshi women had been writing and writing well, they were seriously under-represented in anthologies. For example, the Bangla Academy collection, *An Anthology of Contemporary Short Stories of Bangladesh,* includes only one story by a woman writer; three other collections of short stories published by the Academy are of male writers. Thus a collection of short stories by women seemed to be in order. However, an anthology omitting men appeared to be reverse discrimination. *An Anthology of Contemporary Short Stories* has been out of print for some time, and I would be leaving out some short stories that have become Bangladeshi classics. Hence this collection, containing stories by men and women in equal proportions.

Though Bangladesh has a high rate of illiteracy, people have always given an importance to the written word. The number of books published every year is surprising for a people accused of not buying books. In addition, every daily newspaper has a magazine section which includes short stories. During festival time, special editions of journals and newspapers are published which include short stories and even novels. The short story genre in Bangladesh is thus a rich and varied field and, though many stories have had to be left out from this anthology, the twenty stories in this collection provide an introduction to the genre as well as a glimpse into the social, political, and cultural life of Bangladesh.

The majority of the stories in this anthology have a rural background. This is not surprising as most Bangladeshis have close links to the countryside. Even writers who have dwelt all their lives in the city have chosen to write about life in the country. Thus, the land

and the people who work the land, the monsoon rains, the floods, an unseasonal drought—all these have been the subject of much creative work. However, like Rabeya and her brother in Makbula Manzoor's short story "Flotsam," there is a lot of rural-urban migration, and an increasing number of writers are writing about the life of the city. Thus, Shahed Ali's "Gabriel's Wings," Akhtaruzzaman Elias's "Tarabibi's Virile Son," Farida Hossain's "The Customer," Abu Rushd's "The Driver" portray life in the city.

Most of the writers in Bangladesh are socially and politically conscious and, in their writings, condemn existing class differences, religious and moral hypocrisy, discriminations against women, the absurdity, and sometimes downright cruelty, of communalism. Every political movement has found a place in the short story. This is especially the case with the liberation war of 1971 which forms the focus of many short stories. The four stories that have been included in this volume, Hasan Azizul Huq's "The Homestead Yonder," Razia Khan's "The Night of the Vultures," Makbula Manzoor's "Flotsam," and Rizia Rahman's "What Price Honour," are only a few examples of several short stories that focus upon the liberation war.

As a result of their political and social awareness, many writers are more concerned with the message of the story than with the craft of writing. It is therefore a pleasure to read a writer like Purabi Basu, who turns her story about a woman who refuses to cook into a prose-poem, or Humayun Ahmed, who gives his story a twist that readers of the genre have come to expect. A master of the art of the short story, Ahmed often takes up the slightest of episodes to tell a tale of human interest. This is, of course, not to say that Ahmed's stories, as in the story included in this anthology, "The Man Who Would Not Die," are devoid of social message or comment. Thus, in this story, based in a Bangladesh village, Ahmed describes moral and religious hypocrisy and social constructs and power relations at the village level. The length of the *mullah's* prayer is guided by one eye on his job, and the rich landowner's charity is decided by what time of year it is. Ahmed's humour and wit are tempered by deep sympathy. Not only does the dying man not die—thus allowing a perceptive reader to look at the story as allegory (Is the dying man Bangladesh, poor, sick but resilient?)—but the rich man also changes. So far he has done things because it was expected of him, done things grudgingly. But the resilience of the sick man changes him and leads him to go out of his way to try to save him.

Most of the women's stories explore the relations between men and women in domestic settings and in society at large. Apart from the age-old political and social structures that discriminate against women, natural calamities, political upheavals, and wars add to women's burdens. Makbula Manzoor, Rizia Rahman and Shamim Hamid show how adverse circumstances, natural and man-made, affect the lives of women. Selina Hossain, like Purabi Basu, is not satisfied simply to portray women's unfortunate lives. Thus, in "Motijan's Daughters," Hossain defends the right of a woman to have children outside a loveless marriage. Similarly, Purabi Basu's Radha refuses to do the things a woman is supposed to do—and creates confusion in her family by her behaviour.

The stories in this volume have been written over a period of almost fifty years, beginning with Syed Waliullah's story about the partition of 1947 to Nasreen Jahan's story, published in 1996, about the ambivalent relationships between men and women, mothers and daughters. Taken together, they portray Bangladesh as seen through the eyes of its writers beginning from the partition of 1947 through the liberation war of 1971 to a post-independent Bangladesh. Many of the writers have won national and international awards for their writing, others are less well known as writers; one, for example, is an economist, another an international consultant whose work inspires her to write. While none of the stories is happy or cheerful, and the poverty and the tragedy of human lives in Bengal is only too apparent, stories like "The Rooster," "The Two Singers," "Relief Camp," "The Man Who Would Not Die," describe the strong ties that exist between friends and family, and, even sometimes, between strangers. While these stories do not purport to be social documents, almost each of them gives a small, penetrating insight into a society traditional and changing, static and dynamic, hopeless and hopeful at the same time.

Most of the stories in this volume were written originally in Bengali. The two exceptions are the stories by Razia Khan and

Shamim Hamid. It is possible that, with the growing rise of English language newspapers and journals, a future anthology of Bangladeshi short stories will contain more original stories in English.

Dhaka, November 1997   *Niaz Zaman*

The Tale of a Tulsi Plant

Syed Waliullah

The house stood just past the concrete bridge, which was arched like a bow. It was a huge, two-storeyed building, rising directly from the street. Footpaths were rare in this country, so there had been no need for the graceful gesture of leaving a little space between the house and the street. That was, however, only the appearance from the front; behind the house lay a generous expanse of land. First, there was the courtyard, then the bathroom and the toilet, and finally there were trees, almost a jungle of mango, blackberry, and jackfruit trees. On the weed-covered ground beneath them, even on a sunny day, there lingered the pale gloom of twilight, and a smell of dampness.

With so much land, what would have been the harm in leaving a little plot in the front for a garden? They wondered about that, especially Matin. He was fond of a garden, though so far his garden had bloomed only in his imagination. He planned how he would make a garden if he had his own little piece of land. With great care, he would plant seasonal flowers, *gandharaj, hasnahena, bakul*, maybe a few roses, too. He would sit in his garden every evening when he came home from the office. He would buy a light cane chair or a canvas deck-chair in which to sit comfortably. He would stretch himself out there and talk. Amjad smoked a *hookah*. For the sake of his garden's prestige, he would even buy a proper, handsome *hookah*, with a long pipe. Kader was a lover of tales. His voice would pour out the stories in the gentle breeze. On a moonlit night, filled with the scent of flowers, what would it matter if there were no stories? They would enjoy the soothing calm of the evening, just sitting there quietly, with their eyes closed.

These thoughts crossed Matin's mind as, tired from the day's work at the office, he climbed the stairs, which started from the very edge of the street.

They had moved into the house without a fight. It wasn't that the owner had fled at the threat of their military power. They had been searching day and night for a shelter after they first arrived in the city, during the frenzy of the partition of the country. Then one day they saw this house. There was a massive lock on the main entrance, but a little exploration revealed that there was not a living soul inside. The owner had run away. It did not take long to recognize a deserted house; it was a stroke of luck to get such a place. This sudden good fortune frightened them, but they soon got over their fear.

That very evening, they all came in a group, broke the lock at the gate, and entered the house with a great hullabaloo. Their wild enthusiasm was that of children picking up mangoes after a *Baishakh* storm heralding the coming of the new year. It did not occur to them that they were committing a crime in broad daylight. If a pang of guilt rose in anyone's mind, it evaporated quickly in the thrill of their triumph.

When the news spread around the city the next morning, homeless refugees began to pour in. They came, cluster after cluster, in the hope of securing a roof over their heads.

The first group hid their own exultation and said, "What are you looking at? There's no room anywhere. The whole place is covered with beds. Even in this small room, there are four of them. And now you see only the beds, but when four cots, six feet by two feet, and a couple of chairs and tables are brought in, there won't be enough space on the floor to put your feet down."

Someone added in a compassionate voice, "Don't we understand your misery? Haven't we suffered the same way all these days? But you are just unlucky; that's it, just unlucky."

The disappointed faces grew darker at these words of consolation.

"That room over there?" The room downstairs, near the street, seemed to be empty.

It was not really empty. Looking carefully, one could see, next to the wall, two bedrolls, covered by a carpet. The last place had been taken two hours ago by fat Badruddin of the Accounts Department. He had gone to get his belongings from his brother-in-law. The brother-in-law, too, had set up his quarters on the verandah of a friend's house. If he had not had a family, he would have joined the others.

"Just a matter of luck." Again someone sympathised profusely. "If you had come two hours earlier, you could have beaten Badruddin. There isn't much light in the room, but see that street light near the window? If the electricity fails some night, that street light will be enough."

"Or if one wanted to save money . . . ."

And, of course, all these words stung like venom in the ears of the uninvited who had come to find a refuge.

The police came, in due time, to investigate the matter of the illegal occupation of a house. That was only natural. There was great change and upheaval in the whole country, but it was not yet a land without law.

When they saw the policemen, the occupants wondered if the fugitive owner had appealed to the government to restore his house. But they did not believe this. Surely, one who had left his home and fled the country in two days would now have other, graver problems to handle. They had no doubt that those others, those who had not come here in time and were now wandering about the town trying vainly to find another house, had informed the police. Bad luck was easier to recognize than to accept. A rightful claim was one thing, but sharing illegal booty was another matter. In a case like that, jealousy appears to be not only justified, but, in fact, a duty.

The occupants were defiant now. "We are poor clerks, but we are the sons of gentlemen. We have moved into the house, but the doors and windows have not been broken; nor have the bricks and stones been torn out to be sold in the black market. We know the law, too. Who has made the complaint? If it isn't made by the owner, then it's not in order."

Kader began to wail. "Where shall we go? Do you suppose we came to this house on a mere caprice?"

The sub-inspector and his retinue went away and wrote a complicated, neither-for-nor-against and neither right-nor-wrong report. Their superiors preferred to file it away on a shelf; probably, they were afraid to try to decipher the meaning of the report. Or maybe they realized that in those frantic times, the official rules about illegal occupation were not quite clear.

Kader winked. "What's the harm in telling the truth? The second wife of the sub-inspector happens to be a relative of mine. But don't mention it to anyone."

Nobody believed Kader, of course, but it was easy to forgive him, because the lie was only an innocent expression of his happy relief.

Someone suggested gaily, "How about a round of tea and sweets?"

Overnight, the large house began to bubble with activity. It was not merely that they had found a place to stay which no one could take away from them. It was as if this open, spacious, well-built house had infused a new life into them. Many of these people had lived all their days in the unspeakable stench and filth of Calcutta—in the sailors' quarter of Blockman Lane, in the bookbind-ers' quarter of *Baithakkhana*, among the tobacco merchants of Syed Saheb Lane, or in Kamru Khanshama Lane. In comparison, the vast rooms, the wide windows like those of the indigo traders' mansions, the enormous yard, and the orchard of mango, jackfruit, and berries in the rear—all of these were of a different world. True, they didn't have a separate room for each one, like princes; yet they had never enjoyed so much air and light. Now it seemed as if green grass might sprout in their lives, too, and fresh blood flow vigorously through their veins. The radiance of health and prosperity would light their faces, as it lights the faces of those who earn a few thousand rupees.

Small, scrawny Yunus had already noticed some change in his health. He had lived on McLeod Street. The narrow alley was like a dustbin in the morning, filled with rubbish. There, in a damp room near the kitchen of an unsteady two-storey wooden house, he had lived for four years with a leather merchant from Kutch.

The neighbourhood was permeated with the nauseous smell of tanning hides, so that even the putrid odour of the roadside drain could not reach the nose. If a dead mouse or cat were rotting in a corner of the room, one would never notice it.

Yunus had often had a fever. Sometimes a coughing spell would seize him in the middle of the night. Yet he did not leave the neighbourhood. Someone had told him that the odour of the hides killed tuberculosis bacilli. Not only did he endure the noxious odour without a complaint, but often, after coming home in the evening, he would stand by the window, facing the solid wall of the next house and draw in deep breaths. Not surprisingly, his health had shown no improvement.

There could be no housewarming without a feast; and in Mughal style, the celebration went on for a week. Many unsuspected culinary talents were exposed. Someone's grandmother's recipe for a special cake turned out to be something inedible, but hearty appreciation from everyone made it seem delectable.

Now and then, in the evening, they had a musical *jalsa*. Habibullah had got hold of an off-key harmonium which, accompanied by his powerful voice, provided an indescribable concert, lasting far into the night.

Then one day the *tulsi* plant was discovered, growing on a rectangular brick platform about a foot high, at the edge of the yard behind the kitchen.

It was a Sunday morning. Modabber was pacing the yard, brushing his teeth with a *neem* twig, when he began to shout. He was an excitable man and would raise a frightful uproar over a trifle. But this time it was not easy to ignore him. The other men rushed into the yard.

"What's the matter?"

"Open your eyes and look!"

"What? What is there to see?"

They were probably expecting to find a snake, so they did not notice the *tulsi* plant at first.

"You don't see it? You don't see the *tulsi* plant set up in the ritual way on the platform? It has to be torn out. While we're in this house, no Hindu symbols can be tolerated."

They looked at the little plant dejectedly. It was dying. The green leaves had taken on a brownish colour, and weeds grew thickly beneath it. Probably it had not been watered for a long time.

"What are you staring at?" Modabber cried. "Haven't I told you to pull it out of there?"

They all became very quiet, taken aback by this unexpected discovery. The house had appeared to be empty, deserted, in spite of a few names scratched by an untrained hand on the wall by the stairs leading to the roof. But now it seemed different, as if this half-dead, dried, insignificant *tulsi* plant, caught unaware, had revealed the secrets of the house.

Confronted by this inexplicable silence, Modabber shouted again. "What are you pondering so hard about? Why don't you pull it out by the roots?"

Nobody moved. They were not entirely familiar with Hindu customs; but they had heard that in a Hindu home, the mistress of the house lighted a lamp under the *tulsi* plant at dusk, and, with the end of her sari wrapped around her head, made a *pranam*, bowing to touch the earth with her head. Though it was over-grown with weeds now, someone had lighted a lamp every evening under this abandoned *tulsi* too. When the evening star, solitary and bright, shone in the sky, a steady quiet flame had burned red, like the touch of crimson paint on the bowed forehead.

Today, where was the mistress of the house who had lit the lamp under this *tulsi* plant? Matin had once been a railway employee. Now the picture of many railway colonies passed before his eyes. Possibly that woman had found refuge with a relative in a railway colony in Asansol, Baidybati, Lilua, or Howrah. Now he seemed to see a fine black sari with red borders spread to dry in the sun beside a huge yard. That sari probably belonged to the mistress of this house. The sari fluttered sadly in the breeze. But the woman was sitting near the window of a moving train, looking out as if she were searching for something in the distance, beyond the horizon. Maybe her journey was not finished yet. But wherever she was, when the shadows of dusk thickened in the sky, she would remember the spot under the *tulsi* plant and her eyes would fill with tears.

Yunus had had a cold since the previous day. He said, "Let it stay. We aren't going to worship it. But a *tulsi* around the house is useful. The juice of the leaf is very good for coughs and colds."

Modabber looked at the faces of the other men. Apparently they were all of the same opinion. No one put his hand forth to uproot the plant.

Enayet was something of a *moulvi*; he wore a beard, said his prayers five times a day and recited the Quran regularly every morning. Even he said nothing now. Was he, too, thinking of the woman whose eyes filled with tears every evening?

The *tulsi* stood untouched; it had escaped their hands. But they did not completely forget it. Rather, a sense of weakness lingered with them, an uneasy feeling that they had retreated in the face of a duty. It was because of this that an argument began at their evening gathering. They wanted to wipe out that uncomfortable sensation of impotence by their verbal force. The topic this time was the Hindu community, instead of the usual subjects of politics and economics.

"They are at the root of all this," Modabber said. His well-brushed teeth shone under the unshaded electric bulb. "The country was partitioned because of their wickedness and meanness and fanaticism."

The argument was nothing new. But there seemed to be an extra edge to the words today. In support of their contention, innumerable examples of Hindu atrocities and injustice were related. Soon their blood became hotter and their breath quickened.

The recognized radical of the group, Maksud, protested. "Aren't you going too far?"

Modabber's teeth glistened again. "What do you mean, too far?"

Leftist Maksud was alone now. Perhaps that is why the pendulum of his faith began to move. It shifted doubtfully and finally stopped a little toward the right.

A few days later, Modabber was surprised when his eyes fell upon the *tulsi* beside the kitchen. The weeds that had grown under it were gone. And not only that, the leaves which had grown brown with lack of water were turning dark green again. There was no doubt that someone was tending the plant. Someone was watering its roots, surreptitiously, if not openly.

Modabber had a thin, long bamboo rod in his hand. He slashed it across the plant as if to chop if off. But the branch passed over the plant harmlessly.

Nobody, of course, mentioned the *tulsi* any more. Yunus's cold was gone the next day, so he did not need the *tulsi* juice.

Now they began to believe that they had really left behind the life of McLeod Street, Khanshama Lane and Blockman Lane, and had begun a new life, with abundant light and air. It was not long before they learned their mistake. But it was enough time to let their belief grow quite strong, so that the sudden shock struck them brutally.

That day they came straight home from the office and, according to the plans they had made in the morning, began to prepare to cook *khichuri*. Just then they heard the squeaking of heavy boots on the outer stairs. Modabber peeped outside and hurried back in.

"It's the police again," he whispered.

"Police? Why the police again?" Yunus thought that perhaps a petty thief from the street had taken shelter in the house and the police were after him. But then Yunus remembered the story of the rabbit: when it found no means of escape before a hunter, it crouched on the ground with closed eyes and thought that no one could see it.

Weren't they, themselves, the thieves? Hadn't they refused to admit everything they knew, and weren't they trying to create here a false, beautiful life for themselves?

The leader of the police group was an old-fashioned man. He placed his hat under his arm and wiped the sweat off his forehead, which bore the mark of his hat. He looked like a harmless man. The two constables standing behind him with their rifles seemed to be innocent too, in spite of their big moustaches. Their eyes were turned upward, as if they were counting the roof beams. A pair of pigeons had built a nest in the ventilation hole. They were probably watching the pigeons. Animals and birds caught the attention of good, harmless people, even when they had guns in their hands.

Matin asked politely, "Whom do you want, please?"

The police leader's reply was curt and rasping. "All of you. You have occupied this house illegally."

No one could deny that. They did not protest, but only looked at the policeman with mild curiosity in their eyes.

"You'll have to leave the house within twenty-four hours. Government orders."

They looked at each other silently. At last Modabber cleared his throat and asked, "Why? Has the owner complained?"

Fat Badruddin of the Accounts Office stretched his neck and looked for the owner behind the constables. But no one was there except some people who had come in from the street to watch, always eager to enjoy the spectacle of someone else's humiliation.

"The owner?" The policeman feigned sarcasm, but he did not succeed.

One of the occupants laughed too. Was there a glimmer of hope?

"Then?"

"The government has requisitioned the house."

Nobody laughed this time. For a little while, nobody said a word. Then Maksud came forward. "Aren't we government people?"

The two constables lowered their eyes from the roof beams and the pigeons to look at Maksud. There was wonder in their eyes. The stupidity of people still surprised them.

In spite of all the light and air, a deep shadow descended upon the house. At first, blood rushed into their heads, and they muttered rebelliously. They wouldn't go away, they would stay there, clutching the pillars of the house; or they would move out only in a coffin. But their heads cooled before long and a depression fell over them. Where would they go?

The next day Modabber brought news that their time had been extended from twenty-four hours to seven days. They sighed with relief, but the shadow remained over them, as dense as before. This time Modabber did not speak about his relationship to the second wife of the police sub-inspector.

On the tenth day they all left the house. They had come like a storm and they went away in the same manner. The mementos of their residence—a torn newspaper page, an old piece of rope on which they had hung clothes, cigarette and *biri* butts, the broken heel of a shoe—lay scattered about the empty house.

The *tulsi* plant on the edge of the yard had begun to wither again. Its leaves were tinged with brown. No one had watered it since the advent of the police. Nor had anyone remembered the tearfilled eyes of the mistress of the house.

The *tulsi* plant did not know why it was so. That was for people to understand.

Translated from the original Bengali by the author himself.

"*Ekti Tulsi Gachher Kahini*" was anthologized in *Dui Teer* published by Nawroze Kitabistan, Dhaka, 1964.

The Rooster

Shaukat Osman

Let us begin our story where the southbound highway turns east beyond Chaudyagram.

If you look around you won't find much of human habitation here. Across the untilled plains peasant huts lie scattered like dots, each with a little yard and a few trees—just that bit of green affection in the middle of heartless nature. The hills of Tripura along the eastern sky are only a mile away. Even on a day like this there is no scarcity of colours, but you won't look up, for even the sunflowers close their eyes in the great heat. There are narrow footways separating plots of uneven land and a few palm trees; then a sparse hill forest rises step by step towards the sky, the trees getting taller and thicker. To the east there are a small mosque and a couple of mango trees. This is where the border of the country is, beyond which, the local people will tell you, lies India. The narrow footways which join the highway from many directions bring pious Muslims to the mosque on Fridays. Our story, however, has nothing to do with piety.

When the two of them left the footway to get on to the highway, there wasn't anyone else around. One of them was an old woman of sixty, in a plain piece of cloth and shirt, and a worn-out scarf wrapped around her chest. It would be futile to look for any black strands of hair on her head; the only black object was the umbrella over her head.

That umbrella calls for a detailed description. Its steel ribs looked like the arms and legs of a dead frog. The strips of cloth left on it

were enriched by repeated patches, and the rod was without a head.
Yet it was an umbrella. Not only did it abate the heat of the sun,
it also served as a veil and protected the woman from the sin of
exposure to the eyes of adult males and the consequent fire of
hell. Face to face with a man one could at least hide one's face and
eyes behind the umbrella, as if they were the only things to be
modest about.

The woman's companion, Sajed, was her grandson, aged nine or
ten. He was wearing a Dhaka *lungi*; his upper body was naked,
dark, thin and sweaty.

The two had taken shelter under the umbrella, which somehow
protected their heads. When the unbearable heat made the
grandmother act selfishly for a minute and they walked apart, the
grandson reminded her of her responsibility.

Sajed was carrying a hefty two-kilogram rooster under his arm.
All the colours of the rainbow were neighbours on his wings, where
they played hide-and-seek as the sun shone on them. Even the
crown on his head was enchanting, dark red, serried like the teeth of
a saw, with gleaming pearls of sweat. Even Queen Elizabeth I of
England would have sought the rooster's hand in marriage if she
had seen the splendour of his crown. His legs were smooth yellow
with matching grey nails.

The tarmac highway had borders of grey footpath. The heat of
the sun was so intense that even the eyes of the bird could not
escape its glare. Under Sajed's arm the rooster dozed with its eyes
closed, opening its eyelids now and then for a second or two. Yet it
seemed as if the bird had sunk into a duck-pond of assured comfort,
there was so much love and affection under the boy's arm.

The grandson had fought a battle of wills with his grandmother
before they set out.

"Where are you taking the rooster?" Sajed had said with suspicion
in his voice.

"To your Auntie's."

"Why do you want to take him there?"

Karima Bibi had left the rest of their hens and ducks in charge of
their neighbours. Why was she taking this one? "He's wicked. I
don't want to leave him here."

"I know. You're going to slaughter him, that's why." Sajed stubbornly opposed her.

"You can't go visiting empty-handed. What will people say?" Grandmother had replied foolishly.

"Give him away? I won't let you."

After tantrums and tears, it was decided that Sajed would carry the bird on their journey and bring him back. The old woman had a different idea, but for the time being she was pleased with the compromise.

The rooster weighed two kilograms, but the weight seemed to increase with the fatigue of walking. Yet Sajed refused to part with it. His heart beat fast with heat and sweat; Grandmother's words only irritated him.

"Give me the cock. He's too heavy for you."

"No."

He held the bird even closer to his chest. They had two years of friendship between them.

The bird's eyelids drooped in comfort. When the old woman tried to snatch him away, he showed his disapproval by flapping his wings and raising his legs. Sajed's protest, the bird's disapproval— well, let the boy carry him. The old woman felt sorry for the orphan child who was suffering for no fault of his own.

The ground was hot; it scalded the young feet.

"Grandma, I can't walk any more. Let's sit under that date tree."

But grandma was in favour of walking faster.

"Let's hurry up. We're late already. We should get there by midday."

The heated ground had little effect on the soles of Karima Bibi's feet. The uneven flesh there had long ago cracked and hardened. A thousand pains, whiplashes, labours, worries and anxieties on sweat-slippery life's struggles had accumulated there like wounds, become insensible and then dried up, leaving only their traces. Those soles were the tablets of human history. Karima Bibi walked faster without caring to respond to her grandson's appeal. They had long passed the date tree.

A cloud covered the face of the sun, the heat abating in its shadow; but the sun struck even harder when the cloud passed.

"Grandma," Sajed cried in a tearful voice, "please sit down for a while. I can't go on."

Covering her grandson's head with the umbrella, Karima Bibi looked at his sweaty face. Whatever sediment of pity there was in her, there was an even larger measure of irritation. She did not respond.

When Sajed appealed again, she flashed, "No strength in your body, eh? Don't you eat?"

"Yes, I do. Aren't you ashamed? Have you ever given me a full meal of rice?"

Their conversation had suddenly changed direction. First Karima Bibi got even angrier; then she started grumbling.

"Since my son died all those years ago, I've deprived myself to feed you. Now you say I don't give you enough to eat."

Karima's anger was unusual. The fatigue of walking, the unbearable heat of the sun, anxieties—everything compounded to ruffle her composure. It was for this grandson that she had hung on to life; she would otherwise have died a long time ago.

The two walked on in silence. The bird dozed, its eyes closed. He now seemed to weigh a few hundredweights. As Sajed rearranged his creature friend under his arm, he squawked. Karima Bibi was lost in her thoughts when her grandson submitted an ultimatum: "Tell me if you're going to stop or not?" Sajed stopped walking; he couldn't bear the heated ground any more.

Grandmother had no way out; she softened. "Just a little longer, pet. We'll rest under that banyan tree."

About a hundred yards away stood a shaggy banyan tree by the road. Sajed felt relieved. While wiping the sweat off the boy's body with one end of her scarf, Karima Bibi also quietly wiped off the uneasy distance between them.

The shade under the tree, unpierced by the sun, was cool. Giving the rooster to his grandmother, Sajed lay flat on the ground. The hot wind lost its sting as it murmured through weary leaves. To a tired traveller, heaven and hell lay so close together. Sajed would have loved to rest there for ever.

The sun was lost in the midsky. Karima Bibi's eyes were heavy, but she got to her feet within ten minutes.

"Brother, get up." Her request was softened with affection.

Lying there, Sajed looked at his grandmother. He didn't want to be awkward. Behind Karima Bibi's wrinkled face, there were other faces, a thousand faces of beautiful mothers fused. How could he reject her appeal? He got to his feet with a tired smile. Grandmother held the umbrella over his head. The rooster was under Sajed's arm.

The heat of the sun went up by degrees. They walked on in silence; the rigour of their journey made them silent. Even the rooster didn't make a sound. Now and then a motor car drove past, pushing a steam-roller of cacophony ahead of it.

Grandmother suggested that they walk faster. But Sajed could not cope; he had blisters on his soles. Grandmother's appeals scalded him. He pressed his lips together so that not a word might escape through them.

Now they left the highway to take a country road. After a while Sajed said, "Grandma, I want to sit down for a while. My feet hurt."

Looking at the sun surveying the sky, Karima Bibi realized that it was past midday. They couldn't afford to delay any longer. She responded with a counter-appeal. "Only a little way. We're nearly there."

"I can't. Let's sit down under that tree."

"No, please." There was no irritation in Karima's voice.

Except for some vegetable patches, surrounded by bamboo fences, yawning untilled land lay all around.

Karima Bibi felt sorry as she looked at Sajed's tired face. But they had another mile and a half to go, so his appeal went unheeded. She let him know that no more rest was possible.

Even the bird was being awkward. He was loath to go anywhere for family occasions. Throwing up his arms and legs, he made it known that even he had his rights. Sajed tried to hold on to the rooster, but the latter gave such a show of leg-throwing and squawking that the tired boy failed to restrain the strong bird. Released from the armpit, the bird fluttered on to the ground and scuttled off.

"Catch it, catch . . . ." cried Karima Bibi as she ran all over the place. Sajed gave the bird a chase but he was beyond his reach. The bird was reluctant to be captured.

On other days he readily responded to Sajed's clucking calls, but nothing reached his ear today.

The grandmother and the grandson kept up the chase. While one cornered the bird, the other tried to grab him. But how could the owners, their bodies like jute-stalk, cope with the fatted bird? Running about over acres of land was wasted labour.

Tired, Sajed said, "Grandma, he's gone crazy in the heat. Leave him alone."

"Leave him? What are you saying?"

"Then you go ahead."

Ten yards away the suspicious-eyed bird was resting like his owners. Karima Bibi refusing to give up, the human and the animal started a game of hide-and-seek within a small area. When the old woman was at the end of her tether, she appealed to her grandson, "Brother, let's both try, come on."

"Not me."

"Flesh of my flesh," she said affectionately.

The boy had to respond, and the chase resumed. After half an hour, the rooster ran into a fenced vegetable patch covered with large yellow flowers. The two looked on helplessly; you couldn't chase about in somebody else's vegetable patch. A lot of labour had gone into raising that bit of crop in this desert.

They saw a small cluster of roofs a hundred yards away. Mango trees surrounded the homes of peasants, one of whom doubtless owned the vegetable patch.

The old woman had an idea. "Brother," she said, "keep a watch on the bird. I'll be back in no time."

"Where are you going?"

"I'll go and get a fistful of rice. He'll be caught now."

"Come back soon."

Karima Bibi felt dizzy but she had to keep steady. Before she reached the peasant huts, she saw an elderly woman standing on the roots of a mango tree, watching her.

The curious woman approached Karima Bibi and, as they came close to each other, the latter said without preliminaries, "Sister, give me a fistful of rice. I'm desperate."

"Where are you from?"

"Chaudyagram. Hurry up, sister." There was a great eagerness in Karima Bibi's voice.

"You want rice?"

"Yes."

"Excuse us."

"Just a fistful. Even half a fistful will do."

"I said excuse us. God only knows how he keeps everybody."

"Can't you spare just . . . ."

"The men haven't got any work. There was work on the hills in the east, now that's gone. Who'll give work in the village? Everybody's poor."

Karima Bibi sounded even more impetuous: "Just a fistful, sister . . . ."

"Haven't I said excuse us? The men take their lives in their hands when they go to the hills in the east. Who knows when one of them'll get shot. When they go, I can't eat or drink for worry. If they're late for a day I cry my eyes out."

Karima Bibi had no time for the elderly woman's moaning. She couldn't restrain herself. The heat raised her high voice to an even higher pitch: "What a shameless mean woman is this, won't even spare a fistful of rice," she cried.

Taken aback by this impudence, the elderly woman spat poison. "Restrain your tongue. Begging and yet plying her tongue like a whore. I'll have your face smashed."

"Begging? Who's begging? I've never begged in all my misery and do I come begging now? Aren't I human?"

The elderly woman wouldn't let her off so easily: "Then why do want rice?"

"My rooster's run off into a vegetable patch. We were going to see my daughter, so I took a rooster for them. He's run off."

The elderly woman raised her eyes in surprise and shame, gently slapped herself on both sides of her face and clucked in penitence. She had taken Karima Bibi to be a beggar. It was not unnatural the way she looked in her sweat and fatigue.

The elderly woman more than made up for her misunderstanding. She ran into the house and returned with a dozen children.

"Have you got the rice?" Karima asked anxiously.

"No need for it. Why waste a fistful of rice? It's for this rice the whole country . . . ." She did not finish. She ordered her troops: "Children, this lady's rooster has run away. Let's see if you can go and get it. Don't hurt it though."

She did not let Karima Bibi go with the children but sat her under the tree and fetched her a glass of pitcher-cooled water and a little molasses.

The two women talked about the passports the men needed to go to work across the border, about rice and topics of homely pains and pleasures.

But Karima had little interest in their conversation. Her mind lay in the direction of the noise raised by the children and the rooster. There was a racket round the vegetable patch. About a quarter of an hour passed. The midday sun had long tilted.

At last the children returned, and with them Sajed. One of the elderly woman's grandsons handed the criminal to Karima Bibi.

The cool water, the molasses and the chat in the shade of the mango tree had not soothed Karima Bibi's anger. The moment the rooster was handed to her, she held the bird by the neck and hurled him down on the ground, swearing, "Devil of a bird, wicked creature, you've given me some trouble."

The children had chased him around for a long time, the sun had passed over his head, and he hadn't had a drop of water to drink— the life of a creature, but life all the same. Lying on the ground, the rooster threw his legs spasmodically and breathed with difficulty, Had he been human, one could have said it sounded like the death rattle.

Everybody was dumbfounded, including Karima herself.

Sajed threw himself on the ground beside the rooster and cried: "My cock's dying, it's dying . . . ."

Karima Bibi sat still for a minute and then suddenly stood up to start a theatrical display. She held the elderly woman by the hand and said, "Please go and get a knife—a knife."

"We haven't got a knife."

"A *boty* then, a kitchen blade."

The elderly woman ran back with a blade.

"Sacrifice it," Karima requested the children hysterically.

"We're not *mullahs* or *moulvis*." Of course they were neither. Laughter spattered their ranks.

The rooster's eyes had closed but his yellow legs were still moving. Another death rattle came from his throat.

"I won't let you slaughter him," Sajed cried. "I won't."

Karima did not wait for a mullah; she herself put the blade on the cock's throat.

The small children laughed and cried, "Say 'In the name of Allah'."

"In the name of Allah."

All those colours on the wings of the cock faded away before the scarlet of his blood, which spurted out of his windpipe as he thrashed about, slaughtered.

Sajed could have been sacrificed along with the bird. His tears would not cease.

The elderly woman was very kind. She brought a little molasses and water for Sajed and wiped his tears away with many consoling words.

Then everybody became quiet like the bird. Something unusual had happened all of a sudden.

The grandmother and her grandson got to their feet again. They must move. As she took leave of the elderly woman, Karima Bibi said, "I'll take the cock for my daughter's children. I slaughtered it when it was still alive. It'll be *halal* for the children."

"For the older people too," a cheeky child quipped.

Karima Bibi had the umbrella in one hand and the slaughtered rooster in the other. She held the bird by the wings, his half-severed head twisted round. Blood still dripped and his blue eyes still stared on.

Crestfallen, Sajed walked behind Karima Bibi; walking beside her was abhorrent. He was only following the hearse.

Suddenly Karima said, as if in a state of drunkenness: "Now you won't get anything to eat at your Auntie's house. It's too late."

"Why?"

"It's hard for them too. Ten or twelve mouths to feed. There would have been something for us if we had arrived before meal-time."

"Was that why you were hurrying me?

She had no reply to her grandson's harsh question. Sighing, she said, "They're poor like us. I thought they'd sell the rooster to the gentry for a few rupees, then it wouldn't be too hard on them to feed us, and I'd see my daughter too. Now, look what's happened."

Sajed's eyes moistened at his grandmother's sorrow.

"Then let's go back," he said in a subdued voice.

"No, flesh of my flesh. We'll get back tomorrow morning. We won't stay any longer. Look, there your Auntie's home. Can you see that date tree?"

"Yes," said Sajed in a hoarse voice and then fell silent.

Translated by Osman Jamal.

"The Rooster" is included in *God's Adversary and other stories* published by Penguin Books India, 1996.

The Driver

Abu Rushd

On arriving at Rahmatullah's office in Zindabahar First Lane to collect a debt of taka ten thousand, I learnt that the businessman had left for Chittagong in connection with some urgent work. The news upset me, as I badly needed some money immediately. I had to pay a bill of fifteen thousand taka for my second daughter's hospitalization for a week in a city clinic for a gall bladder operation. A cabin for the purpose at the P. G. Hospital would have been less expensive and safer, I now realized. When I told my name and the purpose of my visit to Rahmatullah's manager, he looked at me with appropriate reverence and informed me, politely, that the master had left a cheque for me. He had tried to phone me several times in this connection but had been unable to get my line. This was by now a familiar complaint. Once my wife decided to make a call, or any of her female acquaintances was on the line, the number was sure to be engaged for at least half an hour. All household titbits, the latest sensational rumour, interesting political happenings, prices and details of the food cooked for the day, were all transmitted with a relish that someone trying to get through was unlikely to appreciate.

The cheque, of course, remedied the initial feeling of disappointment. As I came out of Rahmatullah's office, I found no trace of any rickshaw near about. One was visible at some distance, but it appeared from the rickshaw-driver's leisurely pace and his curiously bandaged head that he was in no hurry for a fare. But the moment I signalled, he proved I was wrong and hurriedly pedalled his rickshaw towards me. Although I felt somewhat curious about the piece of cloth he had wrapped round his head, I was in some hurry to return home. So I directly told him my destination and the fare he might expect. My curiosity was deepened as the rickshaw driver promptly agreed to the fare without the slightest haggling.

As I boarded the rickshaw, the driver loosened the bandage that covered his forehead and I realized that the man was a leper. The thought struck me then that I should at once get down from the rickshaw on some excuse after, of course, paying the rickshaw puller some money. To go all the way back to my house in the company of a leper was a far from pleasing thought, but the look of expectation on his face deterred me from this unkind move. So, despite the fact that the rickshaw was moving rather slowly because of the driver's peculiar deformity, I tried to comfort myself with the thought that leprosy was not necessarily an infectious disease, and one frequently came across lepers on the city streets. There was, therefore, no rational basis for my unease.

On being thus partially and, temporarily, relieved of my anxiety, I tried to concentrate on the surroundings. We had by then crossed the lane, and the main road was still some distance away. Suddenly, a traffic jam caused all modes of transport to came to a stand-still. Not even an inch of further movement was possible. Again, I felt tempted get down from the rickshaw on this very valid excuse and, in compensation, pay the driver a couple of takas, but I heard an inner voice reprimanding me: Don't be such a coward. I resigned myself to my plight and meanwhile tried to buck up, looking at the sights all around. By that time the sunlight had grown more intense and everything was heated up. A noxious smell came from the putrefying objects in the nearby drain. There was such a cacophony of sounds emitted by a bewildering variety of vehicles. Someone commented, "We are all caught in the jam. Uncle, you tried to hurry and unnecessarily got scratched." The day-labourer did not respond to the hilarity and stood looking on disapprovingly. My eyes were riveted on the projecting balcony of the first floor of a new, geometrically designed three-storied house across the road. There, an attractive young woman was bemusedly surveying the traffic jam below, but the sparkle in her eyes had no effect on the disconsolate people caught in the traffic jam.

My unease began to grow as the traffic jam showed no signs of being cleared. All around me life was back in full motion, but I could not take my eyes off the round, wet spots and reddish-black wounds which now became clearly visible on the rickshaw-driver's mutilated body. I found myself alienated from the surrounding scene. I felt the bacteria of that deforming disease entering my nostril and fast spreading to my blood-stream through my tongue. I was being sucked into the clutches of this dreadful disease and my very existence was threatened by that terrible foe. I could easily catch this disease. First, lack of sensation in the affected part of the body. Then inflammation of the skin, that telltale spot, and finally the specialist's frightening diagnosis, "Yes, leprosy, but these days the disease is more or less nothing to feel hopeless about. Of course, you must regularly take medication over several months, the disease will not spread then and your type may not be beyond cure."

That was all very well, but how would I stand in relation to my family? How would my wife react to it? The husband-wife relationship would, of course, be terminated, and gradually my wife's present benevolent attitude towards me would face tremendous pressure and might substantially change. My own conscience would prompt me to avoid close contacts with the members of my family including my wife out of consideration for their health, and I might be forced to live in a corner of the house like an untouchable. Take my wife, for instance. In thirty years of our married life, we had produced four children. My eldest son had earned an M.A. degree in History from Chittagong University and, as a result of a strange concatenation of events, was now employed as an Associate Professor of Folk-lore at a middling American University. My youngest son was still waiting to take the final Chemistry honours examination at the end of the fifth year of what was supposed to be a three-year course. My eldest daughter was living in England with her engineer husband. My youngest daughter was reading for the graduate pass course at Holy Cross College and was now well on the way to recovery after her gall bladder operation. Since the motto of our household was "Business is wealth," we always enjoyed relative affluence. Moreover, my wife belonged to a respectable and well-to-do family. So my wife never did anything which was a deviation from her placid temper. Only when she had difficulty with her bowel movement did her behaviour become somewhat erratic. And she ate at least twenty betel leaves a day which gave her the habit of wetting her lips with her tongue.

But she had a sharp eye for my material needs. My clothes and my shoes were always found in the right place, whenever I needed them. Nutritious and tasty food was never scarce. The absence of our eldest son and eldest daughter, of course, weighed heavily on her and when she particularly missed them, she would express a wish to travel to South India or Nepal or at least Cox's Bazar.

When my wife come to know that I had leprosy what would be her attitude to me? Of course, if the disease proved to be of a mild and non-infectious type and was amenable to treatment, she might not raise much difficulty. At the worst, a separate bed. But if the disease spread fast all over my body and proved infectious and non-amenable to medication, then she would be compelled to avoid any contact with me, and out of fright and frustration might even leave for her father's house. And if that happened, no impartial and fair-minded man could blame her. In that case what would I do with my companionless and unwholesome existence?

In that condition, naturally, even those children of ours who were with us would scrupulously avoid my company and become anxious to send me to hospital. Our eldest son would probably volunteer to bear all my medical expenses. Our daughter who lived in England might pressurize her husband to arrange for my treatment there. Our youngest daughter would probably maintain a non-infectious distance and enquire about how I felt. And our youngest son would mould his behaviour on the basis of the type and severity of the disease. And our relations? Well, why raise that issue? With their own domestic worries and the difficulty about communication, their contacts with me, even in normal times, were severely limited, and when they learned that I had leprosy, they would not even come within half a mile of our house. Some among them might occasionally ring up my wife to discreetly enquire how I was doing.

As the rickshaw driver's pedalling was affected by his physical deformity, we could not come within sight of Yousuf Market though we had been on the move for eight minutes after the traffic jam was over. The road on which we were now moving was astir with human and animal activity with the pedestrians providing some fun because of the disorderly and illogical way in which they made a dash for the other side of the road or suddenly paused in the middle of the traffic. I again felt like getting down from the rickshaw because I wanted to live, but I was deterred by that strange voice within me to stop thinking solely of my own convenience and give some thought to the rickshaw driver too. So I tried to suppress my own apprehension and turn my attention to the man who was driving me to my destination. Really, what was the mental frame of this fellow now? Why should I allow myself to feel panicky at the possibility of catching this disease when this fellow had it and even then was unconcernedly driving the rickshaw although it might be a very painful effort for him. He had not even once turned his face back throughout this time. Like the silent embodiment of a masculine will, he was pedalling the rickshaw through the maze and whirl of an unwieldy traffic, ensuring that the rickshaw got no scratch in the process and proceeding steadily towards the destination I had indicated to him. He needed a living and was desperate to earn it, whatever impediment destiny chose to put before him.

Did this fellow have parents or brothers and sisters? Was he married and had he any children? Did he have a place to go back to? Or did he promise to himself to be self-reliant after buying a rickshaw from his own resources and on being abandoned by everybody? Hats off to him. But I could not prevent a pervading darkness descending on me despite the pity I felt for the rickshaw driver. I felt that all kinds of menace and danger were attacking me from every direction and threatening to engulf me. I realized that whatever had happened in my life till now and whatever I was in this visible world was only a kind of error. Just a clever device to divert my mind. The eerie silence of the rickshaw driver made me suspicious of his real existence. Did he receive any treatment for his disease? Did he regularly take the required medication? Did he feel any urge for a complete recovery? What exactly was his world? Did he have anyone to look after him? We two were playing a game between us: he pretended that I was not aware of his disease, and I behaved as though I did not notice any abnormality in his body. All this was a part of the deception that I was beginning to feel all life actually was. Was the awesome power operating behind this strange phenomenon without any sensibilities that might be comprehended by man or was it a benevolent deity capable of eventually remedying every single human deficiency or lapse? Would the final black curtain descending on the last scene of my life cause millions of worms to crawl on my body and utterly destroy my separate sensibility? Would cobras and other poisonous snakes know about all my lapses and sins and repeatedly bite my corpse with their venomous teeth, after imparting to it a new sensation? Would hideous-looking monsters appear in my grave and tear my still sensitive skin and flesh with sharp weapons? Would the soil on either side of my grave collapse in a sudden frightening movement and reduce what remained of my body to nothingness? No trace of my body would remain, nor the least particle of my particular existence. Only the drum of destruction would be ceaselessly heard. There was, perhaps, another possibility: I had earned redemption for my sins because of this particular rickshaw ride and the rickshaw driver would appear as my saviour at the time of my greatest test. Maybe he was a disguised Christ.

All the time he had been quietly telling me how to avoid the sinuous path of sin and all manner of subtle temptations and instead steadfastly aim at a destination that was without any blemish or blame. What was outwardly ugly was not actually blameworthy if inwardly it was without any blemish. How many times during the anxious rickshaw ride had I felt the temptation to get down from the rickshaw and remove myself to a safe distance from the leprous driver? But some sort of unearthly hesitation had deterred me from carrying out my design. It repeatedly struck me that my leprous and lion-hearted driver had been thrown into a life-and-death struggle and needed this fare desperately to extricate himself from an impossible predicament. And since I was providing this fare, he was silently praying for my welfare. But again the feeling of apprehension returned towards the end of the ride, and I could no longer stand the idea of travelling with a leper. When we arrived at the cross-roads near Gulistan, I instantly decided to complete the rest of the journey on foot. Furtively, I took out my purse from my trouser pocket and found that I had the exact amount in one-and five-taka notes to pay off the rickshaw driver. I did not need to ask him to change a ten-rupee note. I felt completely at ease, as now there was no question of accepting any change from the leprous hands of the rickshaw driver. As I got off the rickshaw, I politely told him—he still maintained his enigmatic silence—that I needed to do some shopping in the Gulistan area. I added the last two words so that what I had said did not sound like a lie. As I looked at the man, something strange happened. The brilliant light of the sun fell on the silent man's face, emphasizing in detail his deformed facial features, but the sight did not repel me. Rather, the strange mysterious light in his eyes, half open under his damaged eyelids, seemed deeply reflected in the mirror of my mind. I looked at him in some surprise, as he pedalled off in a burst of speed as if his legs had suddenly gained some additional strength. He skilfully manoeuvred his rickshaw through the mad congestion and chaos of that immensely busy road so that the rickshaw touched nothing. He soon disappeared from view. I felt a strange reverence for that mysterious, deformed figure.

But the smell of dried fish and indigenous herbal plants brought me back to reality. I became part of the daily animated scene. I had the reassuring thought that there was no possibility of my catching that hideous disease in the near future. My relief led me to buy a seer (the shop assistant had no idea of a kilogram) of crisp and syrupy *jalebis*. The price was a bit high, 38 taka per seer. No matter. My wife was frightfully fond of that preparation.

Translated by the author.

"The Driver" is anthologized in *Selected Short Stories of Abu Rushd*, published by Bangla Academy, 1993.

Haran's Death

Fazlul Huq

I stepped out of the house the moment I heard the news. I had always known Haran to be a quiet, mild-mannered man. how could he do something so terrible? Weighty question; my mind was benumbed under its pressure. I had no strength left to look for an answer, nor was there any hope for one. I felt as if I was forcing one foot in front of the other.

I got back to my senses at the sight of old Bhattacharya, the priest. He was racing away. As he saw me, he cried, "Hell-dweller!" meaning Haran. "Great sinner!" With that he rushed off as if fleeing from a fiend of hell, or pursuing him with out-stretched arms. The old man filled me with bitterness. It would seem as if the sole object of religion was to make man inhuman.

When I arrived at the spot, people from neighbouring villages had already gathered there. A small crowd formed around me. "Have you ever heard a story like this?" Rashid said. "That's a milkman's wisdom for you!" I had heard any number of stories, including the seven parts of the *Ramayana,* but I didn't have a clue about Haran's. I couldn't grasp Rashid's innuendo, though others, judging by their laughter, obviously did.

What had Haran done, that even by dying he was not getting a grain of sympathy?

I would have preferred not to describe the condition in which I found Haran, but the story will be incomplete if I leave it out altogether. Haran was hanging at the end of a cow-rope from a large branch of a mountain pine. The tree had cracked and sagged to the right. Haran's tongue was hanging out, his clenched teeth sunk in the middle of it. Blood and saliva had oozed out of the corners of his mouth and coagulated. Most horrifying were his eyes —raised upward, the eyeballs seemed to be bursting out of their sockets. I didn't have the nerve to look at them a second time.

The police station was one and a half miles away. The village watchmen had gone there with the news. Haran would have to hang until the police sub-inspector had concluded his investigation. The time of his arrival was uncertain. If he came by boat, it would take some time; on his bicycle, he would probably come quite soon. Until then people would hang about in little clusters on the fields of Kailamfula, by the country road, on the verandah of Haran's family home. It wouldn't do to leave the hanging man alone. Unlike the priest, they were not content with simply cursing the suicide. They were dying with frustrated resentment, as if Haran had got off too easily, cheated them. Let his broken neck break even further, the clotted blood in his body turn into leeches and keep sucking into him so he can feel it—it only then would he have adequately expiated his folly.

Haran's wife sneaked out of the house and walked up to the little mound behind the hut. Seeing her husband hanging from the tree, she threw herself on to the ground and howled. Sattar, Rashid and some others, who had gathered there, jeered in a chorus, "Look at the whore's act!" Some relations of Haran's pushed her back into the hut.

By then I had learnt the circumstances of Haran's suicide. When those around me realised that I was in the dark, they all became eager to tell me. Sattar stopped the others and told the story from the beginning to the end; his story did not stop at Haran's hanging rope; through a structure of words, his wife Bindi's whole future clearly revealed itself before the lustful eyes of all. The man had the gift of a story-teller.

I got up to go. I had seen with my own eyes how Haran had hanged himself and I had heard why he had done it; what would be the point of staying any longer? But Haran's uncle Madhu broke into a sob and held me in his arms. Who knew what trouble the police sub-inspector might create; would I not be present when he arrived? If I wanted to go home now, could I come back when the police sub-inspector arrived? "We're ignorant people, Babu", he pleaded.

There was no need to plead with me. I had not realised that the police might give them trouble; if I had I wouldn't have thought of going. As I resumed my seat, I heard the gruff voice of Tamizuddin Bepari. "Now, Madhu, who knows when the police sub-inspector will get here. How about some tobacco . . . ."

As if it was only to protect this unfortunate family of dairy farmers from police harassment that Tamizuddin Bepari was sitting around Haran's body, basking in the winter sun of Kailamfula. Of course, the dairy farmers must provide the tobacco. Perhaps Haran's mother herself would light the charcoal for the hookah!

The police sub-inspector came. He had taken his time. The river, which had dried up, flooded again. There was enthusiasm and liveliness on people's faces. They couldn't punish Haran for the crime he had committed. He was beyond all punishment. But if Haran wasn't there, those related to him by blood, the dairy farmers, were. Let the police sub-inspector get at them—that would somewhat pacify the god of the masses.

The police sub-inspector saw the hanged man. The rope, where it cut against the neck, was glistening. After careful examination, he said, "Waxed. Good, good. The lad used his brains to kill himself".

Then he turned into a proper Sherlock Holmes. "You wouldn't expect to find candles in a dairy farmer's home, would you? The lad spent money to hang himself. Good, good."

Madhu was summoned—he was the head of the family. Putting his palms together in deference, he looked on pathetically, like a sacrificial cow.

The police sub-inspector said, "Do you think your nephew hanged himself of his own free will or do you suspect foul play?"

Madhu couldn't stay a word in reply—he might as well have gone totally dumb. One or two people goaded him, "Come on, say something."

Madhu made an attempt to say something, it wasn't clear whether yes or no; but the sub-inspector laughed indulgently,

"Don't they say a milkman's son doesn't come of age until he's three score years old?"

The remark was greeted with peals of laughter. It was no longer possible for me to keep quiet. "Even by the gentleman's estimate", I said, "Madhu has come of age. He's long passed his sixtieth year."

That was impertinent. The police sub-inspector rolled his eyes, as if to say, "Who's that impudent boy?" But, looking at me, he refrained from saying anything, perhaps because I was nearer thirty and was clearly not a dairy farmer by caste.

The sub-inspector made out a report to the effect that Haran had committed suicide. He was released from the tree. His body wouldn't be fiddled with or cut open, and it wouldn't be necessary for anybody to go to town—a heavy stone was lifted off the chest of the dairy farmer's family. Haran's relations heaved a sigh of relief. The grief at Haran's death was hardly noticeable. I did not know at the time, but heard later, that Madhu's life savings were exhausted paying tribute to the police sub-inspector, Tamizuddin Bepari, and his ilk.

I was thinking of Haran. Sattar said Umesh had turned the whore's head, meaning Bindi, Haran's wife. He probably didn't exaggerate. Umesh, a son of the Talukdar, the master of the dairy farmers, went about in scented muslin shirts; he was fair, doe-eyed, his skin soft and smooth. It was, of course, possible for Umesh to turn Bindi's head. Shotgun in hand, Umesh walked around the dairy farmers' huts in search of quarry—he'd a sudden urge for *shikar*—as if all the wood pigeons in the world had come to the bamboo clumps behind the dairy farmers' huts and to the trees around them. Madhu once asked Umesh, "How much do those cartridges cost, Babu?"

The figure surprised Madhu. Why shoot wood pigeons, then?

Umesh had explained that Madhu would not understand the meaning of shooting for fun.

Yet the meaning was not hard for anyone to understand. But who would dare stop Umesh? Within a few days of his marriage, in Sattar's words, Haran had become glued to his wife. He wouldn't even go out of the hut if he could help it. When he had to, it was only to look for scented oil, hair ribbons and such like. Perhaps

Haran didn't go that far, but he undoubtedly was very much in love with his wife. Within six months of their marriage, Umesh appeared on the scene. There was nothing new about it. No law existed forbidding Umesh from having the young women of the dairy farmers for his pleasure. It was said of Umesh's father that when he, in his time, entered Madhu's hut, Madhu went into the yard to smoke his hookah. But Haran was besotted with Bindi and perhaps it was this condition which prompted Madhu to pluck up courage and ask Umesh, "Why shoot wood pigeons, Babu?"

It's not known if Madhu had spoken to Haran. But Haran regained his composure and the dairy farmers, perhaps assuming that Haran had accepted the inevitable, were relieved. Sattar explained to me that the situation was entirely different. It was Bindi's deception which had reassured Haran. Bindi had persuaded him that he was her all, her husband and god; that going round the farmers' huts, Umesh would only wear out his shoes. That wouldn't be a loss to Haran or Bindi, would it? Then that evening Haran saw them under the pomelo tree . . . . Sattar described the scene in strong language. Briefly, Umesh had no gun in his hand and Bindi had her arms round him.

Haran did not kill either his wife or Umesh; he put a rope round his own neck. For this, there was no abuse which was not showered upon him; all human contempt and hatred were heaped on his hanging corpse, nothing spared. Yet everybody knew Haran loved his wife more than his life and Bindi herself had persuaded him that, if she was faithful, Umesh couldn't do them any harm. Nevertheless, man's hatred brooked no limits.

Translated by Osman Jamal.

Gabriel's Wings

Shahed Ali

The tiny hut stood among the trees on the left side of the street
cutting across Azimpur and going towards Peelkhana Road.
Exposed to the sun, rain and wind, the mud walls of the hut were
not quite intact. Through the holes in the rusty tin window, one
could see bits of the blue sky.

Mother and son lay on the mat. That evening Haleema had
thrashed Nabi very hard. Now seven years old, the boy was appren-
ticed to a *bidi* shop in order to earn his living. His father had died
when he was a baby. To support themselves, Haleema had sometimes
to sit near the cemetery gate to beg when her irregular earnings as
temporary domestic help were not enough for their needs.

People coming to pray over the graves of their relatives would,
now and then, give her a few coins.

Still only an apprentice, Nabi did not get any wages. The owner
of the shop gave him his afternoon meal; that was all. He was
promised five rupees a month, provided he picked up *bidi* making to
perfection. But of late, Nabi had been playing truant; he would
leave the shop on some pretext or other to go to no one knew
where. He would not be seen till dusk. So far, the owner had
complained to Haleema three times. Today he came to warn her
that he would be giving him the sack as he had no use for such
wayward boys.

The whole afternoon Haleema fumed with anger over the boy's
disobedience. The thought of his future troubled her even more.

Having no outlet for her rage, she carried on a silent harangue with herself: Why should that ass of a son work anyway? Isn't his mother there to beg for him, to work as a servant to feed him?

As soon as she saw Nabi enter the house that evening, Haleema gave him another thrashing. She insisted on his telling her where he had been; but no answer came from the boy. All that he did was to sob violently. Afterwards, he fell asleep without taking his meal. Haleema sat down to eat hers but, after a few morsels, which she swallowed unwillingly, she got up. She remembered how the child had opened his eyes only to close them immediately, when she had begged him to eat. She sat down on the mat, her eyes seeking the sky through the broken walls, her hand on the sleeping boy. Tonight her heart ached violently at the thought of having beaten him, though at times she felt no remorse even when the stick with which she beat him broke on his back. She told herself how wrong it was to blame him when he was so young and innocent. She could not help pitying herself when she thought of her double responsibility as both mother and father to the boy. She thought of the days ahead, after her death, wondering how Nabi would support himself then. As her eyes filled with tears, she kissed the child on the brow.

Nabi opened his eyes suddenly and, pointing towards the door, shouted, "O Mother? Who's that?"

"Where?" asked the astonished Haleema.

"There he goes!" Extending his right arm, Nabi again pointed towards the way the stranger had gone.

"There is no one," Haleema said.

"Why do you want to keep it from me?" Nabi was cross. "Didn't I see the handsome man? What a glorious complexion, Mother, and what clothes!"

"Handsome man?" Haleema's astonishment grew further.

"Yes," Nabi said with dilated eyes. "He brought sweets. Haven't you kept them?"

"Yes, I believe your story," groaned the sad Haleema, pained by what she thought to be Nabi's ingenious way of wish fulfillment. "Go to sleep, Nabi. In the morning you shall have sweets."

"Where did the man come from, Mother? Did you see his wings?"

"Wings?"

In the semi-darkness of the half-lit room, she looked at Nabi with eyes sharpened by uncomfortable astonishment.

"Yes, wings—gorgeous ones! Like a peacock's plume."

Haleema hugged her boy and, stroking his back, said in a tender voice. "An angel must have come. Tonight is *Shab-e-barat*, the night when everyone's luck is decided. The angels are going from house to house to see how everybody is."

Nabi's body tingled with expectancy. In his excitement he left the bed. The night was beautiful. The earth was bathed in the bright liquid silver of the moon. Even at that late hour, from the nearby mosque, came voices reciting Quranic verses. The cemetery was still teeming with people. In their belief that they could communicate with the souls of their dead, all forgot their sleep, and stayed awake praying to Allah for their own happiness and the fulfillment of their hopes and desires. Only Nabi and Haleema were wasting the night in sleep instead of telling God's angel who passed by their door about their needs and desires. Haleema lit the lamp to examine Nabi's expressions and movements better.

"Aren't you hungry, dear? Will you have your food now?" she asked without getting an answer. Nabi had forgotten his hunger in a sweet but difficult speculation. If the angels took messages to God, had they told Him about his mother and himself?

"Did you tell the angel anything, Mother?" he asked. Haleema kept silent, wondering at him.

"He passed by our door and you said nothing. Why didn't you call me?" He choked with disappointment.

"You are crazy!" rejoined his mother bitterly. "Why should the angels listen to us? They come to ask after the rich. If one of them passed by our door, it was only to go to their houses."

"Why don't you say your prayers?" asked Nabi in an unpleasant bossy tone, breaking a long silence.

"What will prayers do?" Haleema's voice betrayed supreme disgust.

"Why do you talk like this?" Nabi flared up. "Angels come only to those who pray! And God also listens to them."

"No, my boy, no!" Haleema nearly screamed. "God is sleeping under His quilt. Only those who worship Him with gold and silver are listened to. Our plain prayers cannot move Him."

Nabi got more perplexed, thinking that if his mother was right, then the poor had nobody to look up to. Without gold and silver they could never have their desires fulfilled. This explained why so many poor people constantly prayed and never got rich, and why the rich got even richer with the passage of time. But if God created all, why this partiality? Didn't he ever feel sorry for the poor?

In spite of these thoughts, Nabi could not help thinking of the angel with the golden complexion, with a peacock's multicoloured wings and his whole frame giving out a wondrous perfume. He could visualize the white horse with the swaying waist carrying the angel. If he had only been awake at the time, he would have lain in the angel's way and compelled him to listen to his endless sorrows. If the angel had refused to show interest, he would have clung to his wings till he was carried to God. He would have surely awakened God with his shouts. If He had still slept, Nabi would have scratched Him all over till He bled and woke up. Nabi went back to bed, his brain crowded with thoughts.

Haleema too lay down after putting out the light. Though she could not see Nabi in the darkness, she was aware that he was wide awake and strangely restless. Stroking his back, she said, "It's late, darling. Go to sleep."

Nabi watched the sky in silence while his imagination tired itself trying to find a solution to his problem. There was such a flood of moonlight and yet so much darkness. Then a flash of lighting, as it were, lit up his eyes. He thought he knew it now. He would tie a string to the feet of God's throne and thus shake Him up.

The next day, after eating the left-overs of last night's rice with water, and being bullied by his mother, Nabi went reluctantly to work. Haleema had exhorted him. "You have to build your own fortune; just begging God won't do."

As he bound the *bidi* leaves along with the other boys, Nabi's mind wandered in the quiet woods of Peelkhana bordered by a growth of prickly cactus. Every day he sneaked out of the shop to fly his kite there. None knew of this. A stomach-ache was his excuse for leaving the shop. Today he was more restless than ever.

When he reached home, he was overjoyed to find that his mother was not in. Taking advantage of her absence, he rummaged in the deep and empty cooking pots and found two annas, a wealth equal to seven kingdoms. Grasping his spoil firmly in his fist, he ran to Nawabganj, bought some thread, and started running again with the expectation of a great event stirring in his breast.

Inside the woods was a forsaken, ruined mosque. From one of its dark crevices, he took out his kite and roll of string. It was this kite which often carried him beyond the world to the open regions. Though he was loquacious about all his other exploits, about the kite he did not utter a word to anyone.

After a while he came to the quiet corner in Peelkhana, covered with the thorny shrubs of the cactus. Tying a new length of string to the old one, he flew his kite. As it gained height, an uncontrollable joy made him restless. A smile spread from his mouth to his eyes, now shining with the lustre of his happiness.

He felt today he was going to reach the feet of God's throne.

As the kite grew smaller, he was running short of string. It grieved him to find the kite still within sight, that near. He must be sleeping far away, beyond man's sight. To reach Him, he needed much more thread. Where was the money? Did this mean their sorrows were never to and? Nabi moaned in despair. As long as flying kites remained his hobby, he drew unmixed pleasure from it. But now that the kite had a special significance for him, instead of giving him pure joy, it filled him with a nameless sorrow.

Winding up the bit of thread he had, he put the kite back in its hiding place. He knew that asking his mother for money would mean such a hard thrashing that the skin of his back would come off. He feared what was in store for him once the theft of the two annas was discovered by his mother. He consoled himself with the thought that in order to bring about a change in their fortunes they would have to spend a little money, even bear some losses.

In his mother's absence he looked into all the cooking pans and bundles of old clothes. But desperately trying to provide at least one meal a day, his mother had to spend every bit of the little money she earned as a maid and as a beggar-woman. Saving anything was out of the question.

Nabi had a brilliant idea: he would go the railway station and earn some money as a porter. After waiting for a long time, Nabi saw a train coming. He was quite dazzled by the great number of passengers and the variety of clothes they wore. People shouted for porters. Nabi was unlucky; he could not attract a single passenger. With his eyes fast filling with tears and arms outstretched towards the passengers, he was mistaken for a beggar. Some even gave him a lecture on the dignity of labour and the infamy of begging. One or two pushed him mercilessly out of their way.

When the train left, Nabi sat down in despair, thinking of the many more days they would have to starve, of their inability to wear new clothes even once a year. They were still wearing the clothes his father had bought them, patched and mended a hundred times over. The walls of their hut were crumbling, the slightest rain left pools on its floor. Only if their desires reached God would their sorrows end. But Haleema never said her prayers, and Nabi hadn't had a chance to learn Arabic verses. So he thought it only natural that God did not hear them.

When, after about an hour, another train arrived, he was cheerful again. Beckoned by a strong wrist with a watch on it, he approached a first class compartment. The gentleman pointed towards his hold-all and attaché case saying, "Could you take these to the waiting room?"

"Certainly, sir," Nabi replied confidently. "If you would put them on my back."

"How much do you want?" the passenger asked smiling.

"I need a lot of money. How much can you give?"

The man's eyes grew sharp. Looking at Nabi intently, he said, "What a strange boy! What will you do with so much money?"

"Why, I'll buy string—lots of it for my kite," he said, greatly surprised by the man's query.

The man burst out laughing as he loaded the luggage on Nabi's back. When they reached the waiting room, the passenger took out four annas instead of the usual one anna, saying: "Here you are! You can buy heaps of string now."

"I won't take it." Nabi threw the coin on the floor. "What will four annas do? I need a lot of string. My kite has to reach the end of the sky."

The man picked up the coin and asked good-humouredly, "What good will it do if your kite reaches the sky?"

"Why, I'll shake God's throne. Why should He listen only to you and not to us?" He spoke with some agitation.

The atmosphere in the waiting room suddenly became heavy. Everyone was speechless. The man gave him an eight anna bit. Nabi's eyes were full of gratitude.

"When we have money, you must come to our house. I'll fill your pocket with coins then," the boy declared with perfect sincerity.

The passenger at last laughed. "Of course, I'll come. We'll all come that day," said Nabi's benefactor with enthusiasm.

Nabi did not wait to hear the rest of his speech. When, after buying string, he came home, dust had fallen. He had hidden the string in the crevice of the ruined mosque where his kite was.

Haleema was boiling rice which she had got by begging. Rubbing her eyes, she asked, "Where have you been, dear?"

Her affectionate tone pleased Nabi, but he wondered whether his mother had had time to look for the money. Feeling sure that she hadn't, he thanked God silently.

"I went for a walk, Mother, after finishing at the shop," he lied with perfect ease.

Haleema pushed some more twigs into the oven and said, "Don't you run away from the shop again. Once you have picked up the work, you will earn lots of money, darling. We have no other means but this." Then looking at his face, she asked anxiously, "You are hungry, aren't you, my boy?"

His mother's affectionate tone seemed to take away his hunger. The satisfaction of buying all the string he wanted and such unexpected sweetness from his mother, made it a memorable day for Nabi.

"No, mother, I am not hungry. I had my meal at the shop," he said smiling.

"Good. The less you eat of this begged food, the better for you. It spoils luck."

But when the cooking was done, they both ate the detested rice with relish. The next day, on the pretext of going to the shop, Nabi left the house early. The weather seemed ideal for his chosen activity, and the great quantity of string in his possession made him confident about reaching the sky. With a beating heart, he pressed the kite to himself. As it took to the air dancing, and rose higher and higher, Nabi started trembling in desperate courage. His eyes grew large with emotion. His heart-beat became faster, his lips opened in a strange smile. The bright pupils of his eyes danced to the movement of the kite. When he felt that his bamboo string-holder was not rolling any more— which meant that the thread was finished—he was again on the verge of tears. All that string gone, and the kite still within sight!

He had to bring it down. He wondered why God had His seat so far away. Probably the distance ensured His sound sleep. Wasn't there enough string in the world to reach His throne so that it could be shaken? Nabi's thwarted will now became rebellious. Hiding his kite in the mosque, he went to the station again to earn more money to buy more string, the string with which he intended to shake God's throne and pull Him down to His creatures who dwelt on earth.

He could not earn more than two annas, hardly sufficient for the great quantity of string he needed.

With each day's earnings, he kept buying new string and tying it to the older string. The quiet nook in Peelkhana had become almost his private possession. These days every visit to the place filled him with a terrible sadness as he invariably exhausted his string. But giving up the venture was out of the question. The thought that success was imminent increased his determination. Whatever money he earned at the station or in the market as a porter was spent on buying string which got longer and longer because of constant addition. With the shop, which provided him with the excuse for leaving home, he had no connection whatsoever.

One day when the kite had become a black spot and lost itself in the sky, Nabi trembled as he watched it. A pitiful, expectant smile appeared on the child's lips as his brow perspired and his heart almost stopped beating with excitement. There seemed to be a tug-of-war between heaven and earth. His hand, as it gripped the string, felt the terrible tension, as if someone invisible was pulling at the other end and making its veins swell. Today he was determined not to wind up the string; he would let his kite wander in the sky, following its own will. When it caught the feet of God's throne, there would be a hard pull from above, which Nabi would counteract by pulling it down, so that God's throne would shake violently. Suddenly frightened out of His sleep, God would be forced to look at man, to listen to His creatures' woes.

Nabi's eyes were fixed on the point where the string split the sky, a bridge between heaven and earth. White, black, multi-coloured clouds moved past it and the string vibrated with their pressure. Nabi saw the clouds being divided by the thread. Although he did not know where God's throne was, he felt that he had flown the flag of his revolt towards His throne which could not be very far any more. He had forgotten his hunger and his mother's existence. He clung to the string-holder even after dusk. His string had not caught at anything yet. After some time he brought the kite down and hugged it passionately. Bending down he looked at it, stroking it gently. The kite seemed moist, and had a strange odour. He rejoiced at the thought that God had wept over his sorrows. There was no need then to pull at the throne since God had already wept for His creature. Nabi felt confident about the end of their hardship.

On returning home, he found his mother lying in bed with fever. She had come back in the afternoon without earning a penny. Doubt assailed Nabi all over again: If God had wept for them why should his mother get fever and why should they have no food? Then it wasn't God's tears but Satan's urine. Satan didn't want man's desires to reach God! Possibly to cross the seven spheres of the sky, as described in the Holy Book, he needed more string.

In the morning, though still unwell, Haleema got up to look for some food for the boy. When she came back, she did not join Nabi at the meal.

"Won't you eat, Mother?"

"No," Haleema said in a feeble voice. "You eat and then go to the shop."

Nabi drank the broth his mother had begged for him. Haleema smiled sadly, but did not say anything. When Nabi left in a tired manner, she did not imagine that he was going to the station first and then to his favourite spot to fly his kite.

Nothing could stop him now. He threw up his hands towards Him whose pitiless light had once burnt down Mount Sinai.

One evening, on coming home, he found his mother extraordinarily cheerful. She was wearing a new sari and waiting for him with fresh rice and curry served in plates. Sitting down at once to eat, he asked, "Where did you get all this?"

"Don't you remember that the Kahertuli zamindar's wife died recently? It was her *fateha*. They distributed money and heaps of clothes." Although she had a temperature, watching Nabi eat so heartily, she immediately felt better.

"Look. I even asked for a *lungi* for you."

When she showed the garment to Nabi, he was convinced that God had turned His face towards them, that He was at last awake. With moist eyes, he exclaimed, "Mother, didn't I tell you that we were not to remain poor for long!"

Haleema had never taken her son's speculations seriously, but today she was inclined to believe in what the boy said as Nabi's eyes brightened with the hope of a more blessed future.

But when the days of semi-starvation came back again, Nabi was overcome with bitterness and doubt. Did God play with His creatures then?

One day, in desperate need of more string, he thought of the angels who could carry messages to God. Why had they become so inactive, when they could easily carry his kite to God?

On Monday Nabi left the house without his meal. The sky was cloudy. As the pressure of the string made his body vibrate, he was again filled with an irrepressible joy. His imagination soared upwards like a golden eagle. Suddenly he saw a huge bird circling round the dot which his kite now was. Sometimes the bird got lost among the clouds and appeared again with its huge wings. Nabi's string got entangled in its feathers and he felt a hard pull. He was filled with fear as the bird started going up with the kite at a terrific speed. Suddenly Nabi felt the snapped string falling downwards, while the kite kept circling along with the bird. He realised that his dream of shaking God's throne would never come true. He looked up at the kite with tearful eyes, a pitiful solitary figure in the deserted place. Like a black dot, the kite followed the bird as it soared upwards.

Suddenly it occurred to Nabi that it was not a bird but the angel Gabriel come in the guise of a bird in order to carry his kite to God. Now his tears were those of gratitude and his face shone with a wonderful smile. The shadow of his former disappointment mingled with his new hope. He felt ashamed of his stupid despair.

So while he was crying over his lost kite, the angel had at last come to fulfil his heart's desire. When he looked up again after drying his eyes, he found that both bird and kite had disappeared. Only bits of a blue and brilliant sky could be discerned through the clouds.

He almost danced all the way home in triumph, his smile betraying his happiness.

Haleema was cleaning some leaves she had picked for dinner.

"Mother!" Nabi cried, hugging her.

Haleema's face darkened, she bit her lips and seized Nabi by the neck. "Where have you been all day, you son of an ingrate! Today I'll teach you the lesson of your life!" she shouted.

Nabi could not understand the reason of his mother's anger, and went on to give her the great news, "Mother I've seen Gabriel today. Our miseries . . . ."

Before he could finish, Haleema began showering blows on his back. "I spit on Gabriel's face!" she cried. "Are the angels to feed us while we sit at home doing nothing?"

"Mother, please Mother, don't abuse Gabriel. It is a sin. God will be cross!" Nabi remonstrated.

Angered even more, Haleema let a torrent of abuse flow from her mouth, making Nabi bite her hand.

The owner of the *bidi* shop had come to tell her that from that day Nabi was sacked as he hadn't shown up for a long time. He also told her that Nabi ran to the railway station every now and then and flew kites all day. Choking with anger, Haleema had been waiting for the rascal to return.

Now she got hold of a sharp stick and hit him on the head, on his arms and back. "You ungrateful child. As if all my headache is not about your welfare. And you have been deceiving me! Gabriel will bring you platefuls of rice when I am in the grave!"

His back wounded badly, Nabi cried out in pain and then bit Haleema, drawing blood. Then losing consciousness, he dropped down on the floor.

Haleema ran a temperature in the night.

Nabi had not eaten anything. He lay in one corner frowning and pouting and sometimes casting hostile glances at his mother. When he fell asleep, he dreamt that Gabriel was soaring up with his kite through the clouds. The blue sky parted in order to make way for him. The clouds closed behind him as he sped onwards. As soon as the door of the sixth heaven opened, Gabriel's wings caught fire, but still he sped on with the kite. As the gate of the seventh heaven opened, it let out a bright flash of light which nearly blinded Nabi. Covering his eyes with his hands, he cried, "Mother! my eyes are burnt!"

When he got up rubbing his eyes, the sharp rays of the sun reached through the cracks in the walls of the hut and fell on his face.

Translated by Razia Khan.

"Gabriel's Wings" is included in *An Anthology of Contemporary Short Stories of Bangladesh* published by the Bangla Academy, Dhaka.

The Rains

Alauddin Al Azad

The rains will come. The wind from the south, blowing in the spring night slightly touched with dew, will soon have the wetness of the sea in it. It will blow over parched, furrowed meadows and, raising a tremor in the leafless tree tops, will gather in dark clouds on the distant peaks. And then, tearing apart the entire sky in lightning streaks, the rains, amidst deafening thunder, will fall in multitudinous streams like the blessing of God. In place of the dried branches of the trees, tender young leaves will sprout and the whole field will be covered with layers of green. Gleaming in the jute fields under the mid-day sun, one will perspire profusely but with no weariness. For the dreams of the new harvest will entwine themselves with every drop of one's blood like a powerful flood.

Things, however, were different this year. The month of *Falgun* passed and yet the northern sky did not get even slightly dark. *Chaitra* too was coming to an end. Faint rumblings were heard in the sky and the whole atmosphere grew stuffy but that was about all.

And then came *Baishakh*. Still the sun, scattering sparks of fire, continued to blaze with unabated intensity. The young jute plants that had come up from the bosom of the earth slowly withered and grew listless. There was an utter emptiness above.

And below, it seemed, a vast openness stretched from one corner of the earth right up to the horizon. Further below stretched the sun-burnt, baked earth streaked with strange designs. Standing at noon on the border of the field, strange sensations clutched one's heart. The field was a witch stretching out her burnt, coppery tongue. A burning hunger had made her devour the corn-child she carried at her breast. There was no doubt that next year the curse of God would descend.

But why? There must be some serious cause behind it. The question came up for discussion after the Friday prayers. Standing near the pulpit, Maulana Mohiyuddin said, "Dear brothers, I am only a humble servant of God. I don't know what to say to you. You know everything. It is written in the Book that when the world becomes sinful, the curse of God will fall on men. And what do we see today? On the one hand, sons do not obey their fathers, women do not observe purdah, and the world is full of thieves, swindlers and scoundrels. On the other hand, people neither say their prayers nor fast, nor go on pilgrimage. Brother, let us all pray to Him today and weep before Him. He is most compassionate and, if He please, He can bestow on us a particle of His infinite mercy."

The resonant voice of the Maulana filled the interior of the mosque. Hajee Kalimullah stood up from the pious congregation. He had a tiny white beard on his chin and a white cotton cap on his head. Long and regular prayers had left a callous mark on the centre of his forehead. He cleared his throat and spoke, his voice quivering with emotion, "We shall surely do what the Maulana Saheb has suggested. But, along with this, every one must remember that the evil-doer has got to be punished. Have you ever pondered over the question as to why this drought has been visited upon us? To tell you frankly, some woman is surely big with an illegitimate child. She may be one of the women of the neighbouring villages. She may even be a resident of our own village for all we know. We must seek out the sinners or we cannot escape this curse. We must be very stern with them. The scoundrels should be horse-whipped."

Hajee Kalimullah ran the fingers of his right hand through his beard and, trembling with anger, took his seat. Only one thought burnt in the cells of his brain, to find out the real culprit.

It was decided to hold congregational prayers for rain in the football ground under the blazing mid-day sun. But Maulana Mohiyuddin fell ill on the day before the special prayers.

The villagers requested Hajee Kalimullah to lead the prayers. He politely refused at first but, later, at the request of all, he consented to do so.

After the prayers were said, Hajee Kalimullah turned from the west and stood facing east, surveying the large congregation with complacency. It was good to see that the world had not yet become completely uninhabitable. Even now, once the call was given, you could get a thousand people to offer their prayer before the great God. He looked with satisfaction at the sight of the innumerable caps on the heads of the people in front of him. What if they were shabby and torn, dirty and oily? The helpless people sat close together in the wide open field with hollow cheeks praying for a little mercy. Raising his two hands, Hajee Kalimullah intoned in his deep voice, "O Allah, cast Thy eyes on us, be kind to Thy servants. Thou art the Lord of the earth and of the sky, of the sun and the moon. At the sign of Thy finger the sea swells, the wind blows, the sea rushes forth. At Thy slightest wish this world can blossom with flowers and crops. O God, give us clouds, give us water, give us shade, give us peace!"

"*Allahumma Ameen! Allahumma Ameen!*" the entire congregation wailed. Hajee Kalimullah's grey beard became drenched with tears. Overwhelmed with sobs, he finished his prayers with the words, "*Sobhanaka Rabbika Rabbil Izzate Ammayassefun Assalam Allal Mursalina Alhamdu Lillahe Rabbil Alamin!*"

The children, the young men and the old, they gathered in the field like this on three consecutive days. They prayed to God with one eye on the sky and the other on the dying, withering crops. Tiny boys and girls painted the only son of a mother in black, placed on his head a winnowing-fan with a frog and the twig of a *bishkantali* plant on it, and played the game of the cloud and the rain. They cooked rice-pudding on the bank of the river and served it to beggars on banana leaves. They gazed at the sky hour after hour, developing cricks in their neck, and yet the sky remained as blue as ever. There was not a trace of a cloud anywhere.

Sitting on his prayer-mat after the evening prayer, telling his rosary, Hajee Kalimullah was lost in thought. One could detect signs of weariness and anxiety in his eyes. Well, there were good reasons for that. He had earned a few thousand rupees by black-marketing yarn. With half of that money he had purchased a warehouse at a business port on the river Meghna and with the rest a fair piece of land. If he failed to buy jute and store it in his warehouse, its purchase would be pointless. It was no good getting a monthly rent of a measly one hundred and fifty rupees. It looked as if he would not be able, after all, to use the warehouse for himself this year. On top of it, he had cultivated all his land himself this year. That was stupid. If he had leased out the land he would have got about fifteen hundred rupees in cash. At present he was simply tired to death looking after the land and supervising the work of the hired men. He had already spent a fair amount on the purchase of seeds, preparation of land and other measures. A good deal more would have to be spent in the future, but from the appearance of the sky, there was little possibility of a good crop this season.

It had not been wise to give up the yarn business. Last year he had gone to Makkah by aeroplane. He had planned that, on his return, he would not entangle himself so much in worldly affairs. He would leave the warehouse in the hands of his children and would personally look after the land only. But lack of funds spoiled all his plans. He told himself that, after all, business was business; there was no question of honesty or dishonesty in it. Everything was all right as long as one had good intentions and spent something on charities.

The strong fragrance of mango blossoms came through the window. The twittering of the *shaliks* from nearby bamboo clusters had perceptibly lessened. The beads of the rosary slipped through the fingers of Hajee Kalimullah and he found that his mind was being slowly engulfed in a stupor.

Zaigun came into the room to light the lamp and was surprised to find him sitting there. She exclaimed, "Why sir, I thought you had gone to the mosque."

Looking up at her, Hajee Kalimullah said, "I am not feeling very well. Besides," he added, "Your lady will be back, I think, any moment now." Hajee Kalimullah, unable personally to go, had sent that morning his third son by the first wife to fetch her. As a matter of fact, he had always been averse to allowing his wives to stay at their fathers' places for a very long time. He had allowed his first wife only ten days and that too in the beginning when she was a new bride. The number of days had slightly increased in the case of the second wife. But now he was in his declining years. One could no longer afford to be as strict as before in everything. When his second wife died two years ago he had lost all interest in the world and its affairs. But who could predict God's mysterious ways? What was allotted would surely come to pass. Last year, when he was preparing to go on Haj, only a month before the date of his departure, everybody insisted that he should marry again, if only for the sake of the stability of his prosperous and happy family.

But what about the bride? He was going to be sixty and who would offer his daughter as a wife to him?

"How you make me laugh," Maju Pradhan had cried out, running his fingers through his beard. "You just say the word and I will find the girl. And not any girl. I will find out such a woman that you will only stare at her, speechless with wonder."

Hajee Kalimullah's eyes had brightened with happiness. His heart had beat with a strange emotion. But outwardly he had remained rather sorrowful and indifferent. It would not be right to forget the memories of his former wives so soon. He had swallowed and said, "Look, I have now grown pretty old and this is no time for merry making. It would be enough if some one were there to attend to the household affairs and my few personal needs."

"That I understand," Maju Pradhan had argued. "You can do with a damaged boat and you can do with a new one. But what do we want? Which one is pleasant to cross the river in?"

After all this, the wife that was arranged in exchange for full seven *kanis* of land was none other than a granddaughter of Maju Pradhan. She was about twenty-one or twenty-two years old. Women in this country are said to get old at twenty. From that point of view, the match with Hajee Kalimullah was not an unsuitable one.

Zaigun finished her work in the kitchen and returned. With a meaningful solemnity, she drew a stool and sat near the door. Hajee Kalimullah had not yet finished reciting the Quran. Stopping his recitation for a while, he asked, "Any news?"

"Yes, there is," replied Zaigun.

"What is it?" Hajee Kalimullah's fingers paused. He looked at her eagerly. He had engaged Zaigun to collect secret information whenever she was free from her work. And hence this eagerness on his part.

Zaigun said, "I went to Batashi today. She was gathering mango leaves for her goat. As soon as she saw me, she started talking of all sorts of things but I only gazed and gazed at her figure." Casting a glance at the door, she continued, "Her abdomen looked swollen."

Hajee Kalimullah asked solemnly, "When did her husband die?"

"Seven or eight months ago, I am sure," Zaigun said, after a little calculation, "but it looked as if she had conceived only four or five months ago."

"Is that so? Then there is a gap of quite some time." Hajee Kalimullah's eyes twinkled with hope, as if he was seeing the light of truth at last. He asked in a low voice, "Did you see the man who lives in her room?"

"Yes, I did. He is much better now though not yet fully recovered. I saw from the door that he was lying on his bed in that room."

"Yes, yes," the Hajee remarked impatiently. "What if he were sick? Couldn't one indulge in those activities if one lay sick in bed? What do you say?"

"You speak the truth," said Zaigun and added, "besides, I never liked Batashi's ways. People used to say a lot of things about her even while Rajab Ali was living. Didn't everybody know of the affair when Chamu of Namapara opened the doors of her room? The blame fell on Chamu only because Rajab Ali got wise about the incident. Can any one dare act like that without encouragement from the woman?"

"If this be the truth then everything seems simple and clear. I believe Batashi has done it. Otherwise why should not the rains come?" Hajee Kalimullah resumed counting the beads of his rosary. He said after a while, "Still it is better to wait a little. Let me personally check the matter. Then something will surely have to be done."

Hajee Kalimullah was lost in deep meditation after Zaigun left. The furrows on his forehead grew deeper. His fingers on the rosary moved quicker than ever. Batashi! Batashi! Batashi! None other than Batashi could do this. This was the trouble of being a young widow. For how could a woman, having once lived with a husband, forget that taste? It was like opium. One could give up rice but not the intoxication of sex. Besides, she was in the fullness of youth. Just one man or two were nothing to her. She could make them stumble and fall by a mere meaningful wink. And how clearly she had managed the whole show! A cousin, only a day-labourer, a poor victim to black fever, with none to look after him. And so she simply had to take care of him. Well, no one was going to be fooled by such excuses and more. It was quite clear that the man was taken in because she wanted to share her bed with him at night.

But who should be punished for this and how? If one were to follow the directions of the Book, they had to be buried in the earth up to the neck and then stoned to death. But could one do that sort of thing in this age? The law and the police were there. What then? A beating with shoes? A social boycott? Banishment from the village?

While Hajee Kalimullah was deeply engrossed in such thoughts, Khaled had arrived with his new step-mother on the bank of the dying river.

The full moon had appeared in the sky long before they had left the bride's home. It now rose above the bamboo-thickets in shining splendour. Everything was quiet all around. No wind rustled the leaves of the trees.

The shallow river had only knee-deep water in it. Pushing through the mud was a thin stream. The clear water of that stream flowed smoothly over the sand. The tender paddy leaves of the *boro* fields lifted their blades through the water and embraced each other with affection.

Zohra stooped and took off her shoes with her right hand. She held a young child in her arms. Noticing her inconvenience, Khaled came up from behind and said, "Please let me carry Saju."

Zohra and Khaled were almost of the same age. At first Khaled had felt somewhat embarrassed in addressing her as *apni*, the respectful "you" reserved for addressing elders, but he had got over it by now.

Zohra looked at the face of her husband's eldest son, shining in the moonlight. His beautiful eyes under the long-drawn eyebrows seemed more beautiful than ever. Her heart trembled with an unutterable emotion, like the thrilled river in the darkness of the wood. She asked dazedly, "Won't you find it troublesome?" Khaled smiled. "Oh, no it'll be no trouble at all."

Saju's mother had died two years ago. Saju was only five then. Deprived of love and affection, he turned into a constantly whining, weeping boy. But he was different now. He had come to like his new mother so much that he refused to part with her even for a minute. When Zohra left for her parents' house on the first formal return trip after the wedding, he quietly got into her lap and went with her.

In taking his soundly sleeping younger brother from her arms into his own, Khaled felt, for ever so short a moment, the fingers of his left hand touch something warm and soft, like the breast of a pigeon. His fingers trembled like the leaves of the *champa* tree in a sudden breeze. Instantly his whole body quivered like the passing of lightning in a heavy cloud. For a second he saw the girl blush deeply. Her whole face seemed to be suffused with a flaming red colour. Khaled could not stand there any longer.

Like the vague remembrance of some deep memory of an earlier life, an unknown feeling of pain engulfed his heart. He turned his face away and stepped through the smoothly flowing waters.

But Zohra remained standing there. Gathering her clothes she looked up at the moon and then at the moving figure in front. Then, suddenly, she grew restless. Stepping like a frightened deer through the stream flowing smoothly over the silvery sand, she stopped again at the brink of the knee-deep water. She gathered the folds of her sari between her legs with her right hand and drew them up to her knees. Bending over the dark water shining in the moonlight, she saw her image breaking into minute particles. She saw that with each tiny wave the image of the moon was breaking up along with hers. Suddenly, she raised her face and called, "Khaled!"

Khaled answered from some distance, "Yes!"

"Are you going away, leaving me behind?" she asked, as if in a dream. "I can't walk. Look, how beautiful the water is!"

Khaled retraced his steps. He said, "What's the matter with you? Please hurry up. It is getting late."

"Yes, you are right. It is getting late," she said. Zohra walked a few steps through the water and then suddenly stopped again. Looking at the shimmering waves, she exclaimed, "Look, how sweet the water is! One could gladly die in such water as this."

Khaled did not say a word. He bent his head and walked on in silence.

A bird chanted somewhere on the other bank, *"Bou Katha Kao."* Crossing the river, she dried her feet and put on her new pair of shoes. But a hollow feeling filled her heart. Like some dry, empty, directionless wind, a sense of utter desolation overwhelmed her. She thought of herself and started violently. Then her whole body went soft and limp.

Khaled was walking slowly. He heard an anxious appeal from behind, "Please stop for a minute!"

"What is it now?"

"I don't know. Why are tears springing to my eyes?" Zohra moved up to Khaled in a daze and, planting herself in front of him, looked deep into his eyes. In the light of the moon, Khaled saw tears swimming in her eyes and flowing down her cheeks like drops of pearl.

Khaled asked again, "What is the matter?"

"You don't know anything. You don't understand anything."

Wiping her eyes with the skirt of her sari, Zohra said in a rush, like one possessed, "Give Saju back to me. There is no one here and I am afraid. Let us go on quickly, please."

A slight wind had started blowing. The two stood briefly facing each other. Then they moved on without a word. A small, dark cloud floated up slowly from the south.

Hajee Kalimullah, walking in his courtyard with his wooden sandals on, looked up at the sky and grew excited. So his guess was right.

"Zaigun," he called out. "Come and see. We were right. The clouds are gathering in the sky."

Zaigun stretched out her neck from the threshold of the door and said, "Yet you want to verify further. There is absolutely no doubt in my mind. Batashi is a veritable slut."

Hajee Kalimullah looked up at the floating clouds in the sky and again started walking up and down. He could not decide what judgment to pass in this case.

Zohra arrived after half an hour. Even while talking with her, lying in his bed, Hajee Kalimullah found his mind wandering. The night advanced and yet no sleep came to his eyes.

Making up his mind the next morning, he went to Batashi's house across the mango grove on the east of the village. Batashi was busy cooking rice gruel in her thatched cottage. She saw Hajee Kalimullah and came out into the courtyard with a wooden stool in her hand. She did not know how to welcome this venerable person who rarely called on people like her.

She tried to say something to Hajee Kalimullah, but the Hajee paid no attention to her. He watched minutely from the corner of his eyes her smooth, tender, light-gold body.

Meanwhile in his house, after supervising the breakfast arrangements, Zohra sat gloomily on the corner of her bed. After her marriage this particular spot drew her with a strange fascination. It was here that she was mostly to be found during her free moments. What was this magic? What mystery was there? Zohra did not know herself. The house had probably changed in various ways, but this room remained always the same. Only a few new things had been added over the years. The touch of the former wives was still fresh on many objects.

She seemed to hear their soft whispers when she sat alone, quietly in the darkness of this room. It used to strike her that she had no right to enter this room, that, in possessing all the things of this room, she had acted like a thief.

"But how am I to blame? I did not want this. Grandfather said, 'Don't weep, sister. Have patience for a year or two. The old fellow is about to die and then we will get hold of his property first!'"

Zohra murmured to herself. "Property be damned." Her heart burnt inside her, like the scalding sensation one felt when a hot wind blew over a raw sore. She felt as if she was gradually choking. She nearly cried out once. The pupils of her two eyes burned wildly.

Her brain throbbed. Shaking her dishevelled hair, Zohra stepped outside. When she raised her eyes, her look fell on the *mehndi* plant near the well. The plant flourished in the tender wet earth. Young leaves grew thick on its branches.

She had made up her mind to cut down this plant many times, but had not been able to do so as yet. Today her right hand itched. Quickly entering the kitchen, she came out with a sharp kitchen knife in her hand. She began feverishly to cut off branch after branch with each stroke.

Zaigun came running. "What are you doing, ma' am? What is this? It is an old tree and has many uses. The master will be very angry when he hears about it."

"Oh, shut up. I know better than you who will be angry. I want to cut it down and I'll do it."

"I only work here for my food," Zaigun said. "What is it to me? I was speaking for your own good."

"Strange," Zohra looked up at her. "Do you have to worry about my good? Is there no one else in the world?"

Zaigun dared not cross her master's favourite wife any more. With a darkened face she went about her own chores.

Zohra could not say how the morning turned to noon, how evening came and how night fell and covered the face of the earth. Some one seemed to have cut out a part of her heart with a glittering, sharp knife. The tumultuous wave of everyday life evoked no response there. Only a wild fire burned there, like a piece of live coal hidden under ashes.

Hajee Kalimullah came to bed after saying his night prayers, and said, "You know, Batashi has sinned, just as I thought."

"How do you know?" asked Zohra.

Hajee Kalimullah replied, "You don't need much intelligence to find out these things. I struck the string in the right place and it rang out. Well, now there is nothing to worry about. Once the punishment is meted out, the rains will certainly come." He added after a short silence, "I'll raise the issue next Friday after midnight, and we'll see what happens."

Zohra lay quietly and looked outside. Why was the smell of the mango buds so intoxicating? Why was the night so black, so dark? It would be good if the sun never rose again. She would then be lost for ever alone in a land, all by herself.

Hajee Kalimullah felt a soft touch on his forehead and soon started to snore. But for that sound, Zohra would have felt that a dead man lay beside her with a white piece of cloth covering him from chest to feet. Pushing aside his hairy hand, she lay in silence for a few minutes more. Then she rose from the bed quietly and, carefully opening the door, stepped into the courtyard. She stood silently under the mango tree in the corner.

Just as Khaled was stealthily entering the house, Zohra swiftly crossed the courtyard and stood before him. She asked in a low, urgent voice, "Where have you been all day? You like to go without food, do you?"

Khaled did not even try to say a word. He stood there stockstill. Suddenly Zohra raised her right hand and slapped him hard on the cheek and cried out like a demented woman, "I can't bear this pain any more. Please go away from this house. Leave me alone, for God's sake."

Covering her face with her sari, she almost ran to the verandah, entered her room and barred the door.

Khaled stood rooted to the same spot. Tears trickled down his cheeks. He found his throat choking. He had left the house in the morning before any one was up. He had gone to the river bank and wandered aimlessly along the borders of the paddy fields. Then he had crossed over to the *ghat*, on the other bank, where his two elder brothers worked in a store. Nowhere did he find peace. And at last, drawn by some strange and unknown attraction, he had come back home.

At midnight that Friday, the village elders assembled in the sitting room of Maulana Mohiyuddin. The whole village knew of the affair by this time, thanks to muted whispers. But not everybody had the right to sit in judgment. Tonight only the elders, the pious, and the *alem*, learned in religious scriptures, were present in the gathering, They shut the doors and windows of the room, made the accused sit in the centre, and opened the discussion.

Hajee Kalimullah, after carefully going through the religious books and annotations for the last three days and nights, had come to a decision. With the permission of the Maulana he read out his judgment.

Batashi had been moaning softly for some time past. Now she burst into a loud wail, "Oh, mother, was this what was ordained for me? Why didn't you kill me at my birth, oh mother!"

"Stop crying," Hajee Kalimullah shouted. "You thought at that time it was great fun, didn't you?"

Maulana Mohiyuddin looked very thoughtful. He serene face grew melancholy and grave. Slowly raising his face, he asked in a quiet tone, "Well, do you have anything to say?"

"What shall I say, sir? You won't believe a poor woman. We are not human beings, we are cats and dogs in your eyes. How can we have any prestige?" Batashi wiped her eyes, "Otherwise how could you cast such aspersions on my character?"

"But such aspersions do not fall from the sky!" Hajee Kalimullah thundered. "Why is no one else being accused?"

"My ill fate is to blame for that. Otherwise, why did no one notice before that even while my husband lived I used to be sick frequently, that I could not live without eating tamarind and bits of burnt earth every day?"

Batashi's cousin Rahimuddin sat there wrapped in a dirty quilt and groaned from time to time. When he was questioned, he only stared blankly.

While the trial proceeded, the sky outside was being invaded by swarm after swarm of dark clouds from the south. Every now and then the moon was hidden. Light and shadow played hide and seek with the trees and the houses and the river.

And then suddenly the wind stopped blowing. Nature waited breathlessly for a long time. Deep rumblings of lightning streaked through the sky. Everyone within the room waited anxiously.

Exactly at that hour a human shadow stood under the mango tree behind Hajee Kalimullah's house. It walked on tiptoe, reached the window and looked into the dark room searchingly. Like a haunted building in the midst of an unknown forest, the entire house lay there holding its breath.

The figure moved away from the window, started moving up, keeping close to the wall, crossed the kitchen and stopped at the door of the bedroom. With each lighting flash, he seemed to shiver in fright.

Soon the wind started to blow. The clouds clashed with each other and roared. Everything seemed to break and tremble. The door of the room had not been barred. A sudden gust of wind banged it wide open. The man with quick, frightened steps stepped onto the verandah, looked to this side and that for a second, and rushed into the room in desperation. There was a terrific sound above, below, on all sides. Sound and more sound. With each stormy gust of wind, the corrugated sheets of the roof groaned and twisted. The wooden walls creaked loudly.

The man came near the bed, then hesitated, as if he did not know what to do next. The hair on his body stood on end, his heart beat wildly. The blood rose to his head and his eyes blurred. Where was he? Was this life or death? Was this the anguish of giving up all or the savage joy of intense union? He pricked up his ears and heard the soft jingling of bangles, the sound of a deep serene breathing and the tender rustling of clothes. Oh no, not here! He did not want this. He could not want this.

He was backing out step by step when he suddenly felt a pair of soft, smooth, naked arms drawing him close.

The clouds in the sky above had, by then, engaged in a mad scramble. The world shook with the roar of each thunder clap. The sharp, strong stormy wind tore at the trees in a mad fury. Someone seemed to be bent upon an insane orgy of destruction and chaos. Churned out of the depths of heaven, earth and hell, the wild chorus of primeval chaos arose and engulfed everything.

There was only the protest of the newborn when the rains first came, accompanied by sharp stabs of wind. They blew over the fields and houses in windy gusts. But soon this changed. Like the prolonged tune of classical music, the rain fell in heavy showers as the fury of the wind grew less. After that there was only a regular, rhythmic patter.

No one was conscious of the passage of time. After a while the man opened the door of the room, stumbled across the courtyard in the streaming rain and vanished into a room in the northern corner. Zohra followed him out into the verandah and stood there with her dishevelled clothes. The rain fell on her body and drenched her.

After a while Hajee Kalimullah entered the house with an umbrella over his head. He was panting.

Zohra cried out in fear, "Why are you so late? I felt so frightened!"

"What could I do? Well, it is all over now." Placing the umbrella against the wall, Hajee Kalimullah said, "She is a hardened whore. We couldn't get a confession from her even up to the last. But I am no baby that I can't see through the excuses of a woman like Batashi. Both were soundly beaten with shoes and tomorrow they will leave the village for good. And look at the blessings of God! The rains came immediately."

"So they did. Strange, isn't it?" With these words Zohra stepped down from the verandah into the courtyard despite the heavy downpour. She was acting strangely.

Hajee Kalimullah protested anxiously, "What are you doing? Have you gone mad? If you get drenched so late at night you'll catch cold!"

"Oh no, I never catch cold." Zohra stepped upto the verandah. She pushed back a cluster of damp hair from her eyes with her right hand. Raising her excited face that looked like a blossoming flower, she said with her sweet, laughter-laden lips, "Why, don't you know that it is good to get drenched in the first rains of the year? What a wonderful crop this will give us!"

Translated by Kabir Chowdhury.

"The Rains" was anthologized in *An Anthology of Contemporary Short Stories of Bangladesh.*

Relief Camp

Khaleda Salahuddin

Jaigun lights the earthenware stove. When she came to the relief camp, Jaigun had somehow managed to salvage a few battered pots and pans, some patched clothes wrapped in a quilt, a couple of rusty tins of powdered milk and her old earthenware stove. The stove had given her good service during storms and monsoon rains. People like Jaigun have to move frequently. Sometimes the policemen come and break up their shanties. Sometimes during heavy rains the low-lying roadsides are inundated. Their temporary shelters are flooded. Cellophane and sacking can no longer provide them refuge. And sometimes there are floods, as this time. This was no ordinary flood. It was a deluge. Everything was inundated. Even a small flood is bad enough to uproot them, send them looking for a dry shelter. But wherever she goes, Jaigun is careful to take her earthenware stove with her.

As soon as the floods started, several places of the capital Dhaka were submerged. Relief camps were set up in areas that had remained above flood level. Jaigun came to this relief camp with her pregnant daughter Batashi and her ten-year-old son Abul.

This is a primary school. Many people have taken shelter here. Many have come with their entire family, others have come alone. The place is crowded. It doesn't matter. They are safe from the deadly reach of the flood. They have a place to rest their heads at night. It is true that perhaps they have only one full meal of *khichuri* or bread each day. If they get something to eat for lunch, they might not get something for dinner. But it does not hurt them too much even if they get nothing for dinner. They are used to having nothing to eat. Sometimes they miss one meal, sometimes both. Here they are getting at least a meal a day. Of course, they have only had either *khichuri* or bread for several days and they are all longing to eat rice. Yesterday afternoon some people had distributed relief materials. They had brought a huge truck full of bags of rice, lentils and small packets of salt. They had also given them some candles and matchboxes. Those people were really kind. They had crossed the black flood waters to bring them so many things. How much sympathy they had for poor folks.

Deep in her thoughts, Jaigun takes two more scraps of paper from the bundle that Abul had brought and feeds the stove. The flames brighten. She also throws in the broken leg of a bench. She is cooking rice after such a long time. Batashi is nearing her term. She should be delivering any day now. Before the floods came, Abul used to carry lunch-boxes to offices. Now all work has stopped. How is he going to wade through these waters to do anything? He is such a little boy. Batashi's husband is a rickshaw puller. When the floods came he just disappeared one day—and has not returned. Jaigun's husband was also a rickshaw puller. He used to suffer from asthma. Towards the end, despite his illness, he had to continue pulling in order to feed his family. He died a couple of years ago of asthma. Jaigun had managed to carry on working as a daily woman in several houses. She has the added responsibility of her pregnant daughter now. She can't even go to work now because of the flood waters. What can she do? Everything is God's wish.

Jaigun washes the rice and puts the pot on the stove. The girl had asked for rice the other day. She had said, "Mother, I don't feel like eating *khichuri* any more. If I could only eat some rice. "

Jaigun had given her a good scolding. "Rice, rice, rice! Where will I get rice for you? If I could go to work I could get a little rice for you. But isn't it enough that you are getting some *khichuri* and bread to eat? It isn't in your destiny to eat rice, so how do you expect to eat it?"

But after getting the rice yesterday, Jaigun had thought of cooking it for dinner. But she had been too exhausted to do so.

They had to be satisfied with a little left-over *khichuri* for dinner. Today she will cook some rice and lentils and give it to Batashi as soon as it is ready. After all, she is pregnant. And there are so many things one wants to eat in her state. Jaigun rues her destiny. Not to be able to satisfy her daughter's craving! She heaves a sigh and returns to her cooking.

Jaigun's family used to live in a Rayer Bazaar slum. They had been able to find some shelter on the sloping banks of the dying river. When the floods came, their slum was inundated. During last year's floods at least their bamboo rooftops had remained standing above the flood waters. This time the black swirling flood waters had come so rapidly that, even before they knew it, their entire slum was inundated. The slum-dwellers hurriedly moved to the higher ground near the tiled house. They raised bamboo shelters to keep their humble possessions: patched quilts, bundles of clothes, pots and pans, a few tins of powdered milk. Jaigun also kept her mud stove on the bamboo platform. No, the waters could never reach this high. In a couple of days they would be able to return to their old homes. But that very night the flood waters covered the bamboo platform and all. Much of Dhaka was by then under chest-deep water. Boats were navigating the main streets. Jaigun's family had to carry their bundles on their heads and wade through shoulder-high water to reach this relief camp. People had come from all over for shelter. So many people, so many faces. There was a small field in front of the school house. On the east was a spreading mango tree. Rahima Bibi from Rahmatganj laid out her betel leaf and areca nuts under the tree. She managed to earn a tidy sum selling betel. Naimuddin from Keraniganj sold lentils and potatoes. He used to have a small grocery shop in Keraniganj. The flood had inundated his shop.

Karim Sheikh had come to the camp with his wife and four children. He used to sell baked and steamed rice cakes. He had managed to save some ground rice and molasses from the flood waters. Finding a few dry spots on the footpath, he carried on with his business. Some buying and selling still went on.

Chan Bibi came from Kamrangichar. Harried by the flood, she had finally managed to make her way to the relief camp. Her

wo-year-old was suffering from diarrhoea. A volunteer group had
:ome with some packets of oral saline which she gave the toddler.

All of Bangladesh seems to be floating on a raft. Dhaka is
loating. People are floating. But life goes on, slowly recovering
rom its close embrace by the deadly cold waters of the great flood.

Setting down the rice pot, Jaigun calls out to Batashi. "Come
1ere a little. Wash the lentils and put them on the fire. It is quite
ate. Abul will come and shout, 'Give me my lunch, give me my
unch.' How can I manage everything all by myself?"

Batashi, with her bloated body, is sleeping in one corner. She
sn't feeling at all well. Hearing her mother, she sits up somehow.
5he rolls up the torn mat and sets it upright behind the bundles of
:heir clothing. Then, covering her head with the edge of her sari,
she goes and sits beside her mother.

"What is it? Aren't you feeling all right? How are you feeling?"

"No, I'm not feeling well. Since morning I have been having
:his strange pain in my back and stomach. " Her face is distorted
with pain.

"That's nothing. Go and sleep. I'll put up the lentils myself."
Jaigun tries to comfort her daughter.

"Give me the lentils. Let me at least pick the lentils. I'll manage.
It won't be any trouble." Batashi takes the packet of lentils from her
mother and pours the grains into a chipped enamel pot.

Suddenly, hearing a lot of shouting outside, everyone hurries in
the direction of the noise. Shonaban, the wife of Karim Sheikh, is
shouting at the top of her voice.

"You son of a devil, how dare you steal my ground rice? I'll chop
off your head and throw it into the flood waters. Do you
understand, you beggar's son? Have you never seen a rice cake?
Hasn't your beggar of a mother ever given you any to eat?"

"I'm warning you. Don't insult my parents." Abul protests shrilly.

"Why not? What will you do? Let me hear. The beggar's son
doesn't bother about his parents when he's stealing, does he? Just
wait. I'm going to hand you over to the police." Shonaban tugs at
Abul's hand with all her might. A little powdered rice and molasses
fall to the ground.

Hearing Abul's voice, Jaigun leaves her cooking and runs out.

Like a hawk, she snatches Abul from Shonaban's grip Immediately, all hell breaks loose. Jaigun starts shouting at the top of her voice. "You bitch! You want to hand over my Abul to the police! Before that I'll send you to the dock. Who stole my red towel? Do you think I don't know?"

"Who's a thief? I? Say it, say I'm a thief. " Shonaban pulls her sari tight around her waist and leaps forward.

"Well, if you haven't stolen my towel, your son has. Haven't we seen your son with it? I can still see with both eyes. I have not become blind."

"You beggar! My husband bought my son the towel. Who said that that was your towel? God will not stand such blatant lies. Do you hear?"

"Huh, his father bought it for him. Just because you say so doesn't mean anything. You'll say all sorts of things now. Who took my towel then, you whore?"

This time Shonaban lifts both hands and starts shouting, "Oh my God, this woman is accusing my son of stealing her towel. How could she tell this terrible lie?" She approaches Jaigun and gesticulates wildly. "God will punish you. Your tongue will fall off."

By now a crowd has gathered to watch the fight. Sometimes they put in a word or two to fan the tempers. Sometimes they anger Jaigun, sometimes Shonaban.

Rahima Bibi has by now stopped selling her betel goods and come up panting. "Oh Shonaban, oh Jaigun, why are you fighting? Stop your shouting and screaming. Relief is coming, relief. I had gone to the roadside. That's how I know."

On hearing the word "relief" the furore dies down. The battlefield is soon empty. Everyone quickly collects whatever they can from the school room—chipped pots, pans, dishes, trays, plates, tins, mugs.

On the south of the school field there is a narrow, unpaved lane that meets the elevated concrete street. Some of the destitute rush to see whether relief is really forthcoming. Yes, a group of relief workers are approaching the camp. A truck with a red cotton banner across its bonnet rolls down the street and stops at the head of the narrow lane. A jeep has also accompanied the truck.

Naimuddin runs back and scolds everyone, "Why are you crowding around like this? Queue up—queue up. Make a queue and sit down all of you. If you all behave like this, the sahibs will not give any relief."

No, this time the relief workers have not brought *khichuri* but cans of milk powder and packets of oral saline. The relief has come from the "National Children's Welfare Association." In a little while, the organizers of the relief camp make their appearance. The milk powder is dissolved in three large red plastic buckets that the volunteers have brought with them. As soon as the distribution starts, the video camera that the relief team have brought starts rolling. It is necessary to document the unhappy plight of the people affected by the flood. In about an hour's time the distribution of the packets of oral saline and the milk is completed and the work of the relief workers satisfactorily recorded by the video camera.

Jaigun and Shonaban have completely forgotten their quarrel in the scramble for milk and oral saline. It is quite late in the afternoon. Time has passed so quickly in quarreling and collecting relief that no one has had any time to eat.

Jaigun doles out the rice and lentils in plates and then calls out to Batashi and Abul. "Where are you? Batashi, come here with Abul. Come and eat. It is almost evening."

"I haven't seen Abul. Who knows where he's gone."

Jaigun is furious. The boy is really becoming a nuisance. "Where are you, you rascal? You make my insides burn up."

Abul is sitting quietly behind the school house. He has been upset all afternoon. Why did he try to snatch a handful of rice powder and molasses? Every day Karim Chacha peddles rice cakes. Who knows where he goes? After selling whatever he can, he gives the rest to his children to eat. Abul also feels like eating rice cakes. But how will he ever buy rice cakes? They have no money.

He is feeling very hungry. Very, very hungry. He had left very early that morning to wade through the flood waters to collect discarded scraps of paper. Maghbazar, Eskaton, Elephant Road, who knows where else. Those places have not been affected by the floods. Kalu, Habul, Mintu had also gone with him. If they didn't bring paper, how would the stove be lit? Of course, several people

had broken the chairs and benches of the school to light their fires.
What else were they to do? Most places had been submerged.
Where were they to get dry leaves or scraps of paper?

"Abul, where are you hiding? Won't you eat? Won't you have
some rice?"

At his mother's voice, Abul rises in some trepidation. Hearing
the word "rice," his insides cramp with hunger. He walks quietly
towards the verandah.

Most evenings the relief camp is dark. Unless there is some
urgent need, the refugees have no light. They safeguard the half
burnt stubs of candle as zealously as the wealth of Croesus. Most
nights there is no bother of cooking. If there is some leftover lunch
it is eaten before nightfall. Only those who can earn a little despite
the flood are able to have any dinner.

It is after ages that Jaigun's family have eaten rice and lentils to
their heart's content. Having eaten late, Jaigun doesn't eat anything.
Before nightfall, she gives Abul and Batashi the milk that had been
distributed earlier in the day.

Night descends slowly. Like a woman covering her face with her
sari edge before going to sleep, the relief camp covers its face with
the black darkness of night. The mango tree in the corner stands like
a ghostly sentinel in the night. The lane in front of the school is not
a busy one. By nightfall, the place is silent as a graveyard.

Like the others, Jaigun's family lies down to sleep on a mat that
has been covered with a quilt and waits for morning.

In the middle of the night, Jaigun is woken up by Batashi.
Batashi is groaning with pain. "Mother, mother, wake up. My back
is paining. The pain keeps coming. Oh, God!"

"What is the matter, daughter? Is it paining very much? It's
nothing, it's nothing. Don't be afraid. You'll be all right. All your
aches and pains will soon vanish." Trying to comfort her daughter,
Jaigun gropes in the dark for a candle and matches. She lights the
candle and her eyes fall on Batashi's contorted face. Oh God, what is
she to do now? Candle in hand, she wakes up Rahima Bibi who is
sleeping in a corner of the verandah.

"Oh, Sister Rahima, do get up. Come and have a look at my
daughter. What am I to do all by myself? I am frightened."

Rahima Bibi has always been a light sleeper. She wakes up immediately. She's sixty years old, with graying hair. But she is still firm and strong. In her village she had often assisted at births. She often narrates stories of those days. All the wives and mothers of the village were extremely fond of her. Remembering those days, Rahima Bibi is overcome with emotion. Nevertheless she had to leave the village when the river devoured her home. Like many others of her village, Rahima Bibi joined the floating population. Even then she was able to stand on her own feet. She was able to earn her own living.

Roused from sleep, Rahima Bibi rubs her eyes. Hearing Jaigun, she says, "Don't be afraid. Aren't I here? Back in my village, I helped deliver countless babies. Don't be afraid."

By this time several people have woken up. Chan Bibi emerges onto the verandah from her room. Seeing her, Rahima Bibi says, "I'm going to sit with the girl. Go and heat some water, do you hear? Jaigun, hang up a sari this side. Don't let anyone come in."

Rahima Bibi takes full charge of the situation. On one side of the verandah a sari is hung to give some privacy. Batashi is made to lie down on a mat that has been covered with a quilt. A number of candles are collected for light.

Everyone shares Jaigun's anxiety. What is going to happen? Everyone stretches out hands of sympathy. All of them are after all one large family. From the other side of the curtain, Naimuddin asks, "Oh Sister Rahima, will we have to take her to the hospital?"

"Let us wait a little. If I see any problem, of course I'll tell you all," Rahima replies.

Batashi is groaning in unbearable pain. Her heart-rending cries rend the darkness of night. Roused from sleep, Abul is terrified. Clapping his hands to his ears, Abul runs outside. His eyes streaming, Abul sits on the school steps. He prays desperately, "Dear God, please save my sister. Please save her, God. I will never steal again, dear God."

All the waters of the Ganges and the Jamuna flow down Abul's eyes. His little heart seems to drown in the tears.

Finally, the night comes to an end. The soft touch of dawn lights up the horizon. The mango tree blazes resplendent in the early light.

A gentle rain falls lightly on Abul's cheeks and on his dry, tousled hair. From a distant mosque floats the call to prayer, "*Assalatu khairul minan naim.*" The sudden cry of a newborn lights up the eyes of the camp dwellers.

"Batashi, see, see, what a lovely son you have. Oh Jaigun, fill your eyes with the sight of your grandson." Rahima Bibi cries out joyfully. She is happy that she has been able to help Batashi in her hour of need. Rahima Bib's heart fills with satisfaction.

Jaigun's tired old eyes are streaming like the Brahmaputra. Her heart brimming with joy, she says, "You were a great help, Sister. Without you I wouldn't have been able to save the girl."

"What rubbish you talk, Jaigun. God is the one who saves. How much could I have done? And what did I do after all? Wouldn't I have done the same for my own girl? Isn't Batashi like my own daughter? What do you say? " Rahima Bibi's eyes light up with joy.

"After all, we all are one family. Is Batashi an outsider?" Chan Bibi comes forward. Jaigun, Rahima Bibi, Chan Bibi and Anwara carefully clean mother and child. The men have been waiting outside on the lawn. Now Naimuddin comes forward and says, "Oh, Jaigun, don't you need the *azaan* to be said in the ears of your grandson?"

"Yes, yes, but who will do it?"

"Why, I will do it. In my village didn't I give the *azaan* five times a day?"

Jaigun, Rahima Bibi, and Anwara have a wash and then sit down in the verandah to rest. They have had a tiring night. The birth of a human being is not easy. Pain and labour attend a human birth.

No one notices Abul entering and sitting down beside the new-born. He stares wide-eyed at the baby.

"What are you staring at like that? You are very happy, aren't you, to become an uncle?"

Abul looks up startled. So do the others. Sonaban is standing there smiling with a plateful of *pithas.*

"Abul, wipe your tears. Today is a happy day for you. Here, sweeten your mouth with a *pitha,*" Sonaban says, stuffing a *pitha* into Abul's hands. Then she puts the plate in front of Rahima Bibi.

"Here, sweeten your mouth as well. For the first time a child has been born here. It is a happy day for all of us."

Jaigun is sitting silently a little further off. Sonaban goes up to her, holding out both her arms. "Come, Sister. Come and eat a bite."

Jaigun looks at Sonaban in surprise. Sonaban is smiling. Jaigun holds out her hands to Sonaban.

Translated by Niaz Zaman.

"Relief Camp" was anthologized as "*Baan*" in *Nirbachita Galpa*, published by Palak Publishers, 1991. This English translation was published earlier in *Holiday*, September 22, 1995.

The Poet

Syed Shamsul Haq

Poet Abdur Rab Munshi died on the first day of the Bengali New Year, 1 *Baishakh*, 1370 in his native village of Tamai in Pabna. He was only forty-eight years old.

Today, while presenting his collected poems to the literary world, I am tempted to say a few words. I am no professional critic or editor. I have no training to enable me to say things in a neat and orderly fashion on the technical aspects of literature. I shall, therefore, relate some incidents of Mr. Munshi's life. It wouldn't perhaps be an introduction befitting an editor, but that does not disturb me. For I believe that I have a clearer and more intimate conception of his life than of his work. To me the joy of a little boy building a castle of sand at the sea shore is more precious than his skill as an architect.

This happened about ten years ago. My first book of short stories had just been published. Without mentioning its title, let me only say that it was preeminently a first effort. As I look back today, I recall the many sleepless nights I passed with the book under my pillow and the many wise, well-read, respectable people I presented my book to with a steady hand and a stout heart.

During those days, whenever I went anywhere, I invariably carried a few copies of my book with me. Whoever talked intimately and sincerely with me got a copy of my book as a gift with his name neatly inscribed in it.

It was at that time that I first met poet Abdur Rab Munshi. I had gone to visit my aunt, my father's sister, after many years. In fact, I was more interested in seeing the village than her.

It was a real village, all right. Nearly seventeen miles away from the nearest town. There was no regular road that led to it. During the rains it had one kind of a road and, during the summer, another. My uncle had sent a messenger with a bicycle to the railway station. When I got to the village it was eleven at night. I should have reached by six in the evening, but the cycle broke down midway, and I had to walk the rest of the way. And the walk was far from being speedy. For one thing, I was not used to walking on a rustic path. On top of it, I had to lug along the disabled bicycle.

My uncle's home was on the other side of a canal. One had to cross the canal in a dinghy. As I waited to cross, I saw a few shadowy figures anxiously scanning this bank. When I went over, I found my uncle standing there, anxiety writ large on his face, and my aunt almost on the verge of tears. I immediately told them about the breakdown of the bicycle.

I heard the name of Abdur Rab Munshi that very night. My uncle told me that Mr. Munshi had been waiting for my arrival since dusk. He had come to know that I was a writer, and he wanted to meet me. As we ate, I learnt that Mr. Munshi wrote poems and composed songs. Uncle said, "He will come tomorrow and make your acquaintance."

I remember that I was very thrilled. Perhaps it was because some one was anxious to see me simply because I wrote. As far as I remember, Abdur Rab Munshi was the very first human being who had come forward to meet me as a writer.

But he didn't come the next day. A week went by and still I didn't see him. I asked my uncle about him every now and then, which annoyed him.

"Munshi's words don't mean much. Who knows? Perhaps he is busy reciting his poems somewhere right at this moment. You poets are a crazy bunch."

I smiled sheepishly to take the edge off his banter. I was not aware of the norms of rural social etiquette. I gathered that if I first went to Mr. Munshi's home on my own, it would adversely affect my uncle's social position. Uncle was a man of property, while Mr. Munshi had only a few acres of land. In this situation it was out of the question that I should go and pay him a visit.

The desire to meet Mr. Munshi waxed warmer inside me. One day an unforeseen opportunity come up. Uncle had a cousin brother of his, about the same age as me. I called him Uncle, too. They were rather poorly off. He was studying in the city with great hardship in order to prepare himself to be a druggist's assistant. On that day I had gone out with him in a dinghy. We moved up the canal in a leisurely way without any specific destination. My companion worked at the oar.

I had a bag with me where I carried my writing materials: a few sheets of paper, a pen and two copies of my book. While spending my days in the village, I attended to one thing—I carefully looked at the various trees and shrubs and creepers and birds and wrote down their names and a few descriptive lines about them in my note-book. That was why I had my writing kitbag with me.

We were moving up toward the Baumari Lake. Suddenly my companion—I will refer to him as my young uncle from now on—pointed to a house in the distance and told me that it belonged to Abdur Rab Munshi. I looked at it with interest. It was a house with a corrugated iron roof, pleasantly encircled by betel nut and berry trees. The courtyard of the outhouse came down steeply to the edge of the canal. From my moving dinghy, the picturesque house seemed to be swirling closer to me.

"Hey ! let's go to Mr. Munshi's place."

My young uncle seemed to make a faint gesture of protest, or it was possible that I was mistaken. He asked, "Do you want to go there?"

"Yes, let's."

"Who knows if he is in or not." My young uncle seemed to be doubtful.

Trying my best to keep my voice steady and natural, I murmured, "Let's go and find out. No harm in that, is there?"

By then our dinghy had left the main canal and entered a subsidiary stream. Mr. Munshi's house stood by the bank. My young uncle moored the boat at the landing *ghat* attached to

Mr. Munshi's house. We climbed the steep bank and stood in Mr. Munshi's outer courtyard.

It was a neatly swept courtyard. Two big berry trees grew close to the steps of the thouse. Underneath one of them, a low bamboo platform provided seating accommodation. Under another tree was piled a hay stack. Two cows browsed nearby, lazily munching hay. The silence was unbroken except for the murmur of the water flowing in the canal. The whole house appeared quiet and still.

My young uncle went up to the thatched wall of the house and, raising his voice, called out, "O, Poet-uncle, are you in?"

There was an answering sound. Then a middle-aged man came out. He was wearing a *lungi*, but his upper body was bare. His arms were plastered with mud and rice husks right up to his elbow joints. He made a fleeting appearance, for, as soon as his eyes fell on me, he drew quickly back into his home.

My young uncle asked aloud, "O, Poet-uncle, why did you run away? See whom I have brought."

But there was no response. After a short while, a little girl with a ball of puffed rice and molasses in her hand came out and said to my young uncle, "Father has asked you two to wait."

After nearly half an hour, poet Abdur Rab Munshi came out to meet us. He had put on a freshly laundered *lungi*, a *kurta*— somewhat torn but clean and snow-white—with a yellow-brown shawl thrown over his shoulders, a pair of wooden sandals and a cap on his head. When I raised my hand and greeted him, he felt very embarrassed. He avoided looking at me and smiled at my young uncle without a word, as if I was not there at all. Then he said, "Come in. Please sit down, Doctor."

I was amused to learn that my young uncle had become a doctor even before he had qualified to be a druggist's assistant. I began to scrutinize Mr. Munshi.

He started to talk with my young uncle. He inquired about the progress of his medical studies, commented on the work of the newly recruited Bengali teacher at the local school, pointed to the two cows standing close by and said that they now gave over six litres of milk.

I did not know what to say. I had wanted to meet him, but what exactly should I say now? I could not decide what to do though I clearly felt that I ought to say some thing. At last I murmured, "I have heard that you write poems."

"Oh, no. Who told you that?" Abdur Rab Munshi protested in a startled tone. Then he smiled as if caught in some mischief. "There is hardly any time. Making a living keeps me too busy." Then he thought that perhaps he had not said enough. So he added shyly, "Would you like our writings? I have little education, you know. There was a poet-singer in our village, Jamal Hossain by name. And then I had a headmaster during any childhood who used to write beautiful poems. Inspired by their examples, I started to write on my own. That's all. People for no reason call me a poet. I am nothing."

Now one can read these words, but how can I bring to life the manner in which he had spoken them on that day? Pausing every now and then, making many vague gestures with his hands, without glancing at me, and with his eyes on some figures on the outer bank of the canal, he slowly uttered the above words.

But my young uncle protested. Turning to me he said, "Look, you have not seen his poems. There is no one in twenty villages around here who can write so beautifully. People around here sing his songs all the time, on all occasions. Our students recite his poems in school functions."

I said, "I have brought with me a book of mine. I would like to present it to you." So far I had presented my book to various persons on the basis of only slight and casual acquaintance. That day, while giving away my book, I felt within me an extraordinary sensation of joy and happiness. Poet Abdur Rab Munshi accepted my book with trembling hands. His eyes filled with tears. He rested his eyes for a long time on his name in the book carefully written by me. He leafed through some pages. His eyes grew thoughtful. Then, suddenly closing the book, he stood up and went inside his house without a word.

My young uncle said, "Let's go. It is getting dark."

Mr. Munshi returned with a little pocket-size book in his hand. It had a green cover. He said, "I have published a book. Its title is *Necklace*." There was a picture of a rose at the bottom, the picture that a rural press usually prints on wedding cards. Below the picture of the rose were written these words: "Composed and published by

Abdur Rab Munshi." Eight foolscap folded sheets, carelessly printed, in broken types. Eight pages. Price ten annas. Mr. Munshi's first book.

My young uncle said, "But you have another book, haven't you?"

Mr. Munshi answered shyly, "I don't have it with me now. It's a book of songs. My eldest boy has gone with all the copies to Satbere market to sell them."

I learned that his son went with the book of songs to the market every market day. The boy had a beautiful voice. He sang his father's songs, sold as many copies of the book as he could, and, with the little money that he got, bought vegetables and other items of food and household needs from the market and returned home. The market broke at about eleven p.m. Mr. Munshi said that he would visit me next morning and give me a copy of his book of songs.

We were entertained with puffed rice and sherbet.

That was my first meeting with poet Abdur Rab Munshi. I was young then, but the experience is still so vivid in my mind that it seems that our meeting took place only yesterday.

I read all Mr. Munshi's poems that same night on my return home. Almost all the poems had nature for their subject; some were about the seasons which demonstrated the graciousness of God. Some pieces were addressed to a remote and mysterious woman. The feeling for rhyme and rhythm was amazingly developed.

Next day Mr. Munshi's eldest son, an adolescent boy, came and gave me his father's book of songs. They echoed the tone of the transience of life. At the top of every song there were clear directions about the tune and beat and musical score. I requested the young boy to sing me a song, any that he cared to sing. He declined at first. He said he had no instrument with him. He promised to come back later and sing me a song some other time. But I insisted. Then he began to sing. It was an amazingly open and rich voice. Almost unexpected. Aided by the musical tune, the words seemed in a moment to leave the dusty earth and fly away towards Heaven. The soft murmur of the canal water accompanied the music. The skies, winds, rivers of Bengal, its life, seemed to penetrate the core of consciousness like an intoxicant.

The same evening I went out alone in a dinghy to Mr. Munshi's house. One day's training from my young uncle had taught me a great deal about rowing a boat.

I shall never forget that evening in my life. Everything looked tender and melancholy in the crimson-bluish light of the setting sun. As I approached his house, I saw poet Abdur Rab Munshi seated on the bamboo platform under the berry tree, waiting for me, his eyes fixed on the canal water. When he saw me, he said agitatedly that I should not have come like this, alone in a dinghy. It was not safe.

And then, for the first time, I suddenly had an intimate feeling of oneness with him. My uncle did not approve of my visit to this village poet. When I recalled that I felt a stab of sharp pain in my heart. Everything in the village beside Mr. Munshi appeared strange and false to me.

The two of us sat without a word under the leafy tree. Slowly the whole world grew dark. Then the Great Bear and other stars began to shine in the sky. A few tiny dots of fire appeared in some distant village huts, as though they wanted it to be known that there were homes there with human beings. The two milch cows lowed once. Roused from his reverie, Mr. Munshi called aloud to his son, "Take a lamp and have a look inside the cowshed." Noticing my surprise at his concerned tone, Mr. Munshi explained to me in his usual soft voice that sometimes during the night snakes came into the cowshed to suck milk from the udders of the cows. I felt a prickly sensation all over me.

All the little sounds and incidents of that evening began to weave around me the magic web of the deep and eternal truths of life.

Poet Abdur Rab Munshi himself rowed the dinghy and brought me back to the landing of my uncle's home.

After a few days he called on me. My uncle was a strange person. He was not in favour of going to Mr. Munshi's place, but when the latter came to visit him he was the typical gracious host, welcoming him smilingly. He asked the servant to bring a chair for Mr. Munshi. And then, pulling deeply at his hubble-bubble, he asked, "So, how are you, Poet? Have you met our poet here?"

To prevent the unpleasant truth coming out, I quickly said, "Yes, we met when I went to the market place with my young uncle."

Some villagers came at this point to my uncle with their problems and petitions. Mr. Munshi and I moved away and began to walk quietly along the bank of the canal.

My young uncle came and joined us. Breaking the long silence, he asked Mr. Munshi, "Have you read his book of short stories?"

"Couldn't make time yet. But I certainly will."

However, it seemed to me that he had read my book, or rather had tried to, but couldn't make much progress. I somehow realized quite clearly that the world I wrote about, the language I wrote in, were quite unfamiliar to him. I realized that any talk about my book in the present atmosphere and context would be completely out of tune.

I quickly intervened, "Let's not talk of it." Then I said, "Your poems are beautiful. I liked them very much. The other day I even heard one of your songs sung by your son."

"Yes, he told me. I would like to arrange a session of songs for you."

"How wonderful," said I. "I'll certainly go. You must let me hear your new poems and songs, those that are not in your books."

Mr. Munshi laughed shyly, soundlessly. I haven't been able to forget even today that feeling of tender embarrassment towards his own writings. I don't know why, I suddenly felt a strong urge to drive away that embarrassment of his. I asked him, "Well, I find that you paint the picture of nature in your poems again and again. Why do you do that?"

He was not used to such questions. People liked his poems, or they disliked them. But what kind of a question was that?

For a long time he did not say anything. When I repeated my question, he answered, "I really don't know. You see, when I look around I feel that all those things are no strangers to me. When I am hurt it seems that even that creeper over there cries out in pain. When I am happy, I see the reflection of that joy all around me. I think, my father and his father and his father before him, they had all seen these creepers and shrubs and trees, these clouds and raindrops, this sun and moon. They passed away. We now see all those things. Those who went away scattered their spirit among these things. Whatever I write come from the words I hear, from these clouds and raindrops and sun and moon. I only try to mingle my thoughts with theirs, that's all. You are laughing at my words, aren't you? You say to yourself, what is this crazy fellow talking about, eh?"

"No, no, please go on."

But somehow a barrier had been created between us. Or perhaps he thought that I was an educated city-bred fellow and he a rustic, an unlettered person. In any case he clamped up, and I could not make him talk again freely that night.

The sound of a dinghy being rowed along the canal reached us. The poet called out, "Who goes there?"

From the darkness a cheerful voice came ringing back, "Is that the poet? You want to go home?"

He took his leave.

Two days later I returned to Dhaka. The present becomes the past. The past becomes a memory. And memory lies asleep. Without the touch of a relevant association, her sleep remains unbroken. I forgot all about poet Abdur Rab Munshi.

Then after about four years my young uncle came to Dhaka. He was to appear before an interview board for a government job. He put up at my place.

One day, in course of our conversation, he asked me if I remembered poet Abdur Rab Munshi. "That village poet, you know?"

In a moment, raising a ripple in the stream of memory, the poet came up as fresh as ever. I remembered his first look at me, his furtive withdrawal to change his dress, his anxious waiting for me seated under the berry tree, our mysterious conversation in the dark as we walked along the bank of the canal—all flashed in my memory at the same time. I felt happy and said, "Yes, of course I remember him. How is he? Hasn't he published anything else in the mean time?"

My young uncle picked up the first question and replied to it. I detected a note of sadness in his tone, no, not sadness; more like a sense of guilt. He muttered, "He is all right."

An unknown apprehension made me uneasy. Gradually, I learnt everything.

In the election last year Mr. Altaf Talukdar was a candidate from that area. My young uncle asked me if I had heard the name of

Mr. Talukdar. I said, "No." He said, "Well, he came to your uncle's home one day when you were there. Didn't you see him then?"

I grew impatient and said, "That's not important. Go on. What happened to Mr. Munshi? Tell me about him."

He told me that Mr. Talukdar was a candidate at the election and my uncle was one of his major supporters. "You know that all kinds of amusing propaganda gimmicks are organized during election time, don't you? Dramatic skits are presented, feasts are held, clowns parade the streets, songs are written and sung in market-places. Well, your uncle sent word to the poet, asking him to come and see him.

"He couldn't come that day. Next day your uncle's messengers went to Mr. Munshi's place again and brought him over in a dinghy.

"Your uncle said, 'Munshi, you have to compose some new songs. You know that Mr. Talukdar is contesting the elections. There is no hope for the country's welfare if we can't make him win. Got it? It is a job for the country, but don't think that we won't honour you. Mr. Talukdar knows how to respect a man of merit. Besides, when I am involved there can't be any question about anything, can there? Well! Why do you keep mum? Come on, gird up your loins and write a powerful song for us!'

" 'I have no time for that,' Poet Abdur Rab Munshi's voice sounded like a thunderbolt.

"My uncle roared, 'What's that? What did you say?'

" 'What could I say? I said that I had no time.'

" 'Have you gone crazy or what? You have no time for such an important work? Can you utter those words standing before me like this?'

"The poet remained silent.

" 'Tell me your inner thoughts. Come, now.'

" 'I won't be able to write any song.'

" 'Why not?' My uncle's eyes contracted in anger and surprise, and his voice grew thin like the blade of a knife.

"Mr. Munshi answered, 'Are you asking me to compose songs about one who is not fit to be called a man?'

" 'Control your tongue, Munshi. In the forest one has to salute the tiger. Always. A small fry shouldn't have a big mouth.

Be respectful toward the respectable. You may leave now. I would like to hear a song of yours tomorrow morning.'

" 'Why one? Why don't you hear ten songs of mine? I compose songs for all of you, so that you can all hear them. But, please, don't make this request. I can't write the songs you want me to write now.'

" 'Then you aren't willing to do my bidding?'

" 'No.'

" 'Is there no other poet besides you in the land?'

" 'Of course there is.'

" 'You are making a mistake, Munshi. Think again. What you have said, you have said. There's still time to beg pardon and make amends. Tell us, what are you going to do?'

" 'I have said my say. One who is not a human being, one who has never lifted his hand to help the poor, one who is a mean hypocrite—I to write songs for such a one? Never! How can you propose such a thing, Sir?'

"As Mr. Munshi uttered the last words, perhaps a satiric smile hovered around his lips.

"My uncle kept absolutely quiet for a few seconds, as if he was thunderstruck. Then, raising his eyes, he said, 'All right, you can go?'

" 'Good day.'

"Mr. Munshi left. He didn't even get a reply to his parting salute. My uncle drily murmured. 'You won't ever have to write any song, Munshi. I know the kind of medicine you need.' "

My young uncle offered his own comment as he recounted the events of those days. "Whatever you may say, my dear nephew, my cousin didn't do the right thing. Even if the poet were unwilling to oblige him, what right did he have to persecute the man?"

It was a savage persecution, indeed. Next morning it was discovered that Mr. Munshi's paddy field had been brutally ransacked. The maturing, fully grown sheaves of paddy had been mercilessly uprooted and carried away. On another day his two cows failed to return from their grazing ground. Mr. Munshi was warned that if he ever wrote a poem or a song in future, or if his songs were ever heard anywhere again, he would be banished from the village for good.

I said, "Didn't you, the young people of the village, protest?"

My young uncle answered, "You don't live in the village. You don't know how things are run there. We are just dirt under their feet."

I learnt that Mr. Abdur Rab Munshi didn't write any more. I was terribly hurt. I couldn't believe it.

"Has he really given up writing?"

"Yes. He was a fine poet. Now he doesn't write any more. He doesn't even talk to any one."

Perhaps man has to accept defeat sometime. Poet Abdur Rab Munshi didn't write any longer. On that day I could not think of a greater defeat. I felt a strong urge to go and see him once more. It seemed to me that I was my uncle's partner in this crime. As if I too had moved far away from the poet.

I went to the village along with my young uncle. My aunt was surprised to see me. Her husband said jokingly, "Well, young man, didn't I tell you that rural scenery was important for you? This time spend a few days here. There are so many ideas here that you can write on and on, and still find the storehouse inexhaustible."

The next morning I quietly left with my young uncle for Mr. Munshi's house.

I was shocked to see the dilapidated condition of the once beautiful and serene homestead. The empty cowshed fallen to pieces. The outer courtyard seemed as if it had never been swept. Apparently, no one now sat on the bamboo platform under the berry tree. It was littered with bird droppings.

We learnt that Mr. Munshi had gone to his small farm land.

My young uncle said, "Let's go back."

But something had put my back up. I said, "No, we'll go back only after I have seen him. Come on, let's go to his plot of land."

After finding out the whereabouts of Mr. Munshi's land, we proceeded there. My young uncle led the way and I followed him.

The sun rose quickly. The rays burned down on our heads. My feet began to ache. All around me I could see nothing but the dazzling glare of the sun. On reaching the spot supposed to be

Mr. Munshi's plot of land, my companion looked all around him and then pointed to the figure in the distance. "Look, there Mr. Munshi, ploughing his land."

I looked in the direction he pointed. I wish I had not seen what I did.

The man had nothing on but a *gamchha* wrapped around his loins. The rest of his body was bare. Poet Abdur Rab Munshi was labouriously pulling his plough himself.

I was shocked beyond words. Unable to stay there a moment longer, I turned around and started back. After taking a few strides I stopped for a second and looked back. Silhouetted against the pitiless sky, Mr. Munshi was standing motionless, looking steadily in my direction.

Inspite of the earnest requests of my uncle, I found it impossible to stay in his house more than one day.

I said, "I was passing through Sirajganj. So I decided to stop by and look you up. As soon as I can make time, I'll come again and spend a few days with you."

She was my late father's only sister. She made me promise to come again soon.

I had travelled such a long distance only to meet the poet and the result was this! My young uncle felt very embarrassed. He had gone to the poet's home once again that night. As soon as he brought up my name, the poet said, "No, no, I don't write any more. There is no point in my seeing him. Tell him not to come to me any more."

I gathered from my young uncle that not only did he not write any longer but he also got upset if any one sang his old songs. His poems were no longer recited at school functions. That was stopped quite some time ago. After winning the election, Mr. Talukdar had got hold of two young singers, from who knows where, brought them over to the outer courtyard of Mr. Munshi, posted some muscle men about the place and held a musical session there throughout the night. The songs were nothing but filthy lampoons about Mr. Munshi's past, present and future generations. All night they sang those obnoxious songs to the accompaniment of obscene gestures and earsplitting beating of drums.

I thought, well, he could have easily left the village with his son and wife. Why didn't he do that? It made me angry to think about it all. He might have had to beg in the streets for food, or work as a day-labourer. At worst, he might have died of hunger, but why did he submit to this defeat with bowed head? Why did he permit his writing career to come to a halt?

I left the village with a feeling of deep resentment. However, I got the answers to my questions after about two years, and fortunately for me, from poet Abdur Rab Munshi himself.

I went to that village again after about two years to redeem my promise to my aunt. I wanted to see her and also to take some rest. I was working too hard in Dhaka and it was telling on my health. One day, advised by my doctor, I left Dhaka and went to the village in order to take a spell of well-earned rest.

As soon as I reached the village, I remembered Mr. Munshi. By that time my young uncle, unable to get into government service, had started to practise medicine in the village. And he was not doing very badly either. He came to see me in the morning. He was my only friend in the entire village, the only person to whom I could tell everything without fear, whom I could ask for any information I wanted to get. I learnt from him that Mr. Munshi was seriously ill. He was suffering from acute colitis and was bedridden. The pain was severe and he often cried out, unable to bear it. He was perhaps near his end.

I felt terribly helpless. His agonised shrieks seemed to pierce my ears. I told my young uncle that I wanted to see him.

He said, "Let's not go today. I'll go alone and see him today and let him know about you." He was secretly treating the poet.

That night he came to me after supper. We went out and sat by the same old canal and started talking. But everything felt so empty to me.

My young uncle said, "I have told the poet about you."

"What did he say?"

"He was so happy, you know. He took my hands in his, and asked me if I could bring you over to his place."

My whole being pined to go to him that very moment. All night I kept thinking of him.

Next morning I went to Mr. Munshi's home accompanied by my young uncle. The place was more dilapidated than ever. It looked desolate and abandoned, like an ancient graveyard. The entire courtyard was overrun by wild thistles and nettles.

Mr. Munshi's eldest son came out and escorted us in. The boy had grown quite tall. One could see the hint of a moustache on his upper lip. The tender attractiveness of his face had been replaced by a hungry look.

The poet lay in the room on a tattered mattress. It was difficult to think of him as a living human being. He looked like a living skeleton. On seeing me, he feebly stretched out his hand. I took his lean, eager hand in mine and sat down by his side. He continued to stare at me with hungry eyes. He tried to tell me something but found it hard to breathe, and was unable to say a word.

I said, "You will get well." Pointing to my companion, I added, "He has told me about this complaint of yours. It is nothing to worry about."

But it seemed that my words did not register. He quietly said, almost in a whisper, "How good of you to have come. There are so many things to talk about. When I heard about you from the doctor I was so happy. How are you? Haven't you written other books during this time?"

While he said these words, he gently released his hand from my grip and fondly touched my body all over. My eyes filled with tears.

My young uncle got up. "I am going to a place close by," he said, "to make a professional call. You two talk. Don't cry, Poet-uncle. There is nothing to cry about. You will get well, I tell you. I'll be back soon."

When he left, Mr. Munshi said, "He may have become a doctor, but his senses have not yet developed. Death is coming for me. Who can stop death? The doctor? Don't I recognize my own end? Well, you came about two years ago when I ill-treated you. I didn't even talk to you. Please forgive me, dear brother."

I quickly stopped him and said, "I took no offence, sir. I had heard everything. I even saw that you were watching my retreating figure. You are a great man. One day this village will be proud of you. They will boast that poet Abdur Rab Munshi lived here. They will say that he used to sit under that berry tree over there and compose his songs and write his poems."

I was overcome with emotion. I eagerly wanted to make that picture come alive before his eyes. My voice grew husky. I was almost choking, but still I went on.

As he listened to me, the poet sat up in his bed, his eyes shone as if in a trance. The lines on his face began to throb with joy.

I took his hands in mine and said, "You will see that all this will come true. There is nothing for you to grieve over. One day everybody will come to appreciate your worth, and then they will be sorry for their mistake."

It was as if I was relating a fairy tale to him. A child's bright and eager curiosity shone from his eyes. He thought that I was a messenger, an angel, from the future. He felt me again with his hand as if he could not believe that I was real.

His eldest son brought me a glass of sherbet made with liquid molasses. I saw the poet's wife looking at me from behind a half-open door across the courtyard, shading her face with the edge of her sari like a ray of sorrow.

Mr. Munshi said, "Please drink the sherbet."

He picked up the glass himself and offered it to me. I drained it. He watched me in complete silence.

Then he lay down on his bed again and said, "I called you to let you know that the message I sent through the doctor last time was false. I am nearing the end of my days, I know. Mr. Talukdar can't do me any harm. Now I am not frightened any more to tell you that I never stopped writing. Can any one live without speaking? I composed a large number of songs and poems after that incident. Everything has been written. All neatly packed in that trunk. People will come to know of them, tomorrow, if not today. I sent for you to request you to arrange for the publication of these writings in the form of a book. You can do it. Won't you do it?"

I felt thrilled. An indescribable joy filled my heart. Poet Abdur Rab Munshi had not given up. He had worked all day in the field with his plough under a burning sun, come back home in the evening, and secretly written his poems in the darkness of the night.

He turned to his eldest son and asked him to open the trunk. The boy took out a bundle carefully tied in old cloth and gave it to his father. Mr. Munshi made a sign to me to take the bundle. A moment later, he looked amazingly disinterested and calm. Inspite of all his care and anxiety about his writings, he didn't even touch them once with his hand, didn't even glance at them a second time. Only big drops of tears continued to fall from his eyes.

Turning his face, he said in a cracked voice, "Many a time I thought of going away from this place. Anywhere at all. And then I thought again, where shall I go leaving behind this little patch of earth of mine? Where shall I get these trees, these clouds, this air, this sun and this moon? If I go away, will injustice go away, too? It will stay on here. So what good will my going away do? Therefore I stuck to this place. And I spoke to the earth. So many words, you know! I said, O earth, you are my mother. Do you think I don't know about the pain and suffering that have darkened your colour? You never disowned me. Why should I disown you? As long as you are here, I have everything."

As he said these words, he lowered his head still more. With his face nearly touching the floor, he brought out those tear-filled words from the very depth of his heart. He handed to me the flowers he had raised during the lonely days of his sad and long dedication. His son sat at his head quietly, with dull eyes.

That was the last time I saw poet Abdur Rab Munshi.

I regret only one thing, that he could not see his *Collected Poems* before he died.

Translated by Kabir Chowdhury.

"The Poet" is included in *An Anthology of Contemporary Short Stories of Bangladesh*.

The Tale of the Two Singers

Kayes Ahmed

Pishi, his father's sister, had fondly kept his name Jagannath. Jagannath Baroi. Jagannath is an auspicious name. He had been a normal child, with fine and strong limbs, but when he was twelve he had a bout of smallpox which affected his eyes. Since then Jagannath had been blind of both eyes. However, though his eyes were gone, his voice remained. While his voice was not exactly sweet, he could sustain a tune well and long.

Jagannath was neither short nor tall. Of medium height. He was neither thin, nor fat. Of medium build.

Slinging his out-of-tune harmonium across one shoulder, he would accompany "Dohar" Haridas. They would sing on trains, station platforms, bazaars, and street corners. His themes were sad, pensive, soul-stirring, but his wide mouth and the smallpox scars on his face made his appearance ludicrous, to say the least. His white, opaque eyes added to the strangeness of his appearance; they looked like someone drowning, struggling to escape from a choke-hold of leaves and vines. Any normal person looking at those eyes would find himself gasping for breath. Helplessness merged with the ludicrous. Wearing a bright, printed half-sleeved shirt and a *dhoti* worn high, he would appear with dusty feet at Mantu's tea stall accompanied by Haridas. "Tea please, Mantu," he would say.

No one had ever seen Haridas wearing anything on top. If he felt cold, Haridas would wrap one end of his *dhoti* round his brown, long-necked, skinny body.

Haridas was a healthy young man. He could easily have earned a livelihood one way or another. It was difficult to understand why he should be happy to roam around with the hot-tempered Jaga. Jaga was a rascal. Sometimes, Jaga would start shouting so violently at Haridas for little things that one would assume that they were the worst of enemies. But a little later, when the two of them smoked marijuana or sat side by side and chatted, who would believe that a little earlier Jaga had been kicking Haridas.

Sometimes Haridas would say, "Am I your mistress that you treat me in this manner?" Jaga would reply, "Had you been my mistress would you have stayed with me?" To this question Haridas could give no reply. He would cast a long glance at Jaga's blind face.

Who knew what Jaga understood when he pulled the harmonium towards himself and started singing? "The flute calls out to Radha, it knows no name other than Radha." Haridas would laugh and placing a new pot on his stomach, would drum up a tune with his fingers. He would push the pot from side to side, he would make the pot go up and down, causing little gub, gub sounds to emerge. A crowd would gather to hear them.

One fact should be noted here. Though Jaga was blind, he had been married. *Pishi* had married off the orphaned Jaga with a great deal of difficulty. After keeping house for Jaga for about six months, his bride had eloped with a young man from her own village. It had created quite a scandal.

Not that it had caused Jaga a great deal of sorrow. Moreover, Jaga had been bad-tempered from childhood, so one couldn't blame the scandal for his temper. Nevertheless, on occasion people would blame Jaga's wife for his plight.

Haridas had a mother as well as a wife. Haridas was not too fond of his wife, neither did he dislike her. Because people like Haridas aren't very sophisticated in matters of the heart, it was difficult to understand immediately how things stood between them.

One could never be sure what Haridas's wife's mood would be like. If she was in a good mood she would perform her household chores flawlessly. At this time, she would not let her mother-in-law lift a finger, she would keep her children clean and tidy, their hair would be oiled and combed, their eyes lined with *kajal*.

If, however, she was in a bad mood, she didn't care a fig about he house. She spread out her legs and sat down to stitch a *kantha*. After calling her several times and receiving no response, her nother-in-law would grudgingly go into the kitchen herself. And he three children—who knows why?—would take upon themselves o make life hell for the old woman.

Malati would not even lift her eyes. Humming to herself, she vould merrily keep on sewing her *kantha*.

Khantomoni was fed up. Night and day, her son roamed about vith the blind beggar. He neither saw nor heard anything. While naving his food he would keep his head down and listen to everything she said. God alone knew whether he heard anything. He lid not bother to say anything in reply.

After Haridas left about two or two-thirty, Malati would rise and shout, "Oh good man's daughter, have you finished cooking? You have stuffed your son, and told tales to him, but have you pothered to remember that someone else's daughter is starving?"

At such times, Khantomoni wanted to cry. The poor woman had had to work all morning. She hadn't received any comfort rom telling her son about her insults and suffering. On top of hat if this was how her daughter-in-law spoke to her, how was she o feel?

But the mother-in-law said nothing to her daughter-in-law. What could she say? If she tried to reply, Malati would let all hell oose. Khantomoni was terrified of her daughter-in-law.

To her neighbours Khantomoni would say, "She's mad, absolutely mad." Khantomoni would pretend affection for her daughter-n-law—her eyes seemed to brim with affection—but she burned vith anger inside. But what was she to do? Khantomoni's sense of nonour was profound.

If she wished she could have visited her daughter at Raghunathpur. Her son-in-law dealt in rice and paddy. There would be no problem even if she were to stay there for a month or two. But Khantomoni was hesitant. Just because she was unhappy at her son's house, to go and stay at her daughter's house would be to reveal her helplessness, her impecunious position. Khantomoni was embarrassed.

Strangely, her son was exactly the opposite. He had no shame at all. Khantomoni's troubles had no end.

How many times had her son-in-law said to Haridas, "Come join me. If you want to do business separately, that's fine too. I'll give you the capital you need. If you go around like this, we have to hang our heads in shame."

But who bothered to listen?

Naturally, all her anger was vented on her son. When she did not succeed herself, she begged others to talk to him. Sometimes she would curse Jagannath, "Oh God, please let the blind rascal fall down and die this very night."

But the very next morning, Jagannath would appear in front of their house and call out," Where are you, Hari?"

Hari would tuck the bowl under his arm and join him. Khantomoni's eyes would stream with tears.

Haridas and Jagannath roamed around freely. Some days they would travel on the B. N. R. line to Ramrajtala, Shantagachi, Mourigram, Andul, Shankrail, Abada. On other days they would travel on the Bandul or the Kod line to Shingur or Burdwan.

Jaga had a sound commercial sense. He would not sing more than two songs in one compartment. Jaga and Haridas had quite a large repertoire of songs: *kirtan, ramprasadi, baul,* folksongs. All together, they had a total of about twenty songs.

Among them Jaga had some "hit" songs. He would sing them according to his audience. He depended on Haridas for this. Having travelled so much in trains and mingled with people, Haridas had become an expert at judging people. Immediately on entering a place he knew exactly what song should be sung there.

If there were more young, brash people in a crowd, if there were young women in a compartment, Haridas would whisper, "*Jhilli,* that is, girls present.

Jaga would then sing, "Come, my friend, hold me tight, let us spend the night together."

When Jaga stopped singing, Haridas would pick up and continue. When Haridas stopped, Jaga would pick up the tune once again. The young boys would applaud, "Most wonderful, by God."

The girls would assume a look of indifference. The train would rattle on as the two sang:

> "My longing for Krishna torments me;
> Alone, I weep my pain."

When the second stanza ended, Jaga returned to the first stanza again, "Come my beloved, hold me tight, let us spend the night together."

Thus did Jaga and Haridas sing the complaints of lovesick maidens for their absent Krishnas.

The daily earnings of the two were not bad. Sometimes on alighting from the train, they would proceed to the centre of the town. After walking for some time, Haridas would look around him and say, "There is no pleasure to equal this roaming around freely." Jaga made no reply; he would simply put his hand into his pocket and count the money.

Receiving no reply from Jaga, Haridas would hum," I will go to every home in Mathura dressed like a *jogini*." Suddenly stopping the song, he would ask, "How many days remaining to the *rath*?"

The harmonium sat heavy on Jaga's shoulder. He would clutch the *gamchha* tied to the two rings on both sides of the harmonium and sling the harmonium from the other shoulder. "The Thursday after this Thursday."

Haridas looked at the sky. "The days are changing, by God. It is *Ashar* now, the *rath* will take place in a couple of days. At such a time it is supposed to be raining so heavily that it is impossible to go out of doors. And look at the sky. Cloudless, as if it's the month of *Chaitra*."

Haridas was oblivious of the absurdity of telling the blind Jaga to look up at the sky. Haridas, of course, hadn't even realized what he was saying.

Jaga replied, "Everything is changing, but the rascal of a god, he refuses to change."

" It's being said that there'll be no more poor people in the country any more."

"Why not, which heaven will they be going to?"

Haridas didn't know the reply to this. His wisdom was confined to class three. Roaming around from place to place, somehow managing to make out the writing on the posters or reading the large letters written with coal tar on the walls or listening to what people were saying in shops and marketplaces, Haridas had some vague idea of political promises. But it was not enough for him to be able to explain to anyone else. Moreover, where politics was concerned, for some reason, Jaga would become very angry.

Haridas did not get angry. There was no reason for him to be delighted either. After churning the wall writings in his head, or what he had heard people say, finally he would mutter, "Foh. All this is matter for gentlemen. It has nothing to with me or with Jaga."

Haridas could not think of anything separate from Jaga.

On top of that, with all the things that were happening around them, thinking of everything that was written on the wall really made one dizzy.

Thinking about what had happened last year to the brother of Doctor Lalbehari and Bharat Kol's son made one's blood run cold. Just a few days ago, as they were leaving the station, the entire Begumpur area had been put under curfew and people rounded up.

No matter how indifferent Jaga was to these incidents, there could be no denying that these incidents were taking place. And Haridas, with his two eyes, whether he understood the intricacies of all this or no, could not completely avoid thinking about what was happening. Of course there wasn't much to worry about, except that he travelled about all over the place accompanied by a blind fellow. Who knew what might happen some night.

Nor was it possible to explain all this to the obstinate fellow, so Haridas had to keep his eyes and ears open.

Haridas saw that a wormlike line of sweat was trickling down Jaga's temples. His unkempt, bronzed face had turned all flushed and oily. His nostrils flared wide occasionally. The weight of the harmonium pinched his shoulder. Haridas realized that Jaga was getting all worked up inside. If he spoke anything about parties and politics, Jaga would bark with annoyance. When he reached out an arm to take the burden of the harmonium off Jaga's shoulder, Jaga said, "Never mind. It's all right."

The days they left early in the morning to catch the train, they would have their afternoon meal outside. The days they walked, they did not go far. After wandering about all morning somewhere close by, they would return home, have a bath and finish their repast before setting off to the weekly market at Monirampur or Kharsaray. They would start to sing.

> "My bird of love has flown away,
>   Oh catch it, oh catch it.
> It cut through its shackles and flew away,
>   Giving me the slip.
>   Oh catch it, oh catch it."

Jaga had one very bad habit. He called it "playing *lila*." After every ten, twelve days he went to play *lila*, sometimes at Shaoerapholi, Srirampur or Chunchra. At other times he went to Jonai or Andul. He got down from the train wherever he felt like. "Keshta had sixteen hundred maidens to keep him company; Shyam had several times that number. I should have at least sixteen." That was Jaga's argument.

Haridas did not like Jaga's habit at all. But he couldn't say anything. The fellow was blind, wifeless and hot-blooded. Haridas remained outside the door while Jaga went to play *lila* within.

Jaga's aunt was very fond of Haridas. Whenever Haridas went to Jaga's home, *Pishi* would say, "You're here, my son. Come sit down." There'd always be something for Haridas: sometimes two round balls of sweet coconut *narus*, or a brass bowl full of puffed rice with a couple of sugar puffs, sometimes a couple of cucumber slices.

Pishi was very eager to get Jaga married again. She would draw Haridas aside and ask, "Have you been able to find someone?" Even before she began to speak, *Pishi's* eyes started glistening with tears. Her voice became all throaty as she said, "What will happen to the poor fellow when I die? That's the thought that worries me."

She would tenderly stroke Haridas, "May you live long, my son. You have always kept an eye on the blind fellow. How am I to bless you enough?"

The old woman would keep on muttering. But from where was Haridas to get a girl for Jaga? Jaga would eat him up alive if he found out. But Haridas realized that something would have to be done for Jaga. It was true. What would happen to Jaga, when *Pishi* died?

Much of the time Haridas completely forgot that he himself had a wife. Apart from sleeping in his hut at night, Haridas did not spend much time at home. He hardly exchanged a couple of words with his wife. Sometimes his physical needs would make him draw his wife close, but his need over, he would turn over and fall asleep immediately.

Sometimes he would give her an armful of bangles, occasionally some perfumed oil for her hair. But that too after Malati had asked him several times.

But at least they were husband and wife.

Somehow the singing was not going well. Neither Jagannath nor Haridas seemed to be in the mood to sing.

Jaga had chosen a somewhat strange song. "Don't you remember, that you owe a large debt? How long will you pretend ignorance?"

But perhaps the problem was not so much with the song. Since morning Jaga had been very depressed. Haridas had several times thought of asking the reason but he hadn't. Perhaps Jaga would become angrier if he asked him questions.

Jaga had only said, "Come in the afternoon." Just that. Haridas had realized looking at Jaga that he was not in a mood to talk. So he had spent the entire morning chatting with *Pishi* before returning home. When he returned, he found Jaga still sleeping. Even *Pishi* could not explain the reason for Jaga's depression. The only thing *Pishi* had said was, "Who knows my son? It's not for me to understand his whims and moods. What's the point of asking, when all he'll do is bad mouth me?"

After returning from his bath and meal, he found Jaga was ready, but his face was still as gloomy as before. Taking the harmonium upon his own shoulder, and tucking the bowl under his arm, Haridas took Jaga by the hand and sallied forth. All the way the two of them walked without speaking a word.

At Gobra, the two of them alighted from the train in order to change compartments. Haridas noticed that a wedding party returning to the groom's home with the bride after the ceremony was boarding the train a few compartments ahead. It was not a very rich party—that Haridas made out at one glance—nevertheless, it was a bridal party.

Telling Jaga about the wedding party, Haridas pulled Jaga up the steps. These opportunities did not come very frequently. No matter how much modern young men flirted openly, they were most unwilling to exchange their freedom for a bridegroom's crown. The people in the compartment were in a good mood. They welcomed the two singers and made them sit down. Everyone seemed relatively young. The older folks had gone to the next compartment and the younger folks were turning somersaults in glee.

The compartment was packed. Nevertheless, room was made in the midst for Haridas and Jaga.

The bride was sitting on the floor, her low veil covering her face. But Haridas managed to catch a glimpse of the dark-skinned young girl. Next to her, wearing a silk *punjabi*, sat her groom—a rather incongruous bridegroom.

Haridas glanced towards Jaga. Jaga's face was expressionless. Looking at Jaga, Haridas's spirits fell. He started playing the harmonium without much enthusiasm.

Haridas realized that he could say nothing to Jaga at the moment. What could he say to him anyway? Haridas glanced at Jaga and started stroking the bowl.

"If you cover your ears with your veil, how are you going to hear the song?"

"That's right brother Hari."

"There's some dust in front of the nose. See whether she is breathing. Or is she sitting there without taking a breath?"

In the midst of laughter, the drooping bride drooped even more within her veil. "Let's see, brother, what happens when we present a song." The stocky Haridas prepared to sing.

"Oh my friends, how shall I hide my shame?
My bride goes to another's home crossing my courtyard."

Haridas was startled. He glanced at Jaga, somewhat afraid. What song had Jaga chosen to sing? Whether or not anyone else understood, Haridas clearly realized what thoughts were playing in Jaga's head at the moment.

Lowering his head, Haridas drummed up a tune upon the bowl. The train rattled on. The songs continued to be sung. The compartment was crowded. People did not stop chatting when the singing began. They continued to chat while listening to the songs, and after some time, as they continued to chatter, the singing stopped.

"This is very bad. This is scandalous." Again everyone burst out laughing. Jagannath was impossible. The train halted on reaching Dankuni. The place filled with noise as the commotion of the station mingled with bustling passengers changing compartments. Haridas whispered into Jagannath's ear," Are you feeling bad?"

Jagannath shook his head.

"Have some tea." Someone held out two cups of tea to Jagannath and Haridas.

The guard blew the whistle. The train started to move. Sipping his tea, one of the passengers remarked, "Now sing a lively song."

"Yes, yes, turn this place into a real Brindaban." Gesturing towards the groom, Haridas joked, "Then he will have a tough time. Just one lone milkman, how will he tackle so many eager Krishnas?"

Again the compartment filled with laughter.

The sky was becoming cloudy. When they had left home, the sun had been fierce. Now it was no longer so hot. Haridas held on to Jagannath's hand as they crossed the overbridge. "Oh my friend, hold my hands, I do not know the way." Haridas was still in a musical mood. "I rely on you alone, there's no one else to guide me."

But when one's companion is unresponsive, how long can such a mood last? Haridas glanced at Jaga's face a couple of times, and then thought, "Well, whatever is in store for me . . . ." He finally asked, "Okay, tell me what is the matter with you today?"

Without replying to the question, Jagannath asked, "How much do you love your wife?"

Haridas was surprised. He swallowed and said, "Why do you ask?"

"No, just like that." Jaga's voice was low and casual.

They continued to descend. Haridas helped Jagannath slowly down the steps. Haridas felt that it was an opportune moment to tell Jaga. As they walked on, Haridas explained to Jaga as a father would to a son, "No matter what you say, I think it is essential for you to get married." Saying this he became a little wary. Who knew if Jaga might not get furious and take a smack at him right then.

But wonder of wonders, far from taking a smack at him, there was not the slightest hint of anger in Jaga's face. Lowering his head, immersed as if in deep thought, Jagannath kept walking, holding on to Haridas's hand.

Haridas had been wondering whether or not to tell Jagannath. His heart was beating rapidly. Jagannath was silent. Haridas glanced at Jagannath's face. Just before evening it had rained heavily. There were neither clouds nor moonlight now. Jaga's face could not be seen very well.

They had left the red-light district quite some way behind. Haridas thought he would say something, but, noticing Jaga's unresponsive face, he hesitated. Ah, how wonderful to be blind!

Holding Jaga's hand, Haridas carefully guided him up the rough, pitted road.

At the corner of the road, there was a bamboo clump. The place was dark. From behind, a police jeep drove up and passed by them. It hadn't gone very far when, from the darkness, a sudden shot rang out. The shot was followed by a couple more. There was a loud noise as one of the tires of the jeep burst. Haridas managed to drag Jagannath to the safety of a roadside ditch, under a *neem* tree. By that time the gun battle was in full swing.

Jagannath pulled at Haridas's hand, "What's happening?"

"Sshh. The police have clashed with a group of Naxalites."

By this time the police had taken positions on the slope of the road, behind their jeep. The jeep was on fire.

The *neem* tree was not much protection from the hail of bullets that were coming towards them from the rifles of the police. Haridas hurriedly attempted to draw Jagannath to the shelter of the pond, but collapsed on the ground. He was still clutching his blind friend's hand. Unable to see what had happened, Jaga stumbled on top of Haridas along with his harmonium. Jagannath heard Haridas groaning.

"What's the matter, Hari? Are you hurt?" Jagannath moved his hand over Haridas's body; his hand came away sticky. Jagannath was baffled. He shook Haridas. "Hari, Hari." His voice broke.

Through the sound of firing and bomb blasts, Haridas gasped from far away, "Jaga, don't go to the red-light district of Jonai."

Jagannath did not reply to Haridas. He kept on clutching Haridas's shoulders, and crying, "Hari, Hari."

Haridas could not see Jaga's face, as he continued to call out brokenly, "Hari, Hari."

Haridas gasped. "There . . . ." Haridas again gasped for breath. "There I . . . . I saw your wife today."

Haridas fell back lifeless.

Jagannath kept sitting like a broken statue.

The sound of firing and explosions went on. Suddenly, Jagannath got up angrily, "You wicked sons of pigs, just you wait." Jagannath stumbled up the slopes of the pond. His eyes were streaming with tears. His voice was choking. But there was a fire raging within him, as he cried out, "Oh you sons of dogs, sons of pigs." Jagannath stood up defiantly on the banks of the pond. The burning jeep blazed even more fiercely. Jaga could not see the fire, but he could feel the heat even at that distance.

In his high *dhoti* and half-sleeved shirt, the short stocky fellow was a comical sight as lifted his harmonium like some world-shattering hammer.

Jagannath trembled in his rage. He would burst any moment. His tears had begun to dry on his cheeks. Indifferent to the gunshots all around, he stood like a raging bull and thrust his harmonium in the direction of the blazing jeep. " Come you rascals, come . . . ."

With a cry to split the darkness, Jagannath rose up. Still holding the harmonium up high, he continued his mad dash forward. Suddenly, Jagannath's body twisted. His body arched like a bent bow. Then, from the bow, an arrow seemed to shoot out. It was Jagannath's body piercing the earth.

Translated by Niaz Zaman.

Kayes Ahmed's original, "*Dui Gayeker Galpa,*" has been anthologized in *Lashkata Ghar* published by The University Press Ltd., 1987.

The Night of the Vultures

Razia Khan

The cool February breeze had given place to the heat and humidity of March. It plagued Selina more than it did others as she did not keep servants. Its only blessing came in the form of the first blossoms of her gardenia bush; stimulated and stirred by the hot wind, it burst into creamy-white, pearly petals, glorifying and scenting the driveway. She did not have a minute to spare that day; she was celebrating a secret anniversary. It was exactly a year since she had met Malcolm Archer at a production of Wilde's *Lady Windermere's Fan* at the Goethe Institute. She had sat next to him, newly arrived from somewhere in Africa, as deputy in the British High Commission. Physically dead since her marriage, she immediately felt a strange chemistry working between them as he politely picked up her Spanish fan, which had dropped on the floor.

"Lady Windermere's fan—?" he said with a twinkle in his eyes.

"Thanks. I am Selina, a free-lance journalist."

"Malcolm, British diplomat," he said with a warm smile.

"I —never! I might have taken your for an American . . . !"

"Because I am so friendly?"

"Hush!" scolded her husband, infuriated by the open flirtation going on before his eyes.

That night he had slapped her so hard that she got a black-eye. "You slut, you cheat, how dare you flirt with that foreigner right in front of me! How low can you sink?"

Selina sobbed noiselessly, burying her face in the soft curls of her five-year-old baby boy.

After that bashing she had grown bold and rebellious. He had continued hitting and abusing her but she did not care. She appeared with him at parties, calm and resigned to her fate, knowing her child needed his father. With Bangabandhu Sheikh Mujib out of jail, the entire country was caught in a feverish struggle for its final and ultimate freedom from Pakistani shackles. Mentally Selina associated her husband Nurul Alam with the Pakistani menace because of his family's treacherous role during the language movement. Nuru's father was then Home Minister and the firing on the students' procession took place right under his nose. The students had broken the rule 144 to demand Bangla as the state language. Since the massacre of unarmed Bengalees by the Muslim League Government, Nuru's father had been branded as a traitor. And Selina had inadvertently walked into this poisonous circle when she married Nuru, never guessing beneath the soft, polite surface of that family was hidden an inferno for her.

Malcolm had wanted to go to Bangabandhu's meeting on the seventh of March, his birthday. He had worn the white embroidered high-collared *kurta* she had presented him. On her way back from her son Caesar's school, Selina had dropped in at his office. It was an irresistible urge to see him which made her make this indiscreet visit.

Malcolm took the child on his lap and said to his secretary, "This lady might need your help for her English visa. Two coffees please! And a glass of milk."

Selina, overpowered by his warmth and kindness to her son, said, "Am I going to England?"

"That is entirely up you. Can you keep a flat in England reasonably clean? Now see if my Bangla is improving or not!"

On a note-paper he had drawn a heart pierced with Cupid's bow. Words written underneath made her heart leap with ecstasy: "I love Selina!"

Tonight, the 25th of March, was her own birthday. Her husband had as usual forgotten she was throwing a party tonight. As Malcolm wanted to play the piano before dinner, she had asked the guests to come early.

She picked some half-opened buds of gardenia and arranged them on the dining table, set for the evening's entertainment.

Malcolm's favourite dish, chicken cacciatori, had already been prepared and now she was in the middle of making a huge Russian salad. The mayonnaise was patiently and diligently made at home during the winter when Selina had more energy. For drinks, since she could not afford to buy any wine, she served beet-root and carrot juice.

Malcolm had a way of teasing her! "Your house is like a health-food shop. We sinners need hard drinks after the day's work. So I'll do my own boozing before coming to your party."

Nuru was very generous with drinks, but as he never gave Selina any household money, she had to make do with her own small income from free-lance writing. She would have liked some red and white wine to be served with the meal.

David and Jane from the British Council, Barrister Moudud and his girl friend Janet, Allistaire Campbell of the United Nations, Nawab Omar Jackie Choudhury and Arnold Zeitlin of the Associated Press of America were coming. Arnold's wife Marian was the daughter of a science Nobel laureate. Selina liked Marian and went red with embarrassment when Arnold whispered: "We should have met ten years earlier."

Allistaire was the first guest to arrive, followed by Malcolm who sat at the piano Selina had bought from the famous singer Minna Abbasi. He was in a playful mood and very attentive to Selina's son. But once he frowned and declared, "Things are hotting up. You may have to flee to London with the baby."

"Really! I have just enough money in my account to buy a return ticket for myself and my son."

"What about Alam?"

"He doesn't think of us! He leads his own life."

"Inspite of that your son is more fond of him than you!" teased Allistaire.

"That happens to be the sad truth," sighed Selina, handing the mauve and orange drinks to the guests. She wondered what her life would be like if she gave up Malcolm for the sake of her son, who was so devoted to his father and did not seem to care for her at all.

As Malcolm produced a few mellifluous notes from Rossini, Alam, Selina's husband, arrived with his doting lady secretary,

Mrs. Motilal. Voluptuous and dumb, she reminded Selina of Marilyn Monroe. Her vital statistics were considerable. Selina took satisfaction from the fact that she was celebrating the anniversary of her first meeting with Malcolm who had brought a bouquet of the most delectable yellow roses.

In the hall, as Allistaire went towards the drawing-room, Malcolm had given her an intense look, but she shook her head. telling herself, "Never, never in this house!"

Her old-fashioned scruples had thus prevented Malcolm from kissing her. As she looked at the pointed breasts of Mrs. Motilal and her fawning, fond glances at her husband, she regretted her scruples. As she served the chocolate mousse, Nuru gave her a dirty look which meant: I'll teach you a lesson when every one leaves!

But no one could leave. They had come out in the verandah with the small glasses of cognac which Allistaire had given Selina. Suddenly the sky turned rosy—and then balls of fire were seen shooting up towards the horizon. A great commotion followed. Machine guns, mortars, tanks seemed to transform the suburbian city into a veritable battle field.

David declared, "It's the army-crack-down that everyone's been talking about. Let me ring home!"

The telephone lines had been cut off. Jane sat on the steps of the verandah with her head in her hands, the cognac trickling down her beautiful blue evening-dress.

Caesar, well-up in his knowledge of arms, said to his father, "Abbu, it's a point two-two!"

At other times everyone would have laughed. Now they went inside with grim faces, shutting doors and windows.

"So the hawks have decided to eliminate us. The butchers!" Moudud, usually emotionless, screamed, while Janet stroked his arm, trying to comfort him. Selina had lit olive-green candles on the dinner-table. She blew them out while the excruciating noise of bullets, machine guns and rocket-launchers continued unabated. The guests gradually changed their sitting positions to crouching and stooping postures, some lying down on the sofas, some on carpets, some sobbing openly.

The Homestead Yonder

Hasan Azizul Huq

With measured steps, Ramsharan and his family alighted from the launch and climbed up to the embankment. He had already slipped and fallen three times. The pots and pans, the *hookah-chillum*, the precious seven kilograms of rice, clothes and bedding were all sopping wet. Ramsharan had got a bent pole from the city; from the fruit market he had even managed to obtain two broken wicker baskets to hang on the two ends of the pole. He carried his entire belongings on his shoulder, all snugly contained in the wicker baskets. What he could not carry on his shoulders were his wife, twelve-year-old son, ten-year-old daughter, and his youngest three-year-old girl. They walked and even had to carry little odds and ends. His son carried a half cluster of raw bananas, his older daughter had something too. But his wife carried the heaviest burden of all—on her left hip was their youngest three-year-old, while on her right side was some other household stuff.

Once on the embankment, Ramsharan heaved a sight of relief. Bhanumati too lay down her household baggage and stood to rest a while. But her daughter clung to her and would not let go.

Bhanumati said, "Are you going to chew me dead or what?" In response, the child snatched at her mother's breast and sucked her nipple so hard that tears of pain rushed to her mother's eyes. She slapped her daughter on the back and cried out, "Let go, let go of me, you fiendish creature!" and bared her breasts in front of her husband and son.

Ramsharan watched spiritlessly and said, "Don't beat her—there's nothing in her body anyway. Will she live if you beat her that way?"

Bhanumati retorted, "It would be good riddance if she died. You think that this daughter of yours will ever die?"

It was hard to blame Bhanumati for her anger. For the past nine months she had had to carry this child on her hip constantly. She ripped open her petticoat and showed the deep scar on her waist. The little girl was barely recognizable apart from her mother's waist. She protruded like an ungainly, ugly tumour from her mother's left ribs. The skin sagged at the little girl's groin—there was not a single hair on her head—all over her naked body were dry ringworm-like scars. Ramsharan knew his daughter was dying—so did Bhanumati —but she was their daughter. Maybe it was sheer habit, maybe human affection that they carried her along and could not bear to abandon her.

The sun rose higher and the shade of the palmyra tree shrank like a hunched animal to the tree trunk. The pleasant heat-free shade narrowed in area, but Ramsharan managed to seat his entire family within that small patch of shade. He pulled his eldest son onto his lap. Bhanumati, bunching her saree on her lap, sat with her arms spread towards Ramsharan in an embracing gesture. The elder daughter stuck close to her. It was remarkable that Ramsharan's whole family could rest under that small patch of shade. He brought out his *hookah-chillum* and started to light it.

The hot air blew around them and it became stuffy. Ramsharan looked around and said, "What will you see once you get to the village?"

Bhanumati answered, "What will we see? We'll see nothing. What did we ever have before?"

Irritated, she forced her daughter's mouth away from one breast, but the child at once turned to the other breast and sucked noisily at the nipple. "Just see how it sucks like hell!" Bhanumati remarked, without addressing anyone in particular, as she caressed the child's oily, hairless head as if searching for lice.

Meanwhile, Ramsharan had succeeded in lighting his hookah. He inhaled the puffs with a sense of relaxation. Around him were the deserted fields, the half-dried stream, the fallow, uncultivated land which had not seen crops in the past year, the unwieldy grass, the dry marsh caked with salty water. Under the burning sun, this harsh dryness and desolation bore itself into Ramsharan's consciousness with piercing intensity.

He closed his eyes and asked Bhanumati, "How long have we been married?" Bhanumati quickly covered herself with her saree and gave her husband a startled look. Ramsharan stopped puffing at the hookah, drew his son close and twisted his fingers through his hair. Then he began to count the ages of all his children.

"Jogor is now thirteen, isn't he? Two died before him. Munu died at the age of five—the year all villagers had to live on shell-fish, snails, and water lilies. The younger one, Punnima, died at only three. You conceived Munu during the first year of our marriage. That means we've been married for eighteen years."

Around this time last year, Ramsharan had been evicted from his land. What happened was something beyond Ramsharan's wildest nightmare. The boy called Rashid, who lived next door, had come and untied the milch cow from the cowshed and led her away as if for grazing. Ramsharan asked, "Where are you taking her, son?" Now Ramsharan could not remember if Rashid had even answered his question—maybe he was too ashamed to reply—he had merely turned to look once at Ramsharan.

When Ramsharan sat down to eat that afternoon, word came that Ridayacharan, who lived on the west side of the village, had been burnt to death in his own home along with the piles of stored hay. Before one could even begin to fathom what had really occurred, four or five boys came to Ramsharan's house and said to him, "Uncle, how much more will you eat?" "Why, lads, is there someplace I need to go with you?" Most of the boys remained silent, but one, hardly known to Ramsharan, the one with pox marks on his face, said, "The brass platter, the one you're using, we need it. We can't wait, we need to go elsewhere. Just finish eating quickly and hand over the platter to us."

Big drops of tears fell into Ramsharan's rice and made it salty. Within half an hour, he was stripped of all he possessed and evicted from his home.

Since that afternoon, that sharp, pungent taste of salt had remained in Ramsharan's mouth. Nothing, not the miles of walking, not the crossing of rivers, not the yelling and screaming at the border, not the long waiting lines of stony-faced people which seemed to extend into hell—no, nothing could obliterate the taste of that salt from his mouth. Never, not for a moment, whether standing, sitting or walking could he free himself from that brackish bitter taste which refused to leave him.

Now, a year later, having returned so close to his village, Ramsharan could puff indifferently at his hookah and begin to count the ages of his children.

As layers of memory were peeled off by Ramsharan's queries and remarks, there opened up within Bhanumati the immense howling darkness filled with sorrows of yesteryears. She remembered her six children. Though it was hard to lift up her head in the blazing sun, she saw clearly the face of each child. Her oldest son had a birthmark above his chin, her daughter had an ugly wart on her forehead, and one toe on her younger son's foot was larger than the others. She recalled all these details vividly.

Bhanumati remarked, "God divided his bounty in half. He gave six, but left us with only three."

Ramsharan remained silent, but looked absent-mindedly at his youngest daughter, whom Bhanumati had now covered with her sari to shield from the heat. After a while, he thoughtfully commented, "If the tree is there, it bears fruit again. The tree is still here."

A wave of shyness swept over Bhanumati when she heard this. She looked sideways at Ramsharan. He wore only a faded, dirty *gamchha;* his long, awkward hands were sinewy; his hair had turned grey and not a single tooth was left in his mouth.

"Is our house still there? What will we see when we get there?"

"Maybe it is still there."

"Didn't we hear that the military burned the entire village? But the land will still be there, won't it?"

"Maybe it is . . . ." Bhanumati said again.

"Why maybe? Where will the land go?" Ramsharan asked somewhat angrily.

"Then it must be there," Bhanumati said.

Ramsharan grew angrier, but he didn't want to argue more. "How much we have suffered these nine months! After so much, don't you think we'll now be able to settle once again in our own village?"

This time Bhanumati retorted, "How much of happiness did you get in your entire life? Did you ever have enough to eat, to fill up your stomach? You spent your lifetime slaving away for others, but could you ever give your children good food to eat? Could you ever give them decent clothes to wear?"

Ramsharan replied sharply too, "But the land was ours. After a long day's toil, I could at least come and sleep in my own home."

Bhanumati continued to vent her feelings, "Do you remember how our Munu died? Our eldest, our first-born? She died without any medicine, without any remedy. Remember how Punnima died?"

Ramsharan instantly questioned her, "Then why don't you also mention how Dayal died? Why did you stop? Tell me how your younger son died. It happened just recently, just the other day. Tell me, how did he die?"

Bhanumati remained speechless; she could not utter a single word.

"So?" Ramsharan demanded, "If he had died at home, we wouldn't have had to throw his body away like that of a dog, would we?"

Bhanumati covered her eyes with the end of her sari.

"There's no use crying. We still have three. We fled all the way to India—we could have all died—but see, we're back. We've journeyed long, passed through so many stations and *ghats*, stood in long lines begging for food. Now all that is over, we're back. We can start over and live again on our own land." Ramsharan was getting agitated as he spoke. He re-lit his hookah.

The heat was becoming unbearable. In this damp, humid country, the sun did not burn dry. Rather, a horrible steam seemed to emanate from the damp soil; even the half-dried ditches and gutters exuded a suffocating vaporous fog which filled the air. The blazing sunshine made it impossible to look in the direction of the river. Ramsharan's eyes hurt, his stomach hurt, his head was splitting, but, as he puffed at his hookah, he began to spin a fairy-tale about their future. The sordid, harsh reality slowly faded and instead rose up a solid house, resistant to cyclones and floods, in which there would be no scarcity of food or clothing. There was no lavishness in Ramsharan's fairy-tale; his imagination dwelt only on the simple, basic needs of life.

As if lulled by the fairy-tale, Bhanumati was not fighting her little daughter any longer. She pulled her sari over her head and listened with rapt attention. The hard lines on her face softened—even the dark circles around her eyes caused by sleeplessness, worry and hunger seemed to disappear as she listened wide-eyed.

Ramsharan told tales about his father, his own childhood, and about their children with vivid details and colourful exaggerations. Tears rose to Bhanumati's eyes again and again, but she let them flow freely.

"Why worry? We'll set things right again, "said Ramsharan.

Bhanumati also dreamed to her heart's content. Three rooms surrounded their clean courtyard. Her son and daughter-in-law lived in one, she and Ramsharan used another and the third remained empty for their daughters and sons-in-law when they came to visit. Bhanumati, who had been a wife and mother for so long, knew exactly what an ideal home should be like. A cow-shed, cows and bullocks, paddy-fields, a pond full fish, and a store-house full of grains stirred Bhanumati with their magnetic attractions. Her eyes lit up mysteriously, just like the dark *shravan* sky pregnant with clouds.

Ramsharan started to get up but sat down with a cry of pain. He could not even bear to sit any more, but had to lie down. Recently a pain had developed in his back—whenever he tried to get up after sitting for a while, a piercing pain would stop him.

Bhanumati asked, "What's wrong? Did you get hurt?" Ramsharan grimaced and tried to relax his back muscles. Then he sat up hanging his head. Finally, he held his back with both hands and managed to stand up.

"Ugh! this damn pain!" he muttered to himself. He would not bend his head in pain. He kept standing with determination. Two sinewy muscles started to tremble in his neck, as he stood in the bone-scorching heat and felt his skin singe with pain.

Undaunted, Ramsharan picked up the pole on his shoulders, gave the odds and ends to his family members, and started to move slowly along the embankment.

It was hard to see their village clearly because of the high-walled embankment. Ramsharan wanted to cross the bend as quickly as possible. He quickened his pace as if he were ready just to reach his home and then take his last breath if necessary. Tension and excitement filled him—his heart beat violently like a hen just slaughtered writhing in pain; even his intestines slithered and wriggled like a snake.

They had now crossed the bend. Ramsharan halted and blinked long and hard. It was impossible to see anything in the glittering sunshine.

He turned around and asked Bhanumati, "Where's our village?"

Bhanumati asked, "Have we reached there yet?"

Ramsharan scolded her, "Have you become blind? Where did the village go?"

They came down from the embankment. It was not true that there was no sign of their village. Actually, he could not see clearly from far off. Now he began to see the ruins of houses. The black, burnt dwellings, half burnt pillars, twisted enamel pots and pans, broken baskets, brooms, ashes from fireplaces—what did all these mean? Ramsharan had recognized his village, but he was dumbfounded and could not locate his own house. He wondered, "Was this how small our village was? Just these few houses? Weren't there little paths between these houses—laden with vines of pumpkin and gourd? Weren't there open fields with grazing cows, and ponds? Where did all these go? Has everything vanished except these naked, broken pieces of homes?"

Dangling the pole on his shoulder, Ramsharan said, "Perhaps this is it!"

Bhanumati was searching around for the path which went towards Ridayacharan's house. Ramsharan remarked, "No, this is Tulsi's house—not ours." He kept going back and forth among the ruins. "See this was Ridaya's storage. This one looks like Pollah's house."

After a while, he shrieked in frustration, "Where did our land go? O Bhanu, find it, please!" The heavy pole bit into his bones and his eyes filled with tears.

Bhanumati consoled him, "Why are you searching so hard? Is there a house left that you can go home to and lie down on your bed? The entire village has become one piece of land. Is anyone coming to fight for his share?"

Ramsharan thought carefully and saw that Bhanu was right. Not a single house remained, there was no other person around. Why bother searching for their little piece of land?

But an irrepressible urge forced Ramsharan to locate the burnt patch of earth on which their precious home had once stood. Where could it have gone? It didn't have feet, it could not flee. It had to be somewhere here—somewhere amongst the ravage of tottering pillars, cracked bamboos, twisted tin utensils and grindstones. The sweltering heat of *Baishakh*, the melancholy winds, and the vast desolation—had these hidden his land so that he could never find it again? A house was not supposed to move or could it? By ten o' clock that night Ramsharan's family had resigned themselves to their lot. Even Bhanumati, who had begun her search so fervently, had now given up. It was futile crying out in this wide field of darkness. Your cries led nowhere. Bhanumati seemed to have understood, after wailing and lamenting for long, that it was beyond her to carry her cries to God in the heaven above. Her cries, which had rent the air and Ramsharan's ears, suddenly stopped. Now Bhanumati was calling out in a hoarse cracked voice, "Oru, Oru, where are you, my dear?" The muscles of her face and neck were tense; it seemed she needed to be relieved of her heavy burden which filled her being. When a loved one dies, probably during the first few hours the shock grows within one like a stone.

The little girl's name had been Orundhuti. The little girl with such a lovely name had died without a sound or whimper. In the early evening, Bhanumati had located a fireplace and started a fire to cook the rice they had received in the city as relief food for refugees. The little girl had eaten to her heart's content. Then she fell into a peaceful sleep. The older children ate also and sank down on the ground in fatigue. Just as Bhanumati was about to call Ramsharan and serve him, they discovered that Orundhuti had died in her sleep. An alarmed Bhanumati felt the child's heart, put her hand below her daughter's nose and mouth. But there was no sign of life at all. Bhanumati was speechless with shock. Then she stared wild-eyed at her husband and broke down in howling pain.

Within the next two hours, Bhanumati became quiet—maybe she had managed to relieve herself of some of the intensity of her loss. But where would this profound sorrow ever go?

Ramsharan could not hear her screams any more. Lying flat on a mat, and looking up at the clear starry sky, he listened to Bhanumati's mournful groans. Gusts of wind came from the direction of the river. Under the ashes of the extinguishing fire, sparks blazed red in the surrounding darkness. In that glow, Ramsharan could see his son sprawled asleep, his older daughter lying curled up, and next to them, almost touching, lay their dead sister. Her head was completely bald, her arms and legs were bony, like sticks, her wrinkled skin sagged, and her stomach was still swollen with the rice got as refugee aid. An acute pain cut through Ramsharan as he tried to break out in a wail, but he could produce only some odd shrieks. He became quiet. The only sound now was of the wind that struck against the bridge and rebounded. There were no trees around, the wind did not rustle through leaves; it just rushed back and forth wildly.

Bhanumati's moans continued but had become quieter. Ramsharan felt an acute sense of hunger. He got up and tried to talk to his wife, "She found peace in death. Don't cry, it was just our fate!" His hunger gnawed at him. Would Bhanumati now throw away the rest of the rice? If she did, he would soon have to join his dead daughter.

Bhanumati kept crying. Restless and hungry, Ramsharan lay down again. When you have a house, a home filled with children, domestic animals, crops in the field, then the sky seems smaller, like a low ceiling. But now in this deserted village of uncultivated fields the sky rose up much higher, ominous in the dark vastness of the night.

Ramsharan gazed at that sky and wondered if Bhanumati would give him the cooked rice to eat.

Bhanumati did get up finally. She served rice for both of them. Then she sat in silence and gazed blankly. Ramsharan did not delay any longer. He quickly pulled one earthen bowl towards himself and pushed the other towards his wife. Without saying anything, he began to eat the cold, coarse and stiff rice, received as refugee aid, with salt. As he bit into the green chilli, his eyes watered, but forgetting the loss of his daughter, he continued to eat with absorption. Bhanumati dried her eyes with the end of her saree, but even before she took her first bite, her eyes filled up again. It was no use drying these tears. Unstoppable, they fell into her bowl; and she did not need any extra salt to mix with her rice.

Ramsharan lay down beside Bhanumati. A foul stench mixed with the smell of dry ashes exuded from her body. He asked, "What shall we do now?"

Bhanumati did not answer him. The darkness seemed to engulf them. The wind kept hitting against the embankment and returning. Never will this village be inhabited again, nor will there ever be cultivation in this land of the dead. Ramsharan felt terrified and moved closer to his wife.

"What will we do with her now?" Bhanumati began to cry again. "Won't you give her some fire? Won't my daughter get a little fire?"

Ramsharan observed that the few remaining sparks under the ashes were extinguishing rapidly. "What good will cremation do? Actually there's no such thing as God. Tomorrow we'll dig a hole and bury her. Then foxes and other wild animals will not be able to eat her. She'll just mingle with the elements."

The dead girl's body was becoming stiff. "That little girl was my life! O, please cremate her," Bhanumati wept and begged her husband. "Remember how my Dayal died? He died of starvation in India. We had to throw him in the jungle."

"We've achieved independence!" Ramsharan's voice broke with hate and anger. "What did I gain from independence? All I know is that last year I fled for my life to India. For nine months I lived there like a dog. Now I'm back in my own newly independent country, but that dog-life has dogged me here too! Holding my children by the hand, I've had to journey endlessly to railway stations, to launch *ghats* . . . ." The sharp edge of Ramsharan's scathing words scattered all around. "Freedom, independence! What freedom, what independence? Tell me. I don't have anything to eat, my children die of hunger. Is that what independence is really about? Standing like beggars for refugee aid, going from house to house searching for food?"

Bhanumati said, "How will we live here? What will we eat? O my poor Orundhuti . . . ."

Ramsharan sarcastically remarked, "Why worry? The government is giving land, truck-loads of rice, building houses of bamboos and tin sheets—then from the sky there might even fall down a pair of bullocks!"

Bhanumati continued to weep, "O, my Orundhuti! Where have you gone, my child?" She wailed loudly, then became quieter and kept on droning as if uttering a snake charmer's *mantras* in a monotonous tone.

At one point, Ramsharan could not bear it any more. He said, 'O Bhanumati, listen to what I'm saying! What do I understand of independence or freedom? Before I had a piece of land. Now that has disappeared too. How can I call myself independent?"

Bhanumati stopped crying and asked in a low wan voice, "Won't we get anything from the government?"

"Didn't we get seven kilos of rice and a few blankets in India? That's all we'll get."

"Won't they help us rebuild our home?"

"What do you think?" Ramsharan put back the question to her.

"But don't people say that the government will rebuild houses in all villages?"

"O yes, they surely will!" Ramsharan exclaimed. "You have rice enough for three more days—what will you do after that? Where will you beg for food? Is there anyone here? Will the government people come here to distribute rice after three days? Are they bringing bamboos and fencing materials? If they ever do come this way, by that time grass will have begun to sprout from our bones!"

A peculiarly foul stench emanated from Bhanumati's body. Lying beside her, Ramsharan's sorrow rose to his throat. Bhanumati had collected some large dried branches for cooking. One branch was only half burnt. The dead child lay on a torn mat just beside that branch. She looked no different. Just like another branch herself. Ramsharan choked with sorrow. His pain lay heavily upon him. A pair of foxes roamed nearby.

Bhanumati exuded a dreadful odour of mud, ashes, and bodily stench. When this stench grew more intense, it seemed to overcome

Ramsharan. Oddly fascinated, he was drawn towards Bhanumati and crept close. Bhanumati's eyes flamed in the darkness but, despite the deep wrath and anguish he saw in her eyes, Ramsharan persisted. Bhanumati kicked him violently. As he fell over, she only said, "Have you no shame at all?"

The two foxes took care of the dead child in the night.

"All are God's creatures!" Ramsharan merely commented the next morning.

After Bhanumati's lamentations quietened somewhat, Ramsharan broke the used fire-place and scattered the ash-covered bricks. He put all their belongings in the wicker baskets and took up the pole on his shoulder again. Bhanumati had no burden on her this time—her hands were free and empty. Even the older children did not have to carry anything on them.

Ramsharan climbed up on to the embankment. With mincing steps he and his family moved slowly along the embankment like a row of ants. As they were crossing the bend, at about nine o' clock, a launch roared out of the *ghat*.

But Ramsharan did not board the launch. He had nowhere to go on that launch. But he would definitely go somewhere.

Translated from Bangla by Parveen K. Elias.

Flotsam

Makbula Manzoor

On both sides of the road leading from Nimtali Bazaar to Nilkhet, the Krishnachura trees shamelessly flaunt their flame-coloured blossoms in the hot *Baishakh* air. They seem like fallen women draped in flimsy red nylon saris, their lips a matching scarlet, standing on the roadside to attract customers. These days this comparison springs quite frequently to Rabeya's mind. Specially when she drags her tired body back to these tenements after a long day's work, the sight of the flaming trees makes her think of scarlet women. She wants to curse the trees. The blossom-laden branches sway in their scarlet brilliance in the April breeze. Rabeya curses them involuntarily. Die! Shameless hussies, die!

What is the point of flowers in this tenement, of colour, Rabeya muses. If these trees had not been flower trees but blackberry or plum instead, the slum children would have at least been able to gather the fallen fruit to eat. Instead, these useless red blossoms blaze forth brazenly. Rabeya does not know the names of the trees. Before coming to Dhaka she had never seen trees like these. Before coming to Dhaka, in fact, there were many things that Rabeya had not seen or known. True, her home in Dhanchi village had been a hut, but it hadn't been in a slum. The raindrops would penetrate their broken roof, but the small earth courtyard in front of the hut had always been spotlessly clean. Though the landless villagers had no claim on the green fields, they were free to breathe in the clean air of the fields. They could bathe in the river, wash their clothes in its water. But here, though they pay for the hut they have no right to it, no right to the water tap, no right to their own honour. One has to guard one's honour every minute. Particularly someone like Rabeya, who is not yet thirty-five years old. With her slight build, heart-shaped face, luxuriant hair, Rabeya easily passes off as twenty-five. Her honour is threatened not just here but everywhere. It was those threats that had blown Rabeya, the youngest daughter of Kalimuddin Munshi, out from her hidden corner in the darkened hut of her village home, flung her around like a water hyacinth floating on the water, and deposited her in Dhaka. When the open sky of Dhanchi village had refused to let Rabeya breathe, when the cool water of its river had drawn back from Rabeya, there had been nothing left for Rabeya but to let herself be blown about like a water hyacinth.

Rabeya's father, Kalimuddin Munshi, had hoped to educate his youngest daughter whom he called his little Rabu. Nowadays without education no girl can get a good groom. Her older sisters had neither education nor looks, so Kalimuddin had had to marry them off to petty farmers. Rabeya was not fair, but her olive complexion, her heart-shaped face, her attractive features—everything had combined to make people notice her from childhood. Her voice was melodious. Rabeya the Munshi's daughter was as famous for her recitation of the holy Quran as for her singing. She had sung a patriotic song during the annual prize distribution ceremony at her school. Rabeya Begum of class eight had learned to sing by listening to songs on the radio at the home of the Talukdars. The song she had chosen was also a lovely one: "*Dhana dhanye pushpe bhora*, My land so plentiful and beautiful." A lovely song and a lovely voice. The chief guest, the Sub-divisional Officer, had been highly impressed by Rabeya's song. That a village girl could have such a voice! Such talent! Had she lived in town, she would have become famous in no time. Specially in Dhaka. Well now Rabeya is in Dhaka. Where have her songs gone, her dreams of education? As a village girl it was but natural that her education should have started somewhat late. She was fifteen years old in class eight and well-developed for her age. Friends and relatives of Kalimuddin Munshi had derided him for sending his daughter a mile to school instead of marrying her off. There was no high school at Dhanchi village. The neighbouring village had a high school where boys and girls studied together. Kalimuddin Munshi had Rabeya admitted to that school. Both Rabeya and her younger brother. Brother and sister went to school together.

Kalimuddin Munshi was a poor farmer. He owned a mere five *bighas* of land. The land did not produce enough to last them through a year. Kalimuddin supplemented his income by working as *muezzin* in the village mosque. He also taught children to read the Quran beginning with the *qaida* and *amsipara*. He was thus able somehow to look after his family. A two-roomed hut with a tin roof, a lean-to of a kitchen, a small well—this was his entire wealth. In dry weather the well would dry up. Then the river water supplied all their needs.

The winds that blow through cities also pass through villages. The election of 1970 had caused quite a bit of excitement in Dhanchi village. The illiterate villagers believed that if they cast their vote for the sign of the boat their conditions would improve. They would have plenty of rice to eat, clothes to wear, a tin roof over their heads.

After the elections came the non-cooperation movement. A lock hung on the door of the village school. In front of the Talukdar home, large crowds gathered to listen to the news broadcasts over the radio. Rabeya's school also was closed. Rabeya started helping her mother with housework. She thought to herself that the movement must be a sign of good days to come.

But soon the dream of happiness came to naught. People from the cities started flocking to the village in large numbers. The second son of the Talukdars came home. The eldest son also returned from Dinajpur with his family. There were rumours that Biharis were slaughtering Bengalis in huge numbers. Dhaka was in complete control of the Pakistan army. The streets of Dhaka were strewn with the corpses of Bengalis, and in the rivers corpses floated, instead of boats. Eight to ten youths of Dhanchi village crossed the border to India intending to join the freedom fighters. Aslam, the second Talukdar son, went with them, saying he was going to get guerrilla training.

Aslam told the people who gathered to listen to the news, Keep up your spirits. The country will soon become independent, God willing. We are going to fight. Perhaps we shall return, perhaps we won't. But there are hundreds of thousands of young men like us in the country who will sacrifice the last drop of their blood for the independence of this country.

Aslam lived in Dhaka. His manners, his way of talking, everything was different. Rabeya would watch him from afar. She thought that he spoke to her from another world, the world of her dreams. Rabeya had gone to hear the news from the *Swadhin Bangla Betar Kendra,* the voice of free Bangladesh. She returned hearing a voice from the world of her dreams. Girls of Rabeya's age love to dream.

In a few days, the situation changed. A lot of people had come to the village in search of safety. But, almost immediately, the villages were no longer havens of safety. Soldiers entered the villages in jeeps and trucks and took up their posts in the police stations. Kamarkanda was one and a half miles away from Dhanchi village. The army established a camp there. Every villager was threatened. Some selfish villagers started to collaborate with the soldiers. Some cowardly youths joined the *razakars*. Those who had never done a single good deed in their lives, who had roamed around doing mischief rather than good, now strutted about with rifles on their shoulders. But what surprised Rabeya most of all was when she heard that Aslam's father, Mr Talukdar, had become the chairman of the Peace Committee. He knew that Aslam had joined the freedom fighters. When the army captain came to enquire about Aslam's whereabouts, Mr. Talukdar apologized profusely and whined that Aslam had gone to fight against his wishes. If the captain wished, he was quite willing to disown his son on the spot. The captain said that was not necessary. However, if Mr Talukdar heard any news about his son or about the people he was with, he should inform the captain immediately. He would do what needed to be done.

Aslam heard about his father's actions. He also learned that Kalimuddin Munshi, the *muezzin* of the village mosque, secretly helped freedom fighters.

Rabeya's father was worried about his daughter. If the military attacked the village, Rabeya would not be safe. Despite this fear,

Kalimuddin Munshi did not hesitate to extend his help to the freedom fighters along with his twelve-year-old son Harun.

Rabeya's mother was a timid sort of person. But even she understood that their lives, their possessions, their daughters were not safe from the army. At night she often prepared large quantities of rice and *dal*, occasionally, even a curry. Sometimes, in the middle of the night, young men would quietly enter their hut and quickly gulp down the food and vanish into the darkness. Sometimes Harun would tie the food up in a bundle and take it somewhere.

It was the middle of the monsoon. There was no respite from the torrential rains of the month of *Sraban*. At times Rabeya's mother got fed up of the ceaseless rain and cursed it. Rabeya's father reprimanded her. No, don't curse the rain, he said, the rain is God's blessing. Our boys can fight in the rain, they are good at fighting in the water. These rascals are helpless. They are terrified of water, they do not know how to swim.

The events of that evening are burned into Rabeya's soul. It had been raining since afternoon. As evening approached, the rain increased. The wind blew in gusts. Rabeya's mother quickly finished cooking the evening meal. Darkness set in upon Dhanchi village before nightfall. There was something foreboding in the air. As it was, everyone was apprehensive. The army camp was so near, and the mischief of the *razakars* knew no bounds. At little or no excuse they would swoop down upon the villagers. They would carry off whatever they wished—cows, goats, ducks, chickens—all in the name of the major or captain. No one could go to visit their relations without bringing down the wrath of the *razakars* who believed that the young men had gone to join the freedom fighters. They would threaten the parents with dire consequences. Kalimuddin was lucky that he had no grown up sons. But the *razakars* did not spare him and carried off a pair of goats one day. Kalimuddin did not protest, thinking about Rabeya's safety.

Rabeya herself thought more about the safety of Aslam than of her own. Where was the man of her dreams? Who knew in which jungle he was being soaked to the skin in this downpour? Did he get enough to eat? Did he get time to rest? Time and again freedom fighters had eaten in Rabeya's home. Aslam had never accompanied them. Did that mean that freedom fighters were not allowed to go to their own villages? Who knew? Rabeya's thoughts flew in an unending stream.

Suddenly the whole village was shaken by a volley of bullets. The firing seemed to come from very close. Rabeya clung to her mother in terror.

Kalimuddin called Harun and asked him to climb the coconut palm. See where the firing is taking place, he said. Harun swiftly clambered up the tree. He descended in a little while and said, "It seems the freedom fighters have attacked the army camp at Kamarkanda. I had heard that they were planning an operation soon."

Kamarkanda *thana* was quite close. On top of that, the swollen monsoon streams magnified the sounds of the fighting so that the fighting seemed to be taking place in the village itself. Finally, the barking guns were silent. The tired villagers dropped off to sleep.

At Rabeya's home, no one had gone to sleep. Kalimuddin Munshi was talking in soft tones to Harun. He expressed his hopes and fears about the day's operation. Suddenly there was a squishing sound as if someone was treading on the waterlogged ground. Rabeya was the first to hear the sound. Someone seemed to be walking on the flooded path behind their hut. The sounds of conversation were also audible to their ears. Everyone became alert.

A voice called from the bamboo fence behind the house. Rabeya shivered. Aslam. It was Aslam's voice. Aslam was calling.

Kalimuddin Munshi got up quickly. As soon as he unlatched the door, three young men entered the room. Water dripped from their wet garments. One of them was covered with blood. They were the ones who had attacked Kamarkanda a short while ago. They had destroyed half of the army camp. They too had lost a couple of their men. The young man with them had been wounded in the right shoulder. They could not go back to camp with him. He also needed medical treatment. That is why they had brought him to Kalimuddin's place.

Kalimuddin asked them to lay the boy down on a cot. Then he asked his wife to get a piece of clean old cloth. Unless they put a tourniquet on the wound, the bleeding would not stop. Aslam clasped Kalimuddin's hand gratefully and said," Uncle, you are sympathetic to our cause, that is why we brought him here. Please keep him hidden for a few days. When he improves, I will come and take him away. Tomorrow afternoon a doctor will come to see him."

"A doctor! People will then know about him," Kalimuddin expressed his apprehension.

Aslam replied, "No, no. He will not come like a doctor. He will come disguised, perhaps as a ragseller, perhaps as a *fakir* or mendicant. You will recognize him because he will mention Munir's name."

Kalimuddin was relieved. "That's better, my boy. The *razakars* are getting bolder every day. On top of that your father, I mean Mr Talukdar . . . ."

"I will take care of him, Uncle," Aslam replied in a grave voice. Then he shook his head. "My God, how hungry I am. Fighting is hard work, Harun. Oh, Aunt, give us something to eat. What is this, Rabu? You're standing there like a statue. Go on and see what there is in Aunt's larder."

Rabeya wanted to sink into the ground in embarrassment. How dreadful! She had been standing all this while staring at Aslam. She had been staring speechlessly at Aslam's unkempt wet hair, his dripping clothes stuck to his body, his sparkling eyes, his restless excitement. All she was thinking was, He'll go away, he'll go away. He'll go away in a little while, this man who has sprung from the land of dreams.

It was too late to cook. They had to escape while it was still dark under the bridge at Shialkol. The bridge at Shialkol! Everyone said that there was a serpent's nest under the bridge. Rabeya was frightened. She murmured, "Poisonous snakes have their nest there."

Aslam's eyes brimmed with laughter. "Black snakes? I'm sure they're less poisonous than the Pakistanis ones."

There was a ripe jackfruit in the house. Rabeya's mother broke it open and took out the fleshy segments for them to eat. Rabeya poured a bowl of *moori* from the tin. Aslam and his companion mixed the jackfruit with the puffed rice and ate it with relish. It would have been good to give their companion some warm milk. But where could one get milk at this hour? Rabeya remembered that there was a little rice flour. She made it into a thin gruel with water and a pinch of salt. Despite his pain, Munir was also hungry, and he drank the gruel gratefully.

It wasn't safe to keep Munir in their bedroom. So Kalimuddin carried him into the next room with Aslam's aid. There was no furniture in that room which housed a bamboo platform stacked with pots, earthenware jars for storing paddy, winnowing fans, baskets for measuring rice. Clearing a space under the platform, they spread two thick *kanthas* for Munir to lie on. Putting back the lock on the door, Kalimuddin locked the room up as always. Aslam drew Kalimuddin aside and said something to him. Then he took his leave. "We must go now. Aunt, pray for us. Goodbye, Rabu. Harun, be careful." They slipped out and were swiftly swallowed up in the night. Kalimuddin accompanied them for a short distance, then returned muttering prayers, hoping that all would be well. Rabu hid her tears in her bed.

Hardly half an hour passed. A couple of shots echoed loudly through the village. Kalimuddin said, "That's the noise of a sten gun. I saw a sten gun in Aslam's hand. I wonder what's happened in the village now." Despite his curiosity, he knew it wasn't safe to venture out at the moment. Whatever it was had to wait until morning.

Kalimuddin left the mosque after giving the *azaan* for the dawn prayer. He saw a huge crowd milling in front of the house of the Talukdars. The whole village seemed to have gathered there in fear and apprehension. Even before Kalimuddin could enquire what was the matter, one of the worshippers said that the night before some freedom fighters had shot and killed Mr. Talukdar and the two *razakars* who were guarding his house.

The doctor was supposed to come in the afternoon. But long before then, six or seven Pakistani soldiers drove up in a jeep, splashing mud all around. The villagers at first thought that they had come on hearing about the death of the chairman of the Peace Committee. But they had come looking for Kalimuddin Munshi. Kalimuddin was giving the *zohar azaan*, the call for the noon prayer. His voice floated in the air of Dhanchi village. At the captain's order, two Pakistani soldiers dragged Kalimuddin down the steps of the minaret. They did not allow him to complete the *azaan*. They had confirmed reports from *razakars* that the night

before three freedom fighters had entered Kalimuddin's hut. Only
two of them had left, so the third must still be holed up inside.
Those freedom fighters had murdered Mr. Talukdar and the two
razakars. Their faces were muffled up in sheets, so no one could
recognize them. But Kalimuddin Munshi and his family surely knew
who they were. Refusing to listen to Kalimuddin's protests of
innocence, they ransacked his bedroom. They kicked open the door
of the locked room. They knocked down the storage jars with their
rifle butts and smashed them. Two shots followed in quick
succession, echoing like the roar of a wounded lion. Two soldiers
fell down dead. The captain thrust his rifle through the rear wall of
the room and shot Munir in the back. Still clutching his rifle, the
freedom fighter fell face forward on the bamboo platform. The
razakars signalled to the soldiers who then entered the kitchen.
Cowering in terror was a fifteen-year-old girl, a piece of delectable
flesh. Her mother clung to her. With one kick the soldiers flung the
old woman aside, and carried Rabeya outside. Hiding in the
haystack, Harun realized that something terrible was happening to
his family. But he only realized how very terrible after the soldiers
and *razakars* left. He sprinkled water on the face of his unconscious
mother. Then he dragged the body of Munir—twice his age and
weight—outside under the pomelo tree. There the twelve-year-old
dug a grave and laid the corpse to rest.

Three days later someone came and quietly told Harun that he
had seen the body of Kalimuddin on the banks of the Dhapri river.
Next to the corpse was the battered body of Rabeya. Rabeya's
mother started up with a cry, "Why didn't you bring back Rabeya
with you?"

"How could I do that? And does she have the strength to walk?
The animals have torn her to pieces. But you must bring her back
before nightfall or the jackals will do the rest."

Harun and his mother hurried to the spot. In Harun's hand was
a spade. The youngster understood that he might bring the living
corpse home, but the dead body he would have to bury by the side
of the stream.

Five months crept past slowly. Rabeya's days and nights passed
in a dark corner of the hut. After that terrible night few people came

to their hut. Only a couple of curious women came to look at Rabeya. Rabeya's mother had lost her wits. She would sit quietly most of the time, occasionally breaking the silence to mutter curses. Harun carried on bravely. It was he who looked after his mother and sister.

One day, shortly after liberation, Harun heard that the freedom fighters were returning. He rushed to see them. Under the shady tree in front of the school house, Commander Aslam, recently returned from the liberation war, was addressing the villagers. "I will punish the traitors with my own hands. Perhaps you are aware that I punished my collaborator of a father myself."

Harun wanted to cry out, "Do you know what happened to us after you left the wounded freedom fighter in our house?" However, he said nothing. But when the meeting ended, he pushed his way through the crowd and went up to Aslam. Before he could say anything, someone said, "The army has completely destroyed his family."

Aslam replied, "Everything will be all right. We have liberated our country. Even if we cannot compensate everyone for their losses, we will try to do as much as we can."

Then Aslam boarded the jeep waiting by the side of the road in front of the Union Board. The jeep roared away in a cloud of dust.

Hearing Harun's story, Rabeya's face showed no emotion. The war and her own terrible experience had taught her to forget about dreams. Instead, in front of her eyes passed a procession of dead dreams.

After the death of her mother in the famine of 1974, Rabeya and Harun moved to Sirajganj. When their mother was alive, there was still someone to protect her. But after her death there was no one. At odd hours, the youths of the village would come to her door. If Harun were with her, Rabeya felt somewhat safe, but if he had to go on some errand, they would approach the verandah in twos and threes. They would ask Rabeya for water, they would tell her that there was something important they had to discuss with her. They would come to the back of the house and whistle. Harun guarded his sister like a watch dog, but in the end that was not enough.

One dark night, three young men cut the bamboo wall of the hut and entered the house. They tied up Harun's arms and legs and gagged him. Then they picked Rabeya up and took her into the next room.

Harun approached the village elders for justice. But who could punish those devils? The law was now in their hands.

A few days later when Rabeya went to the river to bathe, the village women rebuked her. Rahima Bibi insulted her to her face, "You shameless hussy, you don't even die! How dare you show your face in public? Don't pollute the water any more. Go home."

For a moment, Rabeya looked longingly at the brimming waters of the river. Then, she walked back to her hut, wondering whether the air of Dhanchi village was also being polluted by her breath.

Sirajganj is a small town. Famine had also caught it in its grip. There was no one willing to employ Rabeya and her brother. Finally Rabeya and her brother moved to Dhaka. Dhaka is a very large city. There are many jobs, and also many people. Rabeya managed to get some domestic work. Harun got a job at a launch *ghat*. At night he would remain at the *ghat*.

Rabeya lost count of the number of houses that she had worked in during the space of the five or six years she had been in Dhaka. She could not stay long anywhere. Her body was her greatest enemy everywhere.

Finally she and Harun decided that they would rent a hut in the slums of Kamalapur. She would stop doing regular work in houses. Instead she would work part-time, and at night she would return to the hut and stay with her brother.

Then one day Rabeya learned some news that she thought would change her life. Girls with a smattering of education were being employed in Saudi Arabia. One of the slum dwellers brought the information. Rabeya had gone to school. If she wished, she could go abroad with a fat salary. Rabeya took the man along with her as a sort of guardian to the employment office. She wore her best sari. She tied her hair neatly in a braid and wore sponge sandals on her feet. She was not going to look for a maid's job in an ordinary home. This was a job in the land of gold. Even if it was a maid's job, the salary was a fat one. It was a respectable job.

As she entered the office, a hammer fell on her. Across a large table in the cool air-conditioned room sat a well-dressed, clean-shaven Aslam. It seemed to Rabeya that her heart was pounding like a rice husker. Even though she tried, she could not raise her head to look up at Aslam.

Someone asked her name and permanent address. Lifting her head to answer, Rabeya saw that neither her name nor that of Dhanchi village caused the slightest change in Aslam's expression.

Emerging from the office, Rabeya told her companion that she would not take the job. Hearing her, the man exclaimed, "You mad girl, what are you saying? Such a good job and you won't take it! If you continue to work in this country, how long do you think you will remain a decent girl? Mark my words, you'll finally land up as a prostitute."

Rabeya looked at the man's angry face and said quietly, "Had I taken the job I *would* have been a prostitute."

The man threatened Rabeya. "Fine. I'd like to see how long you remain a chaste woman." Naturally he was angry. Had Rabeya taken the job, he would have received some commission.

A few days later, Rabeya left the Kamalapur slums and moved to Nimtali. She has been living here for some years now. These days Harun no longer bothers about her. The winds of Dhaka have blown him far away from his sister. They have taught him to look out for himself. One day he went back to Dhanchi village without informing Rabeya. There he sold their home for a song to an uncle. Harun had forgotten the day he had buried a freedom fighter under the pomelo tree of that home.

As she goes to sleep after closing the door of her hut at the end of a tiring day, Rabeya sees only that hut under the open sky of Dhanchi village. She imagines returning there one day when the people of Dhanchi have forgotten her shame.

Translated by Niaz Zaman.

The original, titled "*Kochuripana*," was anthologized in Makbula Manzoor's *Ekush O Muktijuddher Galpa,* published by Narigrantha Prabartana, 1992.

What Price Honour?

Rizia Rahman

The sky was an ominous leaden colour. Leaden, splattered with white clouds. The wind whistled in gusts. On top of a storm-battled palm tree perched a lone eagle. The murky leaden sky was pitiless. Gusty winds rustled through the leaves of the palm tree. The eagle screamed in tune with the wild rustling of the leaves. Halimun was afraid. She was also angry. She wanted to catch hold of the tuft of leaves and stop the terrible cries. She wanted to rent the pitiless leaden drape of the sky with a sharp *dao* and rip out the bright blue day from within. That would punish the sky all right. But below? The river water was rising rapidly. Land and water were indistinguishable. The ravenous, sluggish brown flood had devoured the land, had inundated all the paddy fields. The flood waters dashed against the sides of the huts. The very posts tottered. Any moment now their hut would be washed away, leaf-thatched roof and all. And the water kept on rising. The only noise to be heard was the gurgling and swirling of the flood waters. Halimun shivered, wrapping the frail rag of a sari closer round herself. She was cold. The gusty wind stirred up the dismal drizzle to slash against Halimun, adding to her discomfort. The water bubbled up through the earthen stove in the corner of the hut. The sides of the earthen stove dripped like rotting meat. Her empty rice bowl swirled about on the water. Seeing her bowl twisting around on the flood waters, Halimun shivered. Her stomach twisted with hunger. The pangs of hunger wracked her like pangs of childbirth. Hunger.

Which one could not glare at and subdue. How could the nineteen-year-old Halimun tackle that hunger? For a moment, Halimun forgot about the turgid waters and the leaden sky. The picture of a bowlful of bright, full-grained rice came to her mind, each grain plump and separate. Beautiful, white rice. And golden lentils. What else could any one ask for? No, nothing else. Just one bowl of rice and lentils. At this moment Halimun could ask for nothing more precious than a bowlful of rice and lentils. Halimun was hungry. She had eaten nothing for four days at a stretch. The flooded ditches and canals, the inundated paddy seedlings, the collapsing mud huts, the washed out garden—amidst all this Halimun was conscious of one thing alone: her hunger. She wanted rice. Just one bowl of rice. Halimun whose father, mother, brother and sisters had been killed by the army. They were not men, but bloodthirsty hyenas who had set their hut ablaze. They had not killed the seventeen-year-old Halimun. Instead they had called out to the sloe-eyed Halimun. Come here, little girl. We must get our fill out of you first. Halimun had not understood their words. But she had understood the look in their eyes. The smirk on their lips. She had understood that more than her life was in danger. Spared their bullets, Halimun had leapt into the flames.

The soldiers had been disappointed to lose so fine a prey. When they realized what had happened, they fired some shots into the flames and then left the place. Strange! Even stranger was that Halimun had not died in the fire.

Singed by the fire, Halimun had somehow managed to survive.

A girl who could leap into fire to save her honour was worthy of respect and admiration. At least in those days of enemy occupation. The villagers had looked after Halimun, brought her food and medicine. After liberation, relief workers had looked after Halimun, brought her food and medicine. After liberation, relief workers had come and constructed a hut with *golpata* leaves. Journalists had come from town to take pictures of the orphaned Halimun to print in their city papers. But after that? What had happened after that? The young girl who had burned her feet started doing odd jobs in people's houses in order to support herself. No one came forward to look after her. That was when the whispers started, "That girl has been ravished by the soldiers. That is why she tried to commit suicide by jumping into the fire." Halimun did not heed the whispers. She held her head high. No one had touched her. What did it matter that she had no roof over her head? What did it matter if she had no husband? She hadn't lost her honour. It was true that the fire had rendered one leg shorter than the other, but the fire had not disfigured her soul, it had not distorted her mind. She sustained herself by selling her labour, not by selling her body. How many girls could claim the same? That is why Halimun thought herself one of the most fortunate of women.

It had only been last *Kartik*. The relief contractor, the one who it was said had now become a big businessman at Rajarkhola, hadn't Halimun spurned him roundly? The rascal. He had a wife and family too at home. But in the middle of the night he had come knocking on Halimun's door. Halimun had peered at him through the hole in the bamboo wall, standing there in the fog-dimmed moonlight. No, he had not looked like those bloodthirsty cruel wolves, but like a greedy fox trying to steal chickens in the middle of the night. Halimun had opened the door and flung a fishcutter at him. "Where are you, you son of a whore? Come here. I'll chop off your penis. Come here, you bastard. I'll satisfy your lust for ever." Seeing the sharp fishcutter in Halimun's hands, the terrified man had attempted to flee. He had looked like a fox with his tail between his legs, fleeing from the dogs. Halimun had started to laugh, Hee, hee. Hearing that laughter, two bats were startled out of dark trees in the back. The quietness of the winter night was rudely shattered. The man fled. Halimun continued to laugh as she fastened the door of her hut, "Why are you fleeing now? Why are you fleeing, you son of a dog? If you come near Halimun once more, I shall cut off your head."

After this incident, Halimun had always slept with the fishcutter next to her. The incident did not remain a secret. The villagers heard it and said, "Oh mother, that is no woman. She is a jinn." Halimun would merely smile and hold her head even higher.

Her stomach cramped up once more. From behind the hut, where Asmat Mullah had planted his chillies, came a strange squishing sound. Halimun pricked up her ears. Perhaps Asmat's widowed daughter was wading through the flood waters, looking for some *kochur loti,* some river weeds to cook. Halimun herself had hunted for *kochur loti* and an odd assortment of leaves and boiled them to satisfy her hunger. She had mixed the whole-meal flour with water and eaten that. Finally, in the entire hut, there was neither a handful of flour nor broken rice grains. Ants, cockroaches and frogs had taken shelter in the empty pots and pans. Whom could she ask for food? No one in the inundated village had any rice or paddy husk. And where was there dry fuel to cook wild greens?

The squishing sound came closer to Halimun's hut. Halimun raised herself to peer in the direction of the noise. Asmat Mullah's twelve-year-old son, Ramiz, was sitting in a large bowl normally employed for feeding cattle and using both hands as oars to steer the "boat" towards her. The bowl struck Halimun's hut, and Ramiz alighted. He held onto the bowl with one hand, and, with the other, he clutched the bamboo wall of the hut. The wet bamboo wall collapsed and slipped into the flood waters. Ramiz let go the fence and fell into the water. Ramiz had girded a *gamchha,* normally used as a towel, around his loins. Standing in the rain, he smiled at Halimun and asked, "Have you eaten, Sister? Your hut will collapse any minute now. The hut on the east of our courtyard collapsed early this morning. Father and I cut down an areca nut tree and have supported the big hut with its trunk. Come and stay with us, Sister."

Halimun shivered in the rainy gusts of wind. She glanced at Ramiz through eyes as dark as the flood waters, "Where can I go? Everyone is in the same condition."

After a brief silence, she asked, "Do you think the water is receding a little, Ramiz?"

Clutching on to the bowl with one hand, Ramiz grimaced. "So soon? First the army destroyed half the country. Then poverty added to our suffering. This time the floods have come like Azrael, the angel of death. The floods devoured the paddy and the betel leaves, now they will destroy our homes, only then will the waters recede."

Halimun was silent. She looked at the branches of the tall palm tree.

Ramiz said, "I have brought something for you. Will you eat it?"

Halimun was startled enough to draw back her glance from the palm tree. "What, what is it, Ramizza? Has Chachi sent some rice for me?"

Water plopped down from Ramiz's wet hair. It rolled down his lips, bluish with the cold. Wiping off the water, Ramiz laughed mirthlessly, "From where will she get rice? Day before yesterday we had porridge made of broken rice grains. For two days we have quelled our hunger with all sorts of rubbish. Today older sister went to collect some greens from under the berry tree and found that a fat snake had twined itself around the tree."

Suddenly Ramiz stopped. He bent down and brought out, handful of roasted jackfruit seeds from the bottom of the bowl. Proffering them to Halimun, he laughed, "Here, Sister, eat. Mother roasted these yesterday. I saved some for you. You too have eaten nothing for the past few days."

Halimun's eyes sparkled. She almost snatched the seeds from Ramiz's grasp. She peeled off the white membrane covering the seeds and stuffed them into her month. But it was as if ghee had been poured onto flames, because, after eating the seeds, Halimun's hunger increased. Her hunger turned into a hundred sharp knives and stabbed her stomach. Clutching her stomach, Halimun doubled over with pain. She groaned, "Ooh, I can't bear it any longer." Ramiz got frightened. He clambered up beside her. He shook Halimun's doubled up body and said, "Oh, Sister, what is it? Why are you behaving like this?"

Halimun groaned. "Hunger, hunger, my dear. I can't bear this any longer. Ramiz get me a handful of rice."

Ramiz looked pensive. He thought for a moment and said, "Be patient, Sister. When I was coming, I saw two coconuts floating beside the chilly fields. I'll go get them."

Halimun sat up straight. "No, don't go alone. Who knows where snakes might be lurking. I'll go with you." Halimun stood up. They lifted up the bowl and set it on the roof, then waded through knee-deep water towards the chilli fields. The colour of the sky had become even more ominous. Had the sky ever been blue? It was impossible to believe that a bright sun had once shone in this sky. The wind was blowing even stronger, the rain stung like sharp needles.

Suddenly both of them stopped in waist-deep water. Where were the coconuts? There was nothing. Just the water, churning by rapidly. Dead leaves and pieces of straw floated on the surface. Ramiz looked around him, then said dejectedly, "I saw them right here. Where did they go?"

Halimun started up angrily, "If you saw them, why didn't you get hold of them then? Were they going to wait for you? Where did they go?"

Ramiz shouted abruptly, "See, Sister, see. There's a pot floating by. Wait here. I'll swim and get hold of it."

Ramiz waded through chest-deep water towards the floating pot. Halimun looked at the red painted earthen pot floating by. It was pretty large. What was inside it? Like flashes of lightning, Halimun's imagination caught fire. Maybe there was gold inside it. Maybe rice and lentils and wheat. Ramiz was halfway to the pot when he cried out, "Sister, snake."

Halimun's happy fantasies slipped and fell. Halimun asked in fear and despair, "Where, dear? Where is the snake?"

Ramiz lifted his head above the water and pointed towards the pot, "There, next to the pot. It is swimming alongside it."

Halimun also saw the snake. Yes, there was no doubt about it, it truly was a snake. With its head slightly above the level of the water, the snake, its body stretched out straight, was swimming along the current, next to the pot. It seemed to be guarding the pot. Halimun watched it go by helplessly. It wasn't striped. There were circular markings on its forehead. Most likely it was a poisonous snake. If they attempted to catch hold of the pot, they could not help touching it. Both of them watched the pot, brimming with possibilities, float by their helpless eyes. It was going farther and away. They had been standing in water for so long that by this time their bodies had become stiff. The cramps of hunger had faded into a dull pain. Halimun thought she would slip into the water any moment. She felt dejected. Then she threw caution to the winds and did something foolhardy. She dived into the water near the tail of the swimming snake. She reached out above the snake and caught hold of the pot. Then, holding the pot with one arm, she swam towards the shallow water. Ramiz was astounded. Halimun laughed. She felt courageous, capable of doing anything. Maybe she remembered that in times of danger, snakes do not bite human beings. Or perhaps, not having eaten for four or five days, she was unable to resist grabbing a pot which might contain something valuable. At present Halimun was not thinking of anything. Her stomach cramps had turned into a fast raging fire. Drawing the pot to the shallow water, Halimun opened the lid. She cried out in joy, "Ramizza, come quick and see what I have caught."

Ramiz swam to her side quickly, "What is it, Sister? What is it? Money?"

"No, dear. It's *chira*. A full pot of flattened rice."

"Let me see, let me see," Ramiz bent over the pot.

Seeing Ramiz's joyful face, Halimun's mood changed. She snatched the pot back quickly from Ramiz. She would not relinquish her one hope of sustenance. Clutching the pot close to her breast, Halimun glared at Ramiz. No, she would not share this *chira* with anyone. If she kept the *chira* all for herself, she would be able to survive for fifteen to twenty days. By that time the clouds would surely disperse. The sun would start to shine. The flood waters would start to recede. Halimun would get work again. Her bad times would pass away.

Halimun spoke in a cold, firm voice, "No, I will not give you any."

Ramiz was surprised, "Why not, Sister?"

"No."

Seeing Halimun's angry look, Ramiz flared up, "Give me some, Sister. Give me the pot. There's enough for both of us."

Halimun clutched the pot even more tightly to herself. She screamed violently, "No, I will not. Never."

Hungry and tired, Ramiz was too astounded for a moment to reply. The he jumped upon Halimun. "Why won't you give me some? Why not? Didn't I see the pot first?"

Halimun was unmoved. She clutched the pot tighter to her bosom. Ramiz was thrashing the water. He shouted, "Give me the *chira*. Give the *chira* to me. I have eaten nothing. My stomach is empty."

Ramiz's anger gave way to tears. Halimun held on to the pot with one hand, with the other she held Ramiz by the hair. She pushed his head under the water. Ramiz thrashed about in the water. Even then Halimun did not release his hair. She would not release her claim to the pot of *chira*. This was her only hope of survival. Ramiz continued to struggle desperately under the water, flinging about his arms and legs. Several times Halimun was on the verge of slipping into the water, but she managed to keep herself above the water. She kept a tight hold on to Ramiz's hair. Suddenly Ramiz gave a violent kick to Halimun's stomach. Halimun's sari came undone at the waist. It floated away on the flood waters. Even now, had she reached out, she would have been able to catch hold of it. But one hand was clutching the pot of *chira*. The other was holding her prisoner fast. Halimun started to tire. What was she to do? She tried to push her head forward and draw the sari back with her teeth. Just then Ramiz kicked her again. Halimun swallowed water. Lifting her head above the water, Halimun saw her sari floating beyond her reach. The only way to reach it now was by stretching out her arm. Her numb body was growing weaker. Halimun realized that she had to choose now between the pot of *chira* and the sari. She could not save both. At the moment the pot of *chira* was more important then her sari. But the sari? With her earnings she could perhaps buy some food for herself, but, in these days of hardship and inflation, she would never be able to buy another sari to cover her shame. She had no other clothes. Just this one torn sari. Which was she to save? She stumbled. Her hold on the pot of *chira* grew weaker. At the same moment, Halimun released her grip on Ramiz's head. Ramiz lifted his head above the water, gasping for breath. The pot of *chira* wobbled, filled with water, and sank. Gulping for breath, Ramiz asked, "What have you done? You have let the *chira* sink."

Halimun was silent. She was aware of nothing at the moment but her naked body and her hungry stomach.

Ramiz shouted at her, "Why aren't you saying anything?"

Halimun moaned weakly, "I had just that one torn rag. I lost it because of you. How am I going to preserve my honour now?"

Ramiz screeched, "What honour? Once you leapt into the flames because of the soldiers. At that time you had food in your stomach. So honour had some meaning then. You have nothing to eat now, and you speak of honour? Go, hang yourself, you whore."

Halimun did not respond. She simply watched her ragged sari being whirled away by the flood waters. She could not drag her starved body through the water to save it. Was she to drown and die? But she did not even have the strength to do that.

Halimun turned around and stood up. She pushed back the water and stood on the muddy slope, completely naked. She was tired and wet.

Standing in chest-deep water, Ramiz screamed, "Where are you going? Where are you going to find fire to set yourself alight in this inundated land?"

Ramiz flung his torn *gamchha* at Halimun. "Here, take my torn *gamchha*. Wear it and go and hang yourself."

Halimun paused for a moment. No, she had no need of a *gamchha*. The flood waters had not just swept away her sari, they had swept away all sense of shame. The only sense she had now was of hunger. Her imperative need now was for something to fill her stomach, to get rid of the cramps in her stomach. The home of the contractor was at the end of the path. There was a sturdy home there, supported by strong wooden poles, there was hope of food there, of rice.

Halimun said, "Go home, Ramiz. I am going to the home of Shamsher Contractor. I will take up residence in the marketplace."

Ramiz gazed after her astounded. Then he burst into tears. He sobbed," You whore."

Translated by Niaz Zaman.

"*Izzat*" is included in Rizia Rahman's anthology *Nirbachita Galpa*, published by Muktadhara, 1987. The story was, however, written in 1973.

Tarabibi's Virile Son

Akhtaruzzaman Elias

The drone of his mother Tarabibi's uninterrupted monologue from within the house penetrated Golzar Ali's ears, created a turmoil in his head, and shattered the calm of his evening.

Today everything had gone so well—all microphones from his shop had been rented for a college function. He had been free to enjoy a long afternoon nap—something he could not do too often—and felt fresh and restful. In the evening, he went to Fakir Chand's Azad Restaurant. He was leisurely relishing two well-done barbecued kabaabs when his friend Asadullah entered the restaurant. Pouring his tea into the saucer and lifting it to his lips, Asadullah said to Golzar, "Come on, hurry. I'm tired looking for you all over the place. Let's make a dash to the Moon Theatre."

Golzar stepped out of Moon Theatre in full contentment. He had not enjoyed something like this for a long time. It was an English film. He had not understood the dialogue, but who cares? The blows and the wrestling spoke for everything. Some blows were worth a million taka each. Golzar was not a skilled fighter, but most of his close associates had talents along that line. Nowadays in times of firearms, however, their days were over. Probably their skills had blunted too. But Golzar was fascinated by the power of human hands shown in this film.

As they came on to the main street, Asadullah said, "Come, let's drop by 'Gangajali'—let me initiate you today."

"No, Ustad."

"Come on, man, you can just sit and watch, maybe drink a bottle. I'll finish and come back."

"No, Ustad."

"What! Go, then, suck your wife's teats," Asadullah was irritated. "I can't make a man of you, Golzar."

Whether Golzar really wanted to become a man or not was doubtful. When Asadullah left, he kept walking straight. He could not help recalling the wrestling scenes—he had seen numerous films about violence and fighting—but this pageantry of blows falling one after another, the repeated confrontations, and just the constant "thud," "thud" of blows surpassed anything he had ever seen before. Golzar imagined how he would re-enact those scenes of wrestling in front of his wife Sakina when he went home. Whenever he looked up, he felt as if the sky was covered with a large screen filled with vivid display of movements by pairs of hands. Almost overwhelmed by this dance of fists and the "tock-tock-tock" sound of blows, Golzar reached his house.

The front of the house had a large wooden door framed by a crumbling thin layer of bricks. The door itself was very old, very heavy, and replete with cracks. Golzar was about to peer through the big crack and call Sakina when Tarabibi's complaining voice reached him.

"You're as good as dead!" she shouted to her husband Ramzan Ali. "All your life you've just lain in bed, never knowing what worries I face in running this house. O God! What a son have I borne! How will I face Allah on the Day of Judgment? It's one at night and he isn't back home! I know where he goes and who he fools around with."

Hearing these words, Golzar felt his merry evening, the dance of blows in the street neons—all dissolving into a haze. He no longer wished to control his life; he yearned to abandon all discretion and conscience to the yellowish black drain under the dark lamp-post by the street.

"Ali Hussain's wife—that shameless hussy—don't I know what all that whispering, murmuring to her is about?" Sitting on the high, narrow veranda, the mother who had borne him wove new sentences, each sharper than the former, each revealing a suspicious mind.

"If there's a maid-servant, he must fool around with her all the time: 'Suruj's mother, bring me water; Suruj's mother where's my vest? Suruj's mother, bring my breakfast'—Why? Doesn't he have a wife?"

How much more of this? Putting a hand on his chest, Golzar peered through a crack in the door and called his wife, "Sakina." Saying, "Who is it?" but without waiting for a reply, Sakina came and opened the door but did not linger. Beyond the door were a few yards of grass-patched, muddy, concrete land, and then a high veranda. There was absolute silence in the veranda as Golzar Ali shut the door with his back turned to the veranda. The longer he could spend locking the door, the better. He kept bolting and unbolting the door. The bolting of the door was the only sound in the house right now. When Golzar turned around, he saw that the verandah was empty. Good, the moment of facing his mother had been delayed a little. But the five steps leading up to the veranda were climbed in no time. Then he must enter through a high door and pass Tarabibi before reaching his own room. Tarabibi's room was long. From the dark veranda, her lighted room seemed a hazy yellow. The first thing which struck one on entering it was that far below the high ceiling—the area which seemed like an empty hole— was actually occupied by Ramzan Ali who tossed and turned his twisted, wooden post-like body on a bed. Often, as he turned his eighty-two-year-old debilitated figure, an unseemly cough burst forth. But nothing like that happened now. Ramzan could not endure light, that is why one side of the lighted bulb was covered with paper. In the opposite corner of the room, Tarabibi sat on a low stool preparing betel-leaf. Golzar almost brushed by her side before he went to his room.

From the bed on the other side, Ramzan Ali's hoarse voice filled the room: "Did you shut the back door?"

"Do you have to remind me?" Before Tarabibi had finished her reply, Golzar reached his own room.

"Did you look under the bed?" Before he heard the reply to Ramzan Ali's second question, Golzar quietly closed the door.

In Golzar's room, on a red-bordered mat, was a bowl of rice, a bowl of curry, mashed potatoes, and some jalapeno peppers and salt

in a saucer. Sitting on the mat and eating rice and curry, Golzar
said, "Amma went on and on, didn't she?" Without replying, Sakina
put up the mosquito net, arranged the pillows, and straightened the
bed-sheet over and over again. Sakina's almost fair and round face
was overcast. Hoping to spread a little sunshine over that face,
Golzar said, "Why don't you eat a little with me?" Without expecting
a reply, he started picking out the bones of the *khalsa* fish. While
doing that he asked, "Had the fish gone stale?" But the staleness of
the fish apparently did not affect his appetite. He went on eating for
a long time. His bowed head almost reached his chest. Sakina, who
stood by holding the bed-post, looked out of the corner of her eyes.
Had Golzar fallen asleep or what? Tarabibi had started her incessant
monotone while folding her prayer mat after the *Maghrib* prayer at
dusk, and it had stopped only now. Oh, Allah! What a long speech
it had been! The rumbling noise of the buses plying on the main
street decreased, but the microphone playing popular melodies in
the restaurant around the corner blared louder than ever. The loud
music together with the continued shrieks of madman Khadem in
No. 11 and, above all, the hubbub of the noisy, bustling, busy
area—all mingled in muddled confusion.

Golzar said, "Amma made quite a scene, hunh?"

"Did Amma say anything to you too?" he asked again.

"Take me away to Mir Kadem. Or, else call Mia Bhai to come
and get me."

Even though he had finished eating, Golzar fiddled with a few
grains of rice.

Sakina said, "I don't like this at all. How much more can I take
of this?"

Sakina's words aroused a faint resentment in Golzar's heart: he
was the one most victimized by his mother's behaviour, but even his
wife refused to share his suffering. This reaction helped him recover
from his passivity. He pulled out the basin from under the bed,
washed his hands and mouth, gargled and cleaned his throat,
then sat on the bed dangling his feet and took the betel leaf from
Sakina's hand.

Sakina gathered and piled the dirty dishes in a corner. While
doing this she muttered in a low and bitter voice: "We're more

village girls, coming from low class families. How is it possible for me to hold on to a husband from a noble family like yours?"

Though Golzar Ali had no regrets that Sakina was a peasant girl, he saw nothing wrong in his mother's accusation either. But he did not want to displease his wife. Maybe, he could still salvage his evening.

"Why must you hold on to me? Have I left you? Couldn't you say that?"

"What could I say?"

How could Sakina say anything to her mother-in-law? Golzar Ali had told Sakina a long time ago that being suspicious was part of his mother's nature. Sakina's first experience had occurred three months after their marriage. One day in this very room Golzar, Sakina, Golzar's friend Ali Hussain and his wife Rabeya had spent the whole afternoon gossiping and making merry. Ali Hussain and his wife were both lively company. Ali Hussain was master of mimicry—he could imitate a stammering man, a crying infant, the sounds of cats and dogs, the sound of a cork being extracted from a bottle, or the sound of water being poured from an earthen jar—he could imitate anything. Rabeya was also a very jolly person. Once she interrupted Ali Hussain and told Golzar, "Golzar Bhai, show how your friend snores in his sleep." Then she herself displayed not only how her husband snored in his sleep but also how he ate a banana. For the first time in her life Sakina laughed continuously for a long time. Amidst this laughter evening fell, and Rabeya put on her *burkhah* and left with Ali Hussain to go home. Golzar also went outside with them. As soon as they had gone, Tarabibi called Sakina, "O, *Bou!* What is all this laughter about?" Remembering Ali Hussain and Rabeya's strange antics, Sakina covered her mouth with the end of her sari and laughed again, "Amma, that woman is so funny, you cannot help laughing!"

But Tarabibi's face was grim. She was dark, tall and heavy. She had no blouse on, only the sari that was wrapped around her chest. She panted in the heat. After a while, Sakina realized that this panting was not entirely due to the heat—Tarabibi was actually very angry. "*Bou,* don't dig a canal and invite the alligator, understand?"

"Hunh?"

"Don't you know what a canal is?" Tarabibi could not tolerate any more, "A village bumpkin . . . and you don't know what a canal is? You who grew up pissing and shitting beside ditches and canals, and now you don't know a canal, eh?"

After humiliating her with these irrelevant remarks, Tarabibi come to the real point, "Do you know that shameless hussy?"

"Ali Hussain Bhai's wife?"

"You don't have to tell me who she is. Don't I know Khadem's daughter? Khadem madman tried so hard to trap my Golzar for her! Golzar's eyes were in that direction too. Look, *Bou,* don't ruin yourself. Didn't you see how she laughed with another man, didn't you see?"

That night was very bad for Golzar. Sakina kept silent and did not respond at all. When Golzar pulled her down on the bed and kissed her for a long time, Sakina started crying. In between sobs, in snatched phrases, Sakina related the first sorrowful experience of her married life.

"Is this how you will take care of my future? My father had given me in marriage with a lot of hopes, what is all this you're doing?"

In between Sakina's lamentations, Golzar asked her, "Did Amma tell you all this?"

"Yes."

"Who knows what Amma said and what you madcap understood!"

But this had no effect. Late at night, Golzar woke up and saw that Sakina was sobbing, sometimes hiding her face in the pillow and sometimes sitting up and putting her face between her knees. When she saw him awaken, she turned and lay facing the other side. Her back was heaving—the sari did not cover her back and her blouse was sticky with sweat. As he lay looking, suddenly a continuous sound entered his ears and flung his body out of bed in a single leap. The sound of Tarabibi weeping had crept through the wall and door into this room. When Golzar tiptoed to the other end of the room and quietly opened the door, that sound burst in.

Tarabibi was fast asleep—the rhythmic fluctuations of her snores were transformed into a continuous wail by the time they reached this room. Golzar closed the door and lay down again. The sound of Tarabibi's sobs imposed upon the emptiness of the room. Golzar's late childhood, boyhood, and even early youth had been interspersed with Tarabibi's crying. By now the sobbing of Sakina lying beside him had calmed down a little. Golzar was afraid that the rest of his life would also be marked by somebody weeping. Putting his hand on Sakina's wet back, Golzar's fear somewhat subsided. There was a woman of flesh and blood, full of joys and sorrows lying beside him. Before there had been only a dirty green sheet on a thin mattress. Above was a high ceiling beneath which was this awkward, cave-like room. There were rooms above that ceiling before. At a very young age, Golzar Ali had seen them and recalled them faintly. But the floor creaked and trembled if anyone walked upstairs—that is why since before Golzar's birth no one had lived upstairs. Some of the upper steps of the staircase had crumbled and fallen down, so the way up was closed. Upstairs now was the sole reign of insects and mice. On some nights, the noise of these pests scurrying to and from came through like a stream of rain. With the fall of this waterless rain and Tarabibi's wailing came Ramzan Ali's short rebukes and Tarabibi's grumbling, and all mingled to from one whole and the thrust of it shook the bed under Golzar's body, the wall around, the mosquito-net and the ceiling to render him absolutely insecure. Golzar's blood and marrow would dry up and his body would become a shadow. There was nothing around his body, just shadows.

Above was the mosquito-net on which fell the shadow of the ceiling, on the side were the wall and the shadow of emptiness, the shadow of night and darkness. When all these shadows had full control over Golzar, he fell asleep once again. On other nights, the rough, prickly voice of Tarabibi would wake him, and after a while, he would realize that Tarabibi was trying to awaken Ramzan Ali: "O Golzar's father! You lie there like a corpse! O old man, even the lifeless bed creaks, but there's no movement in you as you lie sprawled all over!" Either Ramzan Ali would keep silent, or he would take up the hand fan by his pillow and start beating his wife: "Brazen hag, you are lusting for manliness! Wait! I'll show you manliness. Come, I'll satisfy your lust!"

Before his words could from properly in his toothless mouth and sleepy voice, they faded and his bony hands drooped in fatigue. He was above sixty-five then. He worked hard the whole day. They had no tenants upstairs now, they did not have any money for repairs. His only brother Moharram Ali had taken possession of their inherited Arzu Decorators. Now his only asset was a mike shop—renting mikes and records was profitable enough, but now-a-days you needed publicity to gain customers. How could Ramzan Ali's health sustain? At times Golzar would feel angry—why did Ramzan Ali have to remarry at such an old age even though his wife died? Tarabibi was Ramzan Ali's second wife; she had been a sister-in-law of some sort to him. The daughters by the first wife still called Tarabibi "aunt." The three sons of those daughters, who were all older than Golzar, two being born before Tarabibi's marriage, often teased him, "O Uncle, when grandpa married again he was already sixty years old. The old man must have a great deal of trouble handling a twenty-five-year-old woman. Isn't it a lot of hard work for the old man?" Ramzan Ali would not have had to suffer like this at night if he had not married again. Late at night, Tarabibi would chant in her shrill, cracked voice, "O old dead log! Have you already crept inside your grave? Wait, let me say a prayer for you, if you go in without a funeral, won't you be damned?" Golzar's heart would break. If his father had not remarried in old age, he would never have been born into this world. His father had done him grave injustice by not allowing him the joy of not being born. He could not even imagine the condition of non-existence, but bitterly regretted being deprived of that prospect. At this moment, though, lying beside his wife, Golzar no longer desired not to exist. Putting his hand on Sakina's wet back, he felt the womanly smell of sweat trickling into the lines of his hand and he fell asleep.

The next day before leaving for his shop Golzar told his mother, "Amma, your *Bou* probably misunderstood whatever you told her yesterday and cried all through the night."

"What did I say?" Tarabibi was hanging clothes on the rope in the veranda. Without stopping her work, she said, "What is there to cry about?"

"With Ali Hussain's wife . . . ." While Golzar thought how he should go on, Tarabibi spread out a sheet and then rescued her son saying, "I said that wife is shameless. Didn't you see how she flirts with other men? There was talk of your marriage to her."

"What, you never told me about that!"

"Why, don't you know? Crazy Khadem's brother asked your father many times. There was even talk of sending a proposal."

"I didn't know that."

"Why? Didn't you go in and out of Crazy Khadem's house?"

Golzar was not only ashamed to hear such a remark from his mother, but also turned pale when he noticed Sakina standing nearby holding the door. Golzar and Rabeya had lived in the same lane and played together in childhood—all this was true. But after growing up it was doubtful whether they saw each other even once in six months. Actually it was Tarabibi who sent Golzar to call Rabeya when she needed help in sewing or in making pickles and preserves. As he grew older, Golzar himself would feel shy and hesitate to go inside their house and preferred to convey his mother's message through Rabeya's brother. Tarabibi would often fuss and get angry at this feminine shyness of Golzar. And now it was Tarabibi who said, "We thought you were the one who told her uncle to speak to your father."

"No, Amma, I don't know anything at all."

Saying "Huh," Tarabibi started for the water-well.

But Golzar did not face much trouble in bringing around Sakina. Just as she believed Tarabibi without any hesitation, so did she put her trust in her husband. Sakina was always cheerful and happy; her curiosity knew no bounds when she went outside. And she was restless and eager to explore the whole city in one day.

But she could also become sullen in an instant. About a month and a half later Golzar returned home about two-thirty or three in the afternoon and Sakina greeted him with, "Why are you so late? Did you go to Rathkhola?"

"Yes, didn't I tell you? That bastard party gave me the go around even today. That motherfucker is troubling me a lot about the bill."

But Sakina said again, "Where did you go in Rathkhola? To your friend Binoy's house?"

"Where?"

"Binoy's house. I guess you were gossiping with his sister. I think I can figure out why you frequent a Hindu home so often."

Golzar felt very irritated. Even after spending a couple of hours he had not been able to get the money they owed him. And he had not been to Binoy's house in over two and a half years.

"Don't talk like a low-bred."

Sakina started weeping. Sobbing, she said, "Yes, I come from a low-bred family, but it was your mother who said, 'He went to Rathkhola. Must be sitting with Binoy's sister. He won't get back until late.' What can I do?"

Golzar decided to settle this matter once and for all. He went straight to Tarabibi's room. Ramzan was sitting on the bed, caressing his bony feet, his *lungi* pulled up to his knees. Tarabibi sat on the floor crushing betel-leaf for her husband.

"Amma, what did you tell her about Binoy's sister?" Golzar asked.

"What did I say?"

"You know what you said."

"What I said and what she tattled to you, how do I know?" Tarabibi took her hands off the pestle. As Ramzan Ali put out his rotten, bamboo-like hands, Tarabibi pushed away the mortar and said, "Not yet!" It seemed that Tarabibi included Golzar in her rebuke.

But Golzar remained undaunted: "You'll make up all kinds of lies, and make my life a hell, won't you?"

"I tell lies?" Tarabibi sat upright. "What was all that intimacy with Binoy's sister?"

Binoy was Golzar's class-mate in high school. Golzar had flunked the 12th grade a couple of times and given up studies while Binoy, after marginally passing in his second attempt, had gone off to Calcutta. At first he came once a year to Dhaka and Golzar would go to visit him. But the past few years Binoy had stopped coming, and Golzar no longer visited their house. Binoy's father, Radhakrishna Basak, was a timid and cowardly person. If there was the slightest indication of communal disturbance, he asked some one to call Golzar, fed him sweets and said, "Son, for the love of all of you, I couldn't abandon my native land. See to our welfare."

But two and a half or three years had passed since Radhakrishna called Golzar and he had not gone there by himself either.

Tarabibi's full attention was now focused on Golzar. She sat on the floor with her legs spread out. Her feet could be seen on both sides. There was the eczema sore on the upper side of her right foot; it seemed like a pet, she scratched it at leisure. It sometimes increased and then diminished. This was the season of its growth. From his mother's pet sore one or two drops of pus stared at Golzar. Tarabibi's headcover had stuck to the bun of her hair; her face was long, dark, full and uneven, and on her broad and smooth forehead were some grey hairs beneath which were the locks of black hair. When her small eyes targeted Golzar, he was totally subdued. Something snapped in his brain; it seemed that it would be no use saying anything, he would not be able to get through to his mother at all.

But Ramzan Ali was feeling better today. After a long time, he had had *tehari*, a rich preparation of fine rice and meat, from Shukkur Mahmud's shop for breakfast. He felt goodwill towards Golzar and said slowly to Tarabibi, "The boy is now married, but your tongue has not straightened yet. When to say what . . . ." In mid sentence, a guttural sound gushed from his chest and he started to cough with his hand on his stomach.

"You're lying in the grave, you better stay there. What do you understand? I've run your house for thirty years. I've never seen you walk straight. How'll you understand the bad intentions of today's youngsters?"

Tarabibi's words accompanied with Ramzan Ali's cough, scorned both father and son. Tarabibi wanted to pierce Golzar with her all-knowing pair of eyes, "I tell lies? Then tell me, Binoy's sister got married in India and yet eight months of the year she stays at her father's, why? Tell me, why?"

Swallowing a few times and adjusting his voice, Golzar said, "What you link with what! That was three or four years ago. There was some trouble with the passport, that's why she couldn't go for a long time."

"Paskoat!" Tarabibi pounced upon the matter of Dipali's passport. "O, the paskoat was there, eh? In the name of paskoat, didn't she sit in your room for two hours? Don't I understand all this?"

Dipali had come to this house only once. To untangle the problems of her passport, she needed Golzar to make some contacts for her. That was almost four years ago. When Dipali came, Tarabibi herself took her to Golzar's room. "O Golzar, look, it's Binoy's sister!" She even brought a chair for Dipali from her own room. Then saying, "You two talk, I'll be back," she went to the kitchen and did not return. When, after fifteen or twenty minutes, Dipali stepped out on the veranda preparing to leave, Tarabibi saw her from the kitchen and said, "Why not stay for a while more? I'll make tea." After Dipali had sat for another half an hour in Golzar's room, Tarabibi called him and sent tea. Golzar chatted with Dipali for an hour about her husband, about Binoy and Golzar's boyhood. The memory of that hour's chat with Dipali often evoked pleasant sensations in Golzar, but he never had to spend sleepless nights over it.

Whether to control her anger or to take time to choose her words, Tarabibi was silent for some time and then spoke slowly, "How could you stay outside until three in the morning fooling around with some lowly woman? You have a wife at home and she is big with child. You should be ashamed of yourself! Because of your infernal actions, no angel will ever set foot in this house. When children commit sins, does God accept the worship and prayers of parents?"

This reproachful tone of Tarabibi failed to intimidate Golzar. Instead her quiet tone strengthened him. Gazing at Ramzan's rusty pair of eyes, he sucked vitality from the core of the dying old man with the fallen head. Gaining strength from his father's nourishment and mother's moderation, Golzar said, "Amma, no mother ever says such things to her son. You've given me a wife. If there's anything wrong in my character, she'll see to it. She doesn't know a thing, but you've fitted a radar, and every minute your radar stirs and creates a meaningless fuss!"

"O Allah, O Allah! All my fate! I've married my son to a country girl, a simpleton. If only she could understand, then I would not have to suffer like this." Tarabibi was gradually losing her fervour.

After pausing a while, she began with renewed zeal, "If *Bou* had that much intelligence, wouldn't she have discovered your flirtations with the maid long ago? Answer that."

Since that day Tarabibi had decided that the part-time maid was really Golzar's main attraction. It did not matter how long during the day Golzar saw Suruj's mother. She came early in the morning before six and left by nine or nine-thirty. She came again at one in the afternoon and worked until two-thirty or three. Golzar saw her after he awoke for about an hour in the morning and then again for an hour in the afternoon. Because she worked hard in different houses, the maid did have a strong and well-shaped body. Well, why keep a girl with such an attractive figure? Ramzan had also remarked on this matter one day, "If you're suspicious, why not dismiss the maid?"

"Why? Why should I dismiss her? Won't I need to hire another one? Will your son spare any of them?"

Nowadays Tarabibi would not raise these matters in front of Golzar. But she would begin as soon as he would leave the house. Today, since he returned a little late after the movie, she immediately grabbed the opportunity to hound him.

Sakina now sat quietly. The piercing thorns targeted a little while ago at Golzar's heart had now been overlaid by the meal of rice and curry, and he felt very sleepy. But if he slept now, he could not share Sakina's humiliations. Golzar Ali sat beside Sakina and said, "Let me write to your Mia Bhai. When he comes you can go to Mirkadem. Let me see if I can find a house, and once the rent and all's fixed, I'll come and get you." This kind of proposal always worked.

Lying on the bed, Golzar felt like sprawling full length all over the bed, but he had to share the bed with another person.

The next day when Golzar returned around two-thirty, he heard that both Tarabibi and Sakina had gone out. This afternoon was his cousin's *gaye holud*, the ceremonial smearing with golden turmeric, and his uncle had come himself and taken both of them. Ramzan said, "Go and get them back after *Maghrib*." Tarabibi was not in the kitchen, nor was Sakina in their room. Humming a popular melody in a slightly distorted tune, Golzar stretched leisurely without changing his clothes.

Suruj's mother came into the room. "Why are you lying down at this time? Shall I bring lunch?"

He paused his humming but the tune still enveloped his being, "You want to bring lunch? Why don't you let me rest a while."

"No, get up. Once you eat I need to wash the dishes and eat myself." Saying this, Suruj's mother adjusted the sari over her bosom.

As his eyes fell on that gesture, all traces of the tune from his eyes, mouth, and voice vanished completely. Instead, independent of any desire, a whirring sound stifled his heart, and blood from all over rushed towards it at a dangerously high speed. Holding the bed-post, Suruj's mother stood by. His olive-coloured, medium-sized body seemed to have a volition of its own, causing Golzar to leap down from the bed. Suruj's mother watched him with knitted eye-brows. Before her frown could disappear, Golzar had grabbed her right hand and drawn her close. Against his chest now was her head with reddish-black hair and its odour of stale coconut oil.

Suruj's mother whispered, "Let go of my hand."

Immediately Golzar let go and moved back. After standing for another moment, Suruj's mother suddenly walked away rapidly through the veranda into the kitchen. The sound of an aluminium pitcher falling from the veranda made Golzar realize that it was three-thirty. He gathered his *lungi* and *gamchha* from another corner of his room.

After his bath, Golzar returned to find the torn mat spread on the floor and his covered lunch served on it. After eating, he picked his underwear and trousers from the rack, but put them back again. About fifteen minutes later, Suruj's mother entered the room.

"I am leaving. Won't you go to the shop?"

Golzar answered as he lay on the bed, "You can go. I'll go after a while." Trying to erase the effects of the hand-grabbing incident, he added brightly, "I'll go and get Amma and everybody."

"They won't be back so soon."

"Hunh!"

Suruj's mother remained standing, holding on to the bed-post. Listening to the slow rhythmic snoring of Ramzan Ali in the next room, Golzar felt stirrings of desire again.

"Will you lend me ten taka? Don't tell Amma. I've got to take my son to the doctor. Will you?"

Silently, Golzar Ali brought out two five-taka bills from under his pillow and extended his right hand. Suruj's mother stood just beside his bed now. With this very right hand holding the bills he could pull her right onto the bed. Across the room was the entrance to the next room. He must look that way for a moment. But when did Suruj's mother close that door? The door was locked from inside. Golzar was totally unnerved. Suruj's mother was just beside his bed, but he stared straight at his feet. He must cut his nails—he had not done that for a long time, there were marks of sandal straps on his feet. Between the toes were thick layers of dirt. When bathing, he had not scrubbed between the toes. There was dirt under his feet too—suddenly there was a noise and all the filth and grime vanished. Ramzan Ali was coughing in the next room. He seemed to be calling someone in between the fits of coughing. From under the fingers of Golzar's extended hand, a five-taka bill fell onto the floor. His hands lay flat on both sides like dead vines.

"Didn't Abba call?" Golzar breathed normally after a long time.

"No, he's asleep." Before Suruj's mother could finish her reply, there was a loud knock at the main gate and Ramzan Ali's shrieks shook the entire house. Under the impact of the tremour even the erect figure of Suruj's mother stooped on the floor. She deftly recovered one bill from the floor and one from the bed and stood for a moment. Then, targeting Golzar's sightless eyes, she threw a "Huh!" sounding shred of laughter and opened the door.

Through the gaping door, the hoarse screams kept falling with a thud in Golzar's room, "I've been calling you for so long! You bitch, you locked yourself in that room to fuck!"

There was the sound of Suruj's mother opening the front door and the entrance of Tarabibi could be perceived. "Were you all dead? I kept shouting in vain. Bitch!" She closed the main gate herself. "Why haven't you gone yet? Did Golzar eat before he went out?"

Suruj's mother replied, "He did."

"Why didn't you leave? It's after four. What were you doing?"

Saying, "I'm leaving," Suruj's mother turned to go, but Tarabibi stopped her, "Won't you take your rice?" Then she came in shouting at Ramzan Ali: "How can you be so deaf as if you were completely dead. I called you again and again, the whole neighbourhood heard, but you did not."

Ramzan just asked, "Where's *Bou*?"

"*Bou*'ll return at night. Golzar will go from the shop to get her. Didn't you tell him?"

Ramzan Ali sat upon the bed, pointed to the other room and said, "Golzar is home."

"Didn't he go to the shop? Why? When I shouted so loudly, why didn't he hear?"

"How would be hear?" Ramzan answered slowly. "How would he hear? He had locked the door and was enjoying himself with the whore. How could he hear?"

Tarabibi dropped down her swarthy, heavy body on one end of Ramzan Ali's bed.

"I feel I'm already dead. You people don't ever want to see me live again!" Thick drops of tears fell from Ramzan Ali's cloudy eyes, as if pus was collecting on a wound. He spoke quietly, "How can my son flirt with a harlot in a locked room just beside my own? You might as well just murder and do away with me!"

With numerous lines of expression on her broad, dark face, Tarabibi watched her aged husband weeping. There was not a drop of blood in his shrunken visage, the flesh on his face appeared like the crust on a drying wound—if you pinched a corner, all of it would burst open and fall apart. Ramzan's forehead was sweating in his agitation. The few reddish-black locks of hair, like the dried-up fibres on an eaten mango seed, clung to his forehead as he perspired.

"I'm going out." Without glancing at either his mother or his father, Golzar said, "I'm going. Close the door."

Looking away from her husband, Tarabibi glanced at her son. His hair was uncombed, and, as he bent, locks of hair fell over his forehead onto his ears. Tarabibi said, "Go to your aunt's house in Lalbag after *Maghrib* and bring *Bou* home."

Without answering, Golzar crossed the veranda and went down the stairs. As he stepped down each step, his bushy hair fluttered like a cluster of leaves on the highest branch swinging madly in the wind. But there were only five stairs—they soon ended. Tarabibi screwed the lines on her face and raised her head to view the fluttering locks of hair on her son's face.

"There's sin inside this house. Devilish activity curses this home. How'll our prayers be heard?" Ramzan Ali whispered in a sagging voice, "We can't prosper. Do you know why? We've Satan's workshop in our homestead! Why do you think I have to lie on the bed day after day all year round? Let the bastard come home tonight. I'll kick him on his buttocks and throw him out!"

"Enough!" Tarabibi stopped her husband as she started to get up. "Enough! Why do you shout and fuss? What did Golzar do? Isn't my son a young man? You're an old haggard and dying with one foot in your grave. How will you understand the doings of a young man?"

Translated from Bangla by Parveen K. Elias.

Published in *"The Daily Star"* in December 1994.

Motijan's Daughters

Selina Hossain

Marriage gives a woman a certain kind of stature in the new household—she becomes a wife, and becoming a wife means the beginning of a new chapter in her life. She has a world of her own made up of joys and sorrows and so many other things, as well as control over the household—that is what Motijan used to imagine. but she could not understand her position in this household. She did not even know if there was any need for her at all in this household. She had a mother-in-law over and above her who was really in charge, and Motijan was no more than a superfluous addition to the family. Her heart was full of the frustration of being superfluous. The sharp words of her mother-in-law often scorched her soul. At such times Motijan felt totally sick at heart of married life. She wished she were a widow.

The mother-in-law's name was Gulnoor, her son's name was Abul. She had lost her husband when her son was just eighteen months and had been a widow for twenty-two years now. She had managed the house and whatever land her husband owned with an iron hand, looked after the family and brought her son up. She had never asked for help from either her husband's family or her own parents. The people of the village said of her: "She's a very hard woman, mind you." Gulnoor was proud of this. She felt that being hard was really a matter of pride and this hardness had a significance for her. As a result, whatever she herself thought or did was the right thing, it could not be anything else. Motijan had expectations from her husband, but she found that her mother-in-law had totally usurped her rights. Sometimes she thought that even Abul was superfluous in his mother's household. When she expressed her acute grievance at not being able to lead a contented family life with her husband, Abul simply escaped from the house. He told Motijan in clear-cut terms: "Don't tell me anything. I know nothing and can do nothing. Mother is all in all. She keeps my heart trampled under her feet." While saying this, Abul waved his hands in the air, spoke out of twisted lips and gave vent to his feelings in vulgar invectives. But his words failed to indicate the target of his obscenities. Motijan looked at her husband with her eyes wide open. His appearance was always bewildered, his eyes bloodshot and he was totally indifferent about family life. He had absolutely no interest in household affairs. He frequented a den be smoked *ganja* with his friends. He was a regular ruffian and thought nothing of spending money on a woman named Rosoi who had a place in the market. Neither his mother nor his wife was of any concern to him. Realizing this truth, Motijan grew hard. She wanted to be as hard as her mother-in-law. Her mother-in-law's reproaches made her stubborn inside.

Nine months of marriage had completely opened her eyes, but no one could guess that. She pretended to look neither to the right, nor to the left—neither below, nor above. But she had eyes for everything around her; not even a tiny piece of straw could obstruct her vision. Did her life in this new household have a very good start, after all? In the beginning she hardly understood anything properly. Looking back upon the past few months now she realized that not even the first seven days after her marriage had passed well. Her mother-in-law's attitude was sullen, she never spoke to her properly. Motijan could look at her face only with fear. She did not understand her husband even. He too did not speak to her in a normal way. He puffed at *bidis* the whole day and night and filled the room with smoke. It was impossible to take a long and relaxing breath in that suffocating air. Motijan could say nothing to him. The sultry atmosphere in the house always frightened her. She was scared to put her foot down anywhere, scared even to sneeze. At mealtimes her fingers would suddenly become paralysed while picking the bones of a piece of *ilish* fish. Raising a ball of rice to her mouth, she would glance surreptitiously at her mother-in-law and find her looking at her with eyes that made her tremble inside. Motijan's heart seemed to beat noisily, almost like the rumbling of the waters of the Mahananda during the monsoon, as though she could feel the sound of the waves touching her body if she listened carefully. When her mother-in-law raised the topic of dowry on the eighth day, she shrank in fear. She had just finished eating, the aluminium plate still bore the marks of gravy. Gulnoor spoke through gritted teeth, "At the time of the marriage your father promised that he would give a wrist-watch and cycle to my Abul. Why hasn't he sent them yet?"

Motijan remained silent. She drew lines on her plate with her forefinger. She knew her father's circumstances well, his household expenses were twice his income. He had made the promise without being sure of his ability to get the money for all those things. What was going to happen now? Gulnoor spoke harshly again, "Why don't you say anything?"

Motijan said tearfully, "I don't know anything."

Gulnoor burst out, "Why don't you know? You must!"

Motijan began to tremble. Her fingers became motionless on the plate. She felt as though the rice she had already swallowed was choking her; any further shouting and she would simply vomit out all she had eaten.

"Don't snivel, now! Go and wash up the plates and pots."

The order to work relieved Motijan. It gave her a wonderful chance to escape. She collected all the utensils and carried them to the pond. It was the middle of the day, blazing sunlight all around. Motijan sat on the edge of the pond, looking at the sunlight with unblinking eyes. She realized that nothing was smouldering inside her, there was neither any burning feeling nor the pain of being scorched. She only felt like bursting into tears out of an acute sense of helpless anger against her father. She buried her face between her knees and gave in to suppressed sobs. Why did father have to make false promises? What harm would there have been if she had not been married off? All she wanted was to join Beli *bua* who worked with the village cooperative making *nakshi kanthas*, fine embroidered quilts. She was bent upon earning her own living. But her father ruled that out. He would lose face and be utterly humiliated if he could not get his daughter married off. So he had to find a husband for her by any means. Why? Why? Motijan wanted to kick all the utensils into the water. What a mockery of a marriage! Where was the good life she had been led to expect? What about her husband? Was this the prestige her father valued so much? The honour and prestige of the poor depended on the food and clothing they had. Motijan kept on staring at the blazing midday sunlight without blinking. Before her eyes, her bedroom darkened with the smoke of countless *bidis*, seemed to turn into a coloured balloon, soaring higher and higher up in the air. She could never reach up and touch it. At that moment the bright day around her began to freeze into a solid mass within her. She thought, I too shall become a hard woman.

Days roll on, as is the nature of days. Motijan's days also rolled on. She came to realize that although she had to live with Abul, he was not really a part of her life. He spent at least half the month with Rosoi at her place. In the beginning Motijan had tried to remonstrate with him and been rewarded with beatings. Now she no longer raised the subject, neither did Gulnoor bother about whether her son returned home at night or not. She supported whatever her son did. In fact, she felt quite comfortable when her son did not come. Then she could torture Motijan to her heart's content, which she could not do when Abul was present. She had to pretend to humour her son—at least for the sake of appearances. Besides, now-a-days Gulnoor directly gave vent to her anger about the dowry. She shouted loudly at Motijan, "Your father is a liar, a cheat. If he couldn't manage to deliver the cycle and the wrist-watch, why did he promise?"

In her agitation Gulnoor was quite abusive and kept on shouting loudly. Abul also followed his mother's example. One day Motijan could no longer remain silent although she felt like choking. In a trembling voice she said, "My father is not a cheat. He's poor. My father is not a liar. He doesn't have any money right now, that's why it's taking him all these days to buy the cycle and the wrist-watch."

"Shut up, you wretched girl! How dare you speak such big words!"

Gulnoor dragged Motijan by her hair and threw her to the ground. She put a rope round her neck and kept her tied to a post inside the room. She was not given anything to eat the whole day. Motijan grew numb. She had no tears in her eyes, no sense of burning in her heart either. Her lack of feelings slowly began to turn into a hard core within her. She wanted to turn into a hard woman. In the evening Gulnoor dragged her by the rope to the pondside and said, "I can no longer feed rice to you. All you'll get now is grass. Go on eat."

Abul joined his mother in laughing at this terrible joke and then went off to Rosoi's place in the market. A little later Gulnoor brought Motijan out on the verandah and gave her a plate of rice to eat. Motijan ate the rice in stoic, dispirited silence. Then she went into her room and closed the door behind her to be alone in the darkness. She could not sleep for a moment the whole night. She tossed restlessly on her bed, rolled on the floor. She tried hard to remain calm but could not. She spoke to the darkness, Tell me, O darkness, how can I take revenge? How? At this moment of ultimate silence she felt the need of a companion, someone very close to her, someone to whom she could open her heart. She craved for a little joy now. No more this tortured life for her. She felt no responsibility at all for a husband who was a drunkard, a gambler, infatuated with another man's woman. She could visualise only one opponent before her, the one who was reputed to be a hard woman in the village. Motijan's fight was against her.

Days roll on, as is the nature of days. Motijan's days also rolled on. Abul came home sometimes, sometimes he did not. When her mother-in-law became abusive about the missing dowry, Motijan listened in silence. She had not been to her father's house for such a long time. No one from her father's house could come to see her either. Her elder brother had come twice. Gulnoor treated him very badly. She had forbidden him to come again without the wrist-watch and the cycle. No one else had come in the last six months or so. On his last visit, her elder brother had told her in private, "Try not to be so unhappy. I tell you, Father and I are trying to get the wrist and cycle."

Motijan had scolded her elder brother with anger in her eyes, "No, you must not trouble yourselves. Father has already been branded a liar and a cheat. So why should you worry about the wrist-watch and cycle any longer? And I? I have turned into a cow. They ask me to live on grass."

Saying that Motijan had burst out in ripples of laughter—her first uninhibited laughter after arriving in this household. Her brother looked on at her stupidly. From the verandah Gulnoor rebuked her sharply for such unmannerly mirth. For the first time Motijan ignored her mother-in-law and kept on laughing.

Made nervous by her abnormal appearance and the loudness of her laughter, her brother slunk away quietly. His escape made her utterly sad; her grief seemed to rend her soul into pieces. Silently, she went into the cowshed. She cleaned the shed and sat there late into the afternoon making cowdung cakes to be used as fuel. She kept at that task, till the blazing sunlight outside grew dimmer. From that time Motijan's power to ignore anything became stronger within her heart.

Very late that afternoon when Motijan felt ravenous with hunger, she came back to the house to eat, but her mother-in-law stopped her at the door of the kitchen. Motijan understood that Gulnoor had sacrificed her midday nap in order to guard over the food. She wanted to punish her for her impudent laughter earlier in the day. Finding her way blocked, Motijan said in a cold voice, "I want to eat. I'm hungry."

Gulnoor said, "There's no food."

Motijan shouted, "Why not?"

Gulnoor bared her teeth in a snarl and raise her hands threateningly, "I won't give you any rice. You can have nothing but grass."

"I do my share of work in this household. I earn my food—I don't just sit idle and eat. You have to give me food. Hasn't a servant got the right to demand food?"

Motijan stepped past her mother-in-law and entered the kitchen. She rummaged through the pots and pans but found no food. There was a covered plate in a *shika* hanging from the ceiling. As soon as she reached for it, her mother-in-law rushed up, "Don't touch that, I tell you. That's Abul's food."

Motijan broke into her unnatural laughter again. Then she spoke through gritted teeth. "Rosoi has cooked for him. Why should you worry?"

"What did you say? How dare you?"

Motijan made no reply. She held the plate of rice and curry close to her chest and started eating. She realized that she must not let go of the plate. Her mother-in-law would get the chance to jump upon her even if she sat down to eat. So she kept standing and eating in such a way that if Gulnoor attempted to come close she could throw the plate at her. Right at her head. A big piece of fish had been kept for Abul and now, what good luck, it was hers to eat! Or was it something she deserved, after all? That's what Beli *bua* used to say: Claim your own rights. The thought brought a faint smile on Motijan's lips. Ravenously hungry, she kept on eating voraciously without even looking at her mother-in-law. She stole a glance at her out of the corner of her eye. No, had not taken a single step forward. She realized that Gulnoor was staring at her with dilated eyes. Such defeat was utterly inconceivable to a hard woman like her. She felt within her heart a surge of victory as though the waves of the Mahananda were tearing a path through a curtain of thick mist.

Later in the afternoon she came to the bamboo grove beside the pond. It was a secluded, shady spot. Sunlight failed to reach the ground through the thick foliage. It was as though a solid layer of glue across the tops of the trees kept the light trapped there. The ground was damp and wet, soft and pleasantly cool. Motijan's mother-in-law had perhaps fallen asleep in her room after her defeat. There was no sound from her. She always had to have a nap in the middle of the day, it was her favourite habit. Motijan sat down beneath the bamboos and hummed softly to herself. This was the first time after her marriage that she was feeling so happy. The young boy named Budhe had taken the cows to graze on the other side of the pond. He was a very restless child, couldn't sit quietly even for a moment. He would frequently come up to Motijan and say, "Why don't you tell me a story, *Bhabi*."

"What sort of story? About a king?"

He would nod in agreement. Motijan would tell him a story about a king, about the seven seas and thirteen rivers. Listening to her, the eyes of twelve-year-old Budhe would gleam with pleasure. Right at that moment Budhe was not anywhere near. Motijan felt as if today her heart was full of stories about kings as if she were travelling across the seven seas and thirteen rivers herself. She longed to tell Budhe about her feelings.

Leaving the bamboo groves, as Motijan approached the house, she met Lokman before the front door. Seeing her, Lokman smiled. He had a tall, slender figure. Motijan trembled when she looked at his eyes. He was Abul's friend and came to this house ever so often. When Abul did not return home for several days, he sent some purchase through him. Lokman also travelled by the house on his way to and from the market. Motijan had never had the opportunity to speak to him, neither did she have the courage to do so. Today Lokman looked surprised to see her at the front door.

"How are you Bhabi?"

"Well," Motijan smiled easily. Her teeth glittered like pearls and Lokman looked somewhat bemused.

"Here—your shopping."

Motijan reached for the bundle. She spoke with an easy manner, "Come, sit in the shade. Would you like to have a *pan*?"

The lilting tone of her voice startled Lokman. He wanted to sit for a while. Yet he hesitated and said, "I have to go now."

"Do come again, won't you?"

"Yes. I'll come again." Lokman's face brightened as he spoke. Motijan went into the house, walking with a natural grace and looking back once at him over her shoulder. The rhythm of her movements startled Lokman once more. Was this the same woman he had seen so many times before? It took him a while to get out of his bemused state.

Motijan put the shopping down on the verandah and sat there listlessly. Gulnoor was still sleeping. As soon as she woke up, she would open the bundle to check the contents. Motijan was not allowed to open the shopping bag. She never wanted to, anyway. Today she felt more at ease leaving it carelessly on one side. If she could, she would have trampled on that bundle and cast it into the pond. But she did not wish to quarrel needlessly with her mother-in-law. She was engulfed in a dejection that seemed to strike at her like gusts of torrential rain. It was more than a year since her marriage, but she was not a mother yet. The bones in her body grated with her suffering. She was surrounded by an all-pervading emptiness while Abul was enjoying himself thoroughly at Rosoi's place. Motijan could not overcome her dejection.

Since her defeat the other day, Gulnoor had been playing a different tune. She tried to provoke Motijan every now and then by her sarcastic remarks and asked her point blank, "Why can't you have a baby?"

Motijan looked stupidly at her. What could she say in reply to a question like that? Once she felt like asking, "Why don't you ask your son?" But the next moment she desisted and, turning her head, went off to attend to her household chores. Behind her back, her mother-in-law raised her voice to complain loudly, "How can my family lines be kept alive, O Allah?"

The tone of her voice made Motijan feel irritated all over. She stopped abruptly and turned back, but saw her mother-in-law passing through the side door into their neighbour's house. She came back and sat down on the verandah. Her mother-in-law would now start accusing her of being a sterile woman. Her whole body felt numb. Why couldn't she bear a child, after all? Motijan's eyes brimmed over with tears of anguish.

Budhe came and stood before her. He had brought a load of *jams* gathered in a corner of his *lungi.*

"Have some, Bhabi. Look. I've brought so many."

Motijan stared at Budhe without saying anything. On another day she would have shouted in glee and said, "Budhe is a real darling!" Not hearing her admiring remarks today, Budhe nodded his head understandingly and said: "I know, Amma has called you names, hasn't she?"

Budhe whispered, "Don't cry. Bhabi. Amma's very bad."

Budhe dropped the *jams* on the verandah and ran off. At that moment Gulnoor was telling Noor's mother next door, "Sister, that daughter-in-law of mine is barren. Otherwise, why doesn't she bear a child?"

Noor's mother giggled, "What if she's barren? Get your son married again. Be sure to ask for a lot of money this time."

Gulnoor smiled happily and did not waste any time in repeating it all to Motijan. She also declared that her life would be meaningless without a child to keep the family line going. Motijan made no reply at all. The world "marriage" was spinning round and round within her head. When Abul returned home after two days, she mentioned the need for keeping the family line going. But Abul reacted to that simply by snarling at her, "I'll kick the family's behind!"

"But your mother wants it."

"Go and tell mother . . . ."

He stopped abruptly and swore under his breath. Motijan was stupefied on hearing the vicious swearing. She felt as though something was moving inside her abdomen and clutching at her entrails. She felt sick. Yet, as she breathed the stench of *ganja* coming from Abul's mouth, she wanted to become angry with her own life. She wanted to kick Abul off the top of her body. But she restrained herself and imagined Budhe calling her. When the stench of *ganja* hardened inside her chest, she could feel Lokman's tall, slender figure coming within her reach. She stretched her hand trying to touch him, and his body seemed to curl into a small bundle and crawl into her fist.

One day, at noon, the sky darkened with clouds, and a strong wind began to blow. There were sudden gusts of stormy wind. Apparently Budhe had not come back from the grazing fields because the lowing of the cows could not be heard from anywhere nearby. Gulnoor had gone to Kansat in the morning to visit the family of her husband's elder brother. Before starting she had said that she would return in the evening. Abul had been away from the house for two days. Motijan sat on the verandah with her legs stretched out, embroidering flowers on a handkerchief. She had to do the work on the sly, keeping it a secret from her mother-in-law. She wanted to give the handkerchief to Lokman as a present. She had developed an easy relationship with Lokman. He knew when Gulnoor would be sleeping, when Budhe would not be around, when the sunlight would be filtering through the shadows of the bamboo grove. At such times Motijan had endless leisure on her hand: she could travel across the seven seas and thirteen rivers.

One day gusts of stormy wind blew dust from the courtyard into Motijan's face, blinding her eyes and dishevelling her hair. As she jumped to her feet to take cover, she saw Lokman running across the courtyard to the protection of the verandah. The rains came just at that moment, falling in torrents. Inside the room, Lokman pressed Motijan to his chest in a tight embrace. For the first time, the very first time in her life, Motijan truly experienced the intense sensation of a man's touch on her body. She realized that there was a great deal of difference between Abul and Lokman.

Days roll on, as they always will, following their course. Motijan's days, however, passed differently now. She was going to be a mother. After that day's incident when Motijan first missed her monthly period, she cried out in astonishment. Alone in her room she tried to come to an understanding with her own self—to come to terms with the surge of emotions throbbing all over her being, as though all the doors that had so far remained closed were now opening before her.

On hearing the news, Abul looked at her askance, "So the family line is saved, after all!" But Motijan's mother-in-law was not happy at first. She remained ominously quiet. It was her second defeat, she had never imagined that it would come so soon. Then she looked obliquely at Motijan and said in a stern voice. "You must not give birth to a girl child, mind you."

Motijan said, "What makes you hanker after a boy child? Your own son does not care for you."

"What if he doesn't, you slut? You must bear a boy, or you'll suffer the consequences, I tell you."

Her mother-in-law's hot breath seared Motijan's face. She knew that it was a year of acute drought—crops were withering, fields were cracking up. Her whole body was heavy with a fatigue that was trying to tear at and devour her entire being. She tried to ignore her physical weakness with the strength of her mind.

In course of time, Motijan gave birth to a daughter. Abul laughed loudly and mockingly, "So the family line is not going to be saved, after all!"

Gulnoor was grave, she even refused to see her grandchild. But Motijan found a release to all the pent-up emotions within her by pressing her daughter to her breast and showering her with love and caresses. Even in the midst of all the indifference and neglect she was subjected to, the ecstasy she felt at the birth of her daughter billowed all around her like the surging waves of the Mahananda. Motijan danced and swung her daughter before her mother-in-law's eyes and sang her to sleep. Gulnoor could not bear Motijan's joy, she became ferocious and threatening. But Motijan grew stronger than before within herself and said, "If I could I would give birth to a hundred daughters." She no longer remained silent but shouted back. This made Gulnoor madder than ever before. Of late Abul had practically stopped coming home. Motijan came to know that he had left Rosoi and taken up with another woman. He was too busy to bother about anything else. All that made Motijan even more stubborn.

In about a year Motijan was with child again by Lokman and gave birth to another girl. This time Gulnoor remained silent for seven days, then she declared that she was no longer prepared to tolerate a daughter-in-law who bore nothing but a girl child every year. When her son returned home, she would make him divorce this useless wife of his and send her off to her father's house.

Motijan silently listened to her mother-in-law's tirade. She had no time to think of anything else now. She was busy throughout the day with her children. On top of that, she had all the household chores to take care of too. She was nearly always overcome with fatigue and exhaustion.

When Abul returned home after about a month or so, Gulnoor wasted no time in loudly announcing her decision to him. At that moment Abul was very much under the influence of *ganja*. His mother's words startled him. He stared blankly at her for a few seconds, then went out of the house again. Gulnoor filled the house with her angry shouts. "I'll throw that wretched woman out right now!"

Quite a few of the neighbours gathered in the courtyard. Motijan appeared before the crowd with her two daughters pressed to her breast. Gulnoor was still shouting; curses flew out of her mouth like fireworks.

Motijan stood her ground and flared up, "Don't you dare to swear at me. I warn you."

Gulnoor screamed. "You'll get no food at my house from today. I'll get my son married again. My family line must be kept going."

Suddenly Motijan burst into mocking laughter, startling everyone. "Your family line?" she said. "Faugh! If had left it to your son, I wouldn't have got these two girls even."

"What did you say?"

Gulnoor, with her reputation of being a hard woman in the village, kept staring at Motijan with dilated, unbelieving eyes. A barely audible murmur spread among the crowd.

Motijan stood there, holding her two daughters close to her. From the safety of their mother's breast, Motijan's daughters glared at everyone before them.

Translated by Sagar Chaudhury.

The original Bengali story is included in *Motijanar Meyera*, published by Shakil Prokashon, 1995.

The Man Who Would Not Die

Humayun Ahmed

Badrul Alam was on his way to *taravi* prayers that Ramzan evening, but paused in front of the bungalow and peeped inside. The room was dark. Badrul Alam was surprised because, just before beginning his *magrib* prayers that evening, he had expressly ordered that lights be placed inside the bungalow. None of his servants ever seemed to obey the orders he gave them. He started trembling in his fury. Recently every time he became angry, he started to tremble.

It was impossible to stand too long inside the bungalow. The smell was nauseating. Who could imagine that when the human body started to rot it would exude this dreadful smell? The smell assailed one's nostrils and went right up to one's brain. The head started throbbing. And one felt nauseated. Badrul Alam covered his nose with his handkerchief. He should have covered his nose before entering the bungalow. He had just eaten and might throw up his entire dinner. He had told his wife not to give him food. He would eat after *taravi* prayers, but his wife would not listen. Nowadays no one listened to him.

With his handkerchief to his nostrils, he called out, "Ai-ee, ai-ee."

There was no response. He wondered whether the man was dead. Strange, that he should still show no signs of dying though half his body was rotting. The doctor at the Upazila Health Complex had written him off. He had said, "What's the point of keeping him in the hospital? Two days at the most? Take him home. He will die in peace among his relations."

And the asses had to bring him and put him inside his bungalow. How ridiculous! Is this his house? He was astounded at their audacity. The bungalow is used for several purposes. People come to visit. And they leave a half-dead man here! The terrible smell exuding from the bungalow wards off visitors. One's gorge rises at the stench.

He called a little louder, "Ai-ee, ai-ee."

There was no response. He tried to listen carefully. There was no sign of any breathing. No sign of any movement.

I do believe he's dead. Strange, the utter callousness of my servants. A man is about to breathe his last any moment, and they have not bothered to give him a light. Despite my having told them, just before *magrib* prayers, to give him a light. Who knows how long ago he died? The place is dark. Maybe dogs and jackals have dragged the body away and eaten it up.

He removed the handkerchief from his nostrils. Immediately the smell assailed him, but he didn't allow the smell to bother him too much. He lit a match. The room brightened up slightly.

No, he's not dead. He's staring at me. The doctor said he would not last more than two days. The doctors of these days seem to know nothing. How can a patient who is supposed to live for only two days, survive for thirteen?

Badrul Alam asked, "Are you alive?"

Yunus replied, "Yes, I'm alive."

"When I called out a moment ago, why didn't you answer?"

Yunus did not reply. He had not answered because he had been afraid. He is very afraid of Badrul Alam. On top of that, he is not even a daily labourer in this house. He used to work in a neighboring village. They had not been willing to keep him, so they had brought him over here. Even Badrul Alam had not been willing to keep him. He hadn't said anything because he had heard that the man would not last more than two days. On top of that, it was Ramzan.

Badrul Alam said in an angry voice, "Didn't they give you any light in your room?"

"They did. It went out."

Kupi lights tend to go out in the breeze. Not many people come to the bungalow, so it's risky having a hurricane lantern. A thief might come and take it away. This man will just keep on staring. He will not be able to do anything.

"Did they give you something to eat?"

"Yes, they did."

"That's good."

Before Badrul Alam left the room, he lit the *kupi* once more. Let the light last as long as it could.

Everyone was waiting for him at the mosque. The *taravi* prayers started as soon as he entered. The prayers themselves did not take too long, but it seemed as if the *doa* would never end. The same *doa* was repeated in Bengali, Urdu Arabic—several languages. The maulana's job had not been made permanent. It would be made permanent after seeing how he performed his duties during the month of Ramzan.

That is why the rascal is trying to impress me through a lengthy, multi-lingual *doa*. On top of everything, at the end of the *doa*, he has burst into loud sobs. How irritating!

Badrul Alam thought of giving the maulana a piece of his mind. He was the chairman of the mosque committee. Though it wouldn't seem proper on his part to say these things, nevertheless, he would have to. People have their own obligations. It wasn't possible for them to spend their whole nights in prayer. The maulana reached the final portion of the *doa*. "Oh dear friend of our dear prophet, if we do not raise our hands to you in prayer, to whom can we turn? You yourself have said in the Quran Majeed, *'Marajal bahraini yaltakian,'* that is, He it is who has maintained the two huge expanses of water. *'Bainahum barzaku,'* that is, between them is a natural curtain."

Badrul Alam grew even more irritated.

It seems as if tonight's prayers will never end. It is necessary to say something to this maulana. Because I have said nothing to him earlier, he is doing whatever he pleases.

Finally, the *doa* came to an end. Badrul Alam said in a sombre tone, "Maulana sahib, I'd like a few words with you."

The maulana felt nervous at the tone of Badrul Alam's voice. Not waiting for Badrul Alam to speak, the maulana quickly said, "I went to him as you had ordered me to. He is unwilling. This work cannot be done by force. If you wish, I will go again today."

"What are you talking about?"

"You told me to administer the *taoba* to him. He is unwilling to do *taoba*."

Finally Badrul Alam realized what the maulana was talking about. He had told him last week to persuade Yunus to do *taoba*. If one does *taoba*, the job is completed within three days. He was under the impression that the maulana had made the man do *taoba*. Now he realized that the maulana had done nothing.

"Why doesn't he want to ask for pardon?"

"He's afraid. He doesn't want to die."

"What relationship does living or dying have to do with his doing *taoba*? Life and death are in God's hands. Come with me immediately. Make him ask for God's pardon. He will not be unwilling to do so in my presence."

"Very well, Sir."

"On top of everything, it would be better for him to die at this time. The gates of Paradise are wide open for all who die during the month of Ramzan. What do you all say?"

Everyone nodded agreement. One piped up, "Sir, even his own father and mother have not done what you have for him. You have done more than twice what his parents would have done."

Badrul Alam asked in a grave tone, "Who am I to do anything? God does everything. We are only the means. The other day Kuddus Sahib came to me and said, 'What are you doing? Go and throw him somewhere else.' I said, 'Kuddus Sahib don't say such things during the month of Ramzan.' "

One rebuke was enough to make Yunus Meah agree to do *taoba*.

The maulana said, "This time God will save you from the tortures of hell. You are now as pure as a seven-day-old child. You will go straight to Paradise. Do you understand?"

"Yes, I do."

"Have you relinquished all claims?"

"Yes, Sir."

"No, no. You must say, 'I relinquish all earthly claims. No one owes me anything.' "

The maulana sahib was staying inside the mosque. The mosque committee was supposed to have built him a house next to the mosque, but it had not been built yet. Of course, everyone was expecting Badrul Alam to build it. If he said, "Yes" once, it would be enough.

The maulana sahib paid a visit to Badrul Alam on his way to the mosque.

Badrul Alam asked, "Has the *taoba* been properly taken care of?"

"Yes."

"What is his condition now?"

"The end is approaching. No one lives more than three days after the *taoba*. But he'll go sooner."

"What is wrong with him?"

"I don't know. What I see is that his body is rotting. The stench is terrible."

"On the twenty-seventh day of Ramzan my daughter and her husband will be coming to stay."

The maulana said confidently, "He'll not last beyond a couple of days."

But Yunus Meah was still alive four days later. If anything, he was even chirpier. But it was clear that his condition was very bad. Previously the stench had only surrounded the bungalow, but now it started to enter the house itself. On the advice of the Sanitary Inspector, phenyl was generously sprinkled around the house. The smell, however, still persisted. Jackals started prowling around the bungalow. They were unable to resist the smell of putrefying human flesh.

Badrul Alam went to see him, handkerchief clamped to his nostrils. "How are you?"

"Well, Sir."

"That's good."

"I feel very afraid at night."

"What's there to be afraid of?"

"Something prowls around at night. I don't see it. I only hear it."

Hearing this, the maulana sahib said, "The time is swift approaching. Azrael is prowling around."

Badrul Alam was disgusted at the maulana's words. What nonsense. Azrael prowling around! Who knew whether the rascal had had him say the *taoba* properly?

"Maulana sahib?"

"Yes?"

"Has the *taoba* been administered properly?"

"Yes, definitely."

"See whether you can have it done once more. I'm only saying this because of the man's suffering. For no other reason."

"I'll make him say it once more today. There is no problem. The *taoba* can even be said twice in one day. There is a *hadith* of our Prophet's in this connection. Our dear Prophet has said . . . ."

"Never mind all that. I will hear you another day."

The maulana sahib said, "Occasionally, when there is some secret longing, the soul does not want to leave the body. It is necessary to find out if there is anything he would like to eat. Or if there is someone he would like to see."

"Very well, I'll find out."

Yunus was astonished when he heard that he would have to repent a second time. He chirped up, "But I've done *taoba* once. I have not committed any sin after my *taoba*."

The maulana said irritably, "Don't be sacrilegious. It is not up to you to judge whether you have sinned or no, but up to God almighty."

The *taoba* was administered once more.

After the *taoba* was over, Badrul Alam visited the dying man. "You there—how are you?"

"Very well."

"Do you feel like eating anything?"

"No, Sir."

"If you do, just say so."

"I'd like to have rice with tamarind water."

He was given rice with tamarind water. As soon as he had finished eating, he started having difficulty breathing. His chest heaved rapidly. His eyes seemed to be popping out. Badrul Alam sent word to the maulana. If anything happened it would be better to have everything done during the daytime.

Nothing happened during the day. At night the breathing became somewhat easier.

The maulana retired for the night. Before leaving, he told Badrul Alam, "We will have to wait for another day."

Badrul Alam said drily, "What will happen after one more day?"

"It will be the dark of the moon. His wheezing will become unbearable then."

Badrul Alam said in an irritable tone, "At times you talk about Azrael, at others you talk of the dark of the moon. Does Azrael see whether the moon is full or no before he appears?"

On the twenty-ninth of the moon the condition of Yunus was really grave. A rattling sound came from his chest. He started foaming at the mouth. It was easy to see that he would not last till morning. Mrs. Badrul Alam also paid him a visit, with her face muffled in her sari *anchal*. His food had been left uneaten on his plate. He had not even touched it.

Mrs. Alam said, "Give him some water to drink. Can't you see that his lips are parched? Poor soul."

Towards morning Badrul Alam came to see how he was.

"You there—How are you?"

Yunus chirped up, "I'm fine, Sir."

"No difficulty breathing?"

"No, Sir."

Badrul Alam's face grew grave.

Yunus said, "At night a jackal entered. He bit my hands and feet. Please tell them to keep a stick near me. A hurricane lantern also."

Badrul Alam said not a word. As it was, during Ramzan his temper was always high. Today his temper rose to the high heavens.

During *iftari* he told Majnu, "See that a stick is kept by Yunus's bedside. And a hurricane lantern."

Majnu is a worker in Badrul Alam's household. His work is to tend Yunus. This work is not to his liking because by this time Yunus cannot feed himself. He has to feed him. Majnu feels like vomiting in disgust.

Majnu said, "That Yunus is a rascal."

Badrul Alam looked at him. "Why?"

Majnu replied, "The maulana sahib made him do *taoba* twice, but the rascal did not say the *taoba* even once. Whatever the maulana asked him to say, he said the opposite in his mind."

"Who told you this?"

"He told me so himself. One dies after saying the *taoba*, that is why."

"What are you saying?"

"He is a real rascal."

After *magrib* prayers, Badrul Alam dropped in to see Yunus. There was a stick next to Yunus. The hurricane lantern was lit.

"How's everything? I hear you haven't said the *taoba*."

Yunus remained silent.

"Why didn't you say it? Are you joking with God? You're a real rascal."

Yunus murmured softly, "I don't wish to die."

For a long time Badrul Alam kept looking at Yunus. One of his legs had swollen up like a bolster pillow. Most likely the jackal had bitten that leg.

Yunus said, "If you insist, I'll say *taoba* once more. Properly."

"Never mind, there's no need for that any more. If you are so eager to live, let me see what I can do. Come, I'll take you to Mymensingh . . . . Let's see what happens."

Yunus did not quite understand. He kept staring blankly.

Badrul Alam arranged for a bullock cart that night. First they would have to go to Netrakona. From Netrakona to Mymensingh. If the doctors couldn't do anything there, they would have to take him to Dhaka.

The bullock cart started at eight that night. Badrul Alam surprised everyone by accompanying the cart himself. A lot of running around would have to be done. It would not do to rely on others.

"Yunus?"

"Yes?"

"Hang on there. Don't give up. I'm here."

Yunus's eyes grew wet. He tried to hang on with all his might. The cart started to gain speed.

Translated by Niaz Zaman.

From the original titled *"Ayomoy,"* anthologized in *Ayomoy* published by Anupam Publishers, 1990. Despite having the same title, the short story has nothing in common with the popular Bangladesh television serial.

The Customer

Farida Hossain

As was his wont, Raju, the young salesman of Grand Stores, laid out the stack of saris. "What would you like?" he asked. "Striped, check, or printed? A lot of new stuff just came in this morning."

Mili swallowed and kept quiet. Her eldest sister-in-law and elder sister had accompanied her to the shop.

Her sister-in-law said, "Not these. Please bring out some heavy, expensive saris."

Raju brought down some expensive saris. "These are the most expensive saris we have in cotton, Madam. Just see them. She always buys things from me."

Mili started fidgeting in her embarrassment.

Her sister said curtly, "Put away all this stupid cotton stuff. We have come to buy a wedding sari. Show us what you have in *katan* silk and tissue, please."

Raju gulped, "A wedding sari . . . ." The next moment he burst out laughing. "Why won't we have wedding saris? Of course we have wedding saris. Look at this one." He brought down a stack of saris from another shelf: *katan* silk, gossamer-like tissue, richly woven brocade.

Her sister-in-law said to Mili, "See which one you like."

Raju glanced at Mili's face. "Yes, yes. We have all varieties of saris. This light gold tissue will suit her remarkably."

Mili's sister held up the sari and ran the material through her fingers. "Not bad. What do you say? Shall we take it?"

Mili inclined her head gently.

They bought the tissue, along with several other saris.

Raju was surprised. Strange. The girl was getting married. Raju did not know her name. But she was a regular customer. She had come several times to buy saris accompanied by a younger brother or a friend.

Whenever she came she would say, "Let's see what sort of new saris you have this time. Stripe, check, plain. Something absolutely new."

Raju knew what she would ask for by heart now. When new saris came into the store, Raju would often feel like keeping them aside for her.

When Mili came he would say, "Some new varieties of saris have come. Absolutely different. I know that you will like them very much."

Mili would laugh, "All right—let's see them first."

And she never left the store empty-handed.

Raju liked it very much. He got a lot of pleasure if he could persuade Mili to buy two new varieties. The day would pass as swiftly as a merry song.

If Mili ever returned to the shop wearing one of the saris he had sold her, he would look at her again and again.

Mili would understand and occasionally remark, "Yes, bought from here."

Raju would laugh. "Of course, where else will you buy them from? You will always get the latest collection from Grand Stores."

This was the sum of their relationship.

o o o o

A couple of months later Mili came again. Her husband, Jamil, was with her.

Raju recognized who the man was immediately. He smiled and welcomed them. "Come in, come in. Today just one will not do. You will have to buy at least two."

Mili laughed.

Jamil also laughed. He had a warm laugh.

Raju thought to himself that his customer had managed to get a nice and pleasant husband. It was a pleasure to him just to think of it.

No, Jamil didn't buy just two. He bought all of five saris for Mili.

Raju was overjoyed.

Mili returned to his store several times after that. Sometimes she came alone, sometimes with her husband. Not just striped and checked saris, but saris of all sorts of designs.

Raju dreamed his own meaningless dreams. A young man's dreams. He was happy with his dreams.

Lots of girls had visited Grand Store during his three years as a salesman.

They'd laugh with him.

They'd talk to him.

Several of them had made him open out one crisply folded sari after another, but then gone away without buying a single one.

Several had haggled over the price and been downright rude to him. Sometimes, Raju too had lost his temper and replied back rudely.

But Mili . . . .

He had liked her somehow from the very first day he had seen her.

She had a very lovely way of wearing her sari.

Her manner of speaking was also very attractive. There was a childlike innocence about her. Raju was quite charmed by her.

There was an intimate manner in which she addressed him, "Don't forget to keep aside any uncommon sari that comes."

And then . . . .

And then she got married.

Raju knew that it was senseless for a salesman to think in that way. But even then, Raju liked thinking those thoughts.

He counted the days. When would that special customer of his come again? When would Raju again be able to put a couple of saris that she admired into her arms?

o o o o

Several days passed.

Raju was sitting in his Mirpur home reading the newspaper. It was a holiday.

It was a rainy evening.

The window of the small tin shed faced the roadway. One could see a long way down the narrow road.

Most of the homes in this area are more or less of the same type. Normally, people of small means live in the area. The rents are low. Most people rent one or two rooms at the most.

The rain increased in spurts.

Raju glanced casually out the window. Suddenly he sat up straight.

In the dismal light of the rain-swept evening, he clearly saw a woman, drenched to the skin, run up the lane to shelter behind the huge banyan tree in front.

A suspicious-looking ruffian came running up, casting his eyes left and right, searching for the fleeing woman.

Raju wondered what had happened.

The man was moving towards the tree, carefully looking everywhere. In a moment he would come up to where the woman was hiding behind the banyan tree.

The doors were closed. Raju was sitting beside the open window.

It was a wet evening. There was no chance of any one coming to visit him. But it was his habit to sit that way.

The lights had not been switched on. Everything seemed to have been washed in the rain.

The girl could no longer be seen. She had been behind that huge tree.

The man was creeping past a boundary wall.

The lights of the main street came on. But there was no one to be seen on the road.

The door was suddenly thrown open and the girl seemed to be blown into the room.

She crumpled in a faint to the floor. The man was still moving stealthily towards them.

Raju dragged the girl inside, then kicked the door closed so that the man would not catch sight of her.

Raju did not know what to do. All he knew was that he had to save this helpless girl from the clutches of the ruffian.

The man was still coming towards them.

The downpour continued. In the darkened room, Raju held the terrified, wet girl close.

Who knows how much time elapsed in this way?

As soon as the girl regained her senses, she shrieked in terror.

Raju was startled. He felt the wetness on his chest where he had held the girl close. He moved slightly back.

He tried to calm the girl and lay her down on the bed.

The girl screamed in terror. "Who—who are you? Please let me go."

Raju said softly, "There is no need to be afraid. Just get better. I will not harm you."

"Then who are you?"

Raju said, "Let me light a candle. Then we can talk."

Raju lit a candle. Then, bolting the door, he said, "It's better to be careful. There's no knowing whether that ruffian is still hanging around."

The girl sat up in bed.

Raju had just turned towards the bed when he started back as if he had seen a ghost. "You . . . ?" Raju could not believe his own eyes.

Mili could not believe what she saw either.

Raju seemed to have turned to stone. He stared at Mili's face.

Mili covered up her face and burst into loud sobs. She tossed from side to side in her anguish.

Raju stood speechless, unmoving. There was nothing for him to say. Nothing for him to do. He had no strength to do anything.

Mili continued to cry. Great, wracking tears.

Raju pulled himself together with great difficulty. He came forward and placed a hand on Mili's forehead. Hesitantly, in an unsteady voice, he asked, "Why are you crying . . . ? Please . . . don't cry. No harm has come to you. Believe me."

With some difficulty Mili brought herself to dry her tears and ask, "Truly . . . ?"

"Yes, truly. You fainted out of fear. That ruffian did not see you."

Mili shivered again. Her head was throbbing. "I am in great trouble. I must leave immediately." Mili tried to rise, but started to sway in her weakness.

Raju held her firmly and seated her back on the bed. "What I can't for the life of me understand is what you were doing in this area."

Mili wiped her eyes with her sari *anchal*. "My husband is very ill. Liver cirrhosis. The doctors have given up hope. Someone told me that there is an old *kabiraj* who lives here. He has performed many miraculous cures. I had left my car on the corner and was looking for the *kabiraj*."

Raju said, "Surprising. How can an educated girl like you believe in things like that? On top of that you came alone?"

Mili said, "I . . . didn't . . . think things out carefully. Hearing about the old *kabiraj* I was desperate . . . ." She burst into sobs and could not continue.

Raju was embarrassed. "I'm sorry. I shouldn't have said that."

A little later, Raju added, "God has been kind. You are safe."

Outside, night had fallen. The rain had come down to a drizzle.

Raju held out his right hand to Mili. "The rain has almost stopped. Come, I'll see you home."

Mili didn't move.

This time Raju smiled a little. "Don't be afraid. Raju, the salesman of Grand Store, is not a bad man. You can trust me."

Mili held on to Raju's hand and pulled herself up on her trembling legs.

Raju was still surprised at everything. It seemed like a dream. A happy-and-sad dream. He just couldn't believe it had really happened.

○ ○ ○ ○

Several days passed.

Raju thought about that evening several times.

Raju thought about Mili's husband.

In the midst of his work, Raju would grow wistful. At times, his heart seemed to ache strangely. His eyes longed to see a familiar face.

Many more days passed.

It was nearing Eid, and the whole market was packed with eager shoppers. The salesmen were all very busy.

Suddenly, Raju was startled once again.

He was busy with customers, folding and unfolding a whole range of new saris to their whims. He had no time to remember a special voice, a special face. But, from one end of the store, he heard a known voice ask, "Do you keep plain, white sari lengths?"

Even in the midst of all that chaos, his ears caught her words. He looked in her direction. She was standing in front of one of the other salesmen. She was wearing a plain white sari. Her unoiled hair was pulled back into a hurried bun. She looked sad and lost.

Perhaps even Mili was unaware how she had wandered into the store packed with Eid shoppers.

Raju understood that his special customer who had asked for striped, checked, brightly printed saris in cotton or *katan* and tissue saris in silk would now be buying only plain white saris, widow's saris.

Did that mean that her husband had not recovered from his illness? That monsoon evening, looking for medicine to cure her husband, she had come to Raju's home. Why did he keep remembering that episode again and again?

Raju's heart seemed to twist in pain. He could not bear it any longer. Why did she have to come to Grand Store to look for a plain white sari? Or had she wandered into the store by mistake?

Raju suppressed his feelings, and told her curtly, "I'm sorry. We do not keep plain white sari material. Why don't you visit the shop next door?"

Mili looked up startled to hear a voice coming from another saleman. Raju avoided looking at the surprised face of the salesman whom Mili had addressed and turned back to the customers he was dealing with.

Mili did not have to say anything else. She left Grand Store silently. She had no idea of the thoughts that racked the handsome young salesman. But Raju understood that Mili had left. Perhaps she would indeed buy a plain white sari from the shop next door.

Suddenly Raju welcomed the noise of the shoppers all around him. It was as if cymbals were clashing around him.

Bells were ringing . . . .

Translated by Niaz Zaman.

The original "Sari" has been anthologized in Farida Hossain's *Nirbachita Galpa,* published by Anjum Publishers, 1994.

Radha Will Not Cook Today

Purabi Basu

Morning hovers on the edge of night. A cool breeze swirls gently
in the dawning.

Reclining in bed, Radha breathes in the fragrance of the white
and orange *shefali* blossoms.

Last night was unusually calm, free from the frequent quarrels
with husband, mother-in-law, sister-in-law.

Her body temperature is quite normal—she has no fever. There
is nothing physically wrong her, she is not even tired.

It is not raining outside. The sky is clear. A beautiful blue.

It is neither too cold nor too warm. Radha's only child, Sadhan,
is perfectly healthy.

Husband and son are still sleeping soundly beside her.

Nevertheless, Radha suddenly decides that she will not cook
today.

She will not cook, no, she will not cook.

Radha will not cook today.

Radha calls the sun and says, "Do not rise yet. Today I will stay in
bed for a long time."

She has no chance to talk to the night. Night had slipped away
before Radha made up her mind.

Radha calls the birds and says, "Continue to sing your early
morning songs. Today I want to stay in bed and listen to you sing."

She calls the clouds and says, "Help the sun. Hide him in the *anchal* of your sari."

She calls the *shefali* and says, "Do not shed your blossoms any more. Imagine that day has not yet broken."

To the dew she says, "Keep on falling in little drops onto the grass below."

The sun listens to Radha. For a long time he does not appear in the sky.

The clouds stretch and cover the blue sky.

The birds continue to sing ceaselessly.

The *shefali* blossoms cling more strongly to their stems, and continue to adorn the branches.

The dew drops keep on falling and embrace with their loving wetness the grass below.

Radha yawns and stretches on her bed.

Meanwhile there is commotion in the whole house. Everyone has woken up late today.

Forgetting his maths tables and his spelling, Sadhan gazes outside.

It is time for Radha's husband, Ayan, to go to market.

It is time for Radha's sister-in-law to go to school.

Radha's mother-in-law has completed her morning devotions and is awaiting her first meal of the day.

But Radha is still in bed.

Radha will not cook today.

She will not cook, no she will not cook.

Radha will not cook today.

"What's happened? What's wrong?"

"Will everyone starve today?"

"I can't understand what the matter is."

Mother-in-law, sister-in-law, husband are all amazed.

Radha is unconcerned.

She slowly leaves her bed.

She picks up the water pitcher from its corner and moves leisurely towards the pond.

"Will my son go to work hungry today?'

Radha does not reply. Her mother-in-law is angry.

"I'm asking you, where did you learn to be so high and mighty? What is the matter?"

Radha does not reply. Her husband is perplexed.

"Sister-in-law, it is time for me to go to school."

Radha does not reply. Her sister-in-law is sad and surprised.

Radha sits down quietly by the pond, and dips her feet in the water. Behind her there is commotion. With her loud wails, mother-in-law has gathered people around her. Radha is unconcerned. She sits gazing at the water.

The small fishes—*puti, bojuri, kholsa, kajali*—come in shoals and gather at Radha's feet.

"Go away, leave me now. I haven't brought any food for you today."

But the fishes continue to turn joyous somersaults. Radha's presence is enough. They want nothing else.

Radha looks up at the sky. The sun laughs down at her.

"Are you angry?" the sun asks.

"Why, couldn't you wait a little longer?" Radha asks, hurt and angry.

"If you look at the fields you will realize what would happen if I delayed any longer."

From where she sits by the pond, Radha glances at the wilted fields. Radha is worried. "Will they survive?"

"Just smile, and all of them will come back to life."

Radha stands up. Twirling around, she laughs and laughs. She stretches out her arms.

Radha laughs. And laughs. And laughs.

The grain stalks seem suddenly to rouse up from sleep. They give themselves a little shake and stand up tall.

Suddenly Radha finds her husband shaking her by the shoulders.

Her mother-in-law is glowering with rage and cursing her bitterly.

Her sister-in-law stands weeping in dismay.

But Radha is still laughing. Laughing. Laughing. Radha is still laughing.

The wind rustles through the leaves in tune with Radha.

The water of the pond ripples delightedly in laughter.

The birds chirp melodiously in unison.

The fishes dance and float and dive.

The flowers softly nod their heads in harmony with the leaves.

Radha laughs. And laughs. And laughs.

Her angry husband shatters the empty rice pot and leaves for the market hungry.

Her mother-in-law continues to wail and curse at the top of her voice.

Her sister-in-law steals in gentle steps to a neighbour's house.

Her son Sadhan comes slowly to the pond and stands beside Radha.

But Radha will not cook.

She will not cook, no, she will not cook.

Radha will not cook today.

Radha turns her head slightly.

For a moment she wavers. Then, she steels herself.

Radha sits down on the ground. Then she gets up immediately. She is aware that she is not ill. She realizes for a moment that the most normal things in life can make one ill. So she is not afraid.

"Mother, I am hungry."

The cry is repeated, as if from far away. "Mother, I am very hungry."

There is a turmoil in Radha's heart. The smooth sea is suddenly racked by a storm. Holding her son close to her, Radha continues to gaze at the water.

Then she looks up at the sky. Up at the sun.

She looks at the trees, at the birds, at the flowers, at the leaves.

Radha looks longingly at everything around her.

A small crow comes from nowhere and, plucking a small ripe papaya, casts it into Radha's lap. Picking it up with both hands,

Radha peels it and feeds her son. Sadhan's hunger is not assuaged. Radha calls the kingfisher and says, "Bring me the lotus pod from that lotus cluster in the middle of the pond."

The pod is huge—it is sufficient to satisfy any hunger. But Radha's son eats only a little of it.

"Mother, I am very hungry. Aren't you going to cook?"

Sadhan is just four years old. He feels very hungry. How is a small fruit going to satisfy that hunger?

"Mother, aren't you going to cook?"

Her heart wants to burst. She almost succumbs.

Still, somehow, Radha manages to say, "No."

Radha will not cook.

She will not cook, no, she will not cook.

Radha will not cook today.

Clasping Sadhan to her breast, Radha walks to the orchard. Sitting cross-legged on the grass, she lays Sadhan in her lap. Then she looks carefully around her. There is no one anywhere near. The leaves of the star apple and jackfruit trees move gently in the breeze and create a soft canopy for Radha. Radha gently uncovers her breasts. Her firm, well-rounded breasts gleam in the light of the sun, under the open sky. Radha lifts her left breast and pushes the nipple into her son's mouth. With her right hand she caresses Sadhan's head, his hair, his forehead, his eyes. For a few moments, Sadhan is bewildered at this unusual occurrence. Then slowly, very slowly, he sucks at the budding nipple of his mother's breast. At first he sucks gently, then he starts sucking harder, till he finally tries to suck with all his strength this nectar from his mother's body.

Radha is pensive. Radha is eager. But nothing happens. What is she to do now? Straightening her back-bone, stretching both her legs in front of her, Radha seats herself more comfortably. She glances once all around her. She clenches her teeth, she bites her lips. She is asking for something, praying for something. And just then it happens. Cascading like a waterfall, overflowing both sides like a swollen river that floods its banks, causing her whole body to tremble violently, something bursts forth from Radha's breasts.

Radha looks at her son's face.

Sadhan bubbles with laughter.

From the sides of his active mouth the white milk foams in little drops to the ground.

Radha laughs.

Sadhan laughs.

The cloud comes and covers the face of the sun.

The *shalik* bird rests on one leg. A cool breeze swirls gently.

Radha laughs.

Sadhan laughs.

Radha has decided that she will not cook today.

She will not cook, no, she will not cook.

Radha will not cook today.

Translated by Niaz Zaman and Shafi Ahmed.

"Radha Will Not Cook Today" has been translated from "*Arandhan*," anthologized in *Ajanma Parabashi*, published by Prateek Prakashani, 1992. The story, along with its English version, was included in *Infinite Variety: Women in Society and Literature,* edited by Firdous Azim and Niaz Zaman, published by the University Press Limited, 1994.

The Matchmaker

Shamim Hamid

It was just after the *azaan* call for the dawn prayers, the first of the daily five for the followers of Islam. For Rokeya it was the nicest time of the day. The sky only faintly light and the air still cool before the sun's heat sucked it all away. You could smell the earth damp with the night's dew and you could hear the rustling and the stirring of the birds making ready to fly out at first light. But the cuckoo was already calling urgently as Rokeya stretched pleasurably and took up the spiky broom made from the spines of dried coconut fronds and prepared to sweep the hard, mud-packed courtyard. Dry leaves drifted down from the many trees surrounding the little homestead and littered the yard, mingling with stray bits of straw and chicken droppings.

Rokeya bent from the waist down and, tossing her thick, black, oiled and braided hair over her shoulder, started to sweep methodically around the yard. She collected the debris, threw it into the undergrowth and stood the broom in its usual corner by the chicken coop. She lifted the large dome-shaped cover made of latticed bamboo and freed the ducks and chickens it housed during the night. The birds bustled out, indignant at being cooped in for so long and made for the area where Rokeya and her mother usually cleaned the day's portion of rice grains of husks and small pebbles in *kulas,* horseshoe-shaped trays made from the ubiquitous bamboo. A cock crowed from somewhere nearby and a cow lowed plaintively, anxious to be milked.

In a little shed at the side of the house, Rokeya started the fire in the *chula* in which cracks had begun to appear. She made a mental note to plaster the earthen stove the next time she plastered the courtyard with a mixture of clay and cow dung. As she put the old tin kettle on for making tea, the household began to stir. Rokeya's father, Rafiq, came out yawning with a green and red checked cotton *gamchha* on his shoulder and sat near the *chula* on a *piri*, a wooden slab barely raised off the floor, waiting for his morning cup of tea. Rokeya's mother, Amena, soon emerged and, taking the cup of tea that Rokeya had prepared, handed it to her husband together with a shallow earthen bowl filled with puffed rice and a small piece of crystallized molasses. Rafiq ate and drank in silence. Then, tying the *gamchha* round his waist, he picked up his basket and shovel and disappeared round the corner of the house, brushing against the softly nodding leaves of the *kakrol* vine climbing along the earthen walls of the little house. Rokeya's father was a day labourer and he had to get to the marketplace early to ensure that he got hired for a full day's work.

Rokeya quickly doused the fire, because the leaves and twigs gathered from the nearby mango orchard must be made to last. Besides, no one else except her father was allowed to have tea. It was too expensive. By now Rokeya's three younger brothers had come out rubbing their eyes and demanding to be fed. They were each given a handful of puffed rice and a bowl of water from the earthen pitcher standing in a shady corner of the courtyard. The squat black pitcher, covered with the dry shell of half a coconut, kept the water cool and sweet even on the hottest of days.

Rokeya and her mother drank just water and prepared for the day's work. They would eat later when Rafiq came home with rice and some vegetables purchased from the day's wages. In the meantime there was plenty of other work to be done. The water had to be fetched from the pond a mile or so away, leaves and twigs had to be collected, and, if there was time, Amena would take the boys and go down to the flooded paddy fields to trap some small fish to add flavour to tonight's dinner which as usual would be meagre.

Rokeya was thirteen and too old to go wading in paddy fields. She would stay at home and apply a plaster of clay and water to the courtyard which had begun to crack in places and was raising a lot of dust in the slightest breeze. Later she would walk to the nearby field where cows were usually grazed and pick up pats of cowdung. These she would mix with bits of straw and make flat round cakes to slap on to the walls of the house which received the most sun during the day. These dark brown cakes, with the four finger marks making ridges down the centre, would dry out to be used as fuel when slow burning was needed. If she was lucky, she would find a stray guava or two to fill her stomach for she was always hungry and found it hard waiting so long for her first meal of the day.

As the sun reached the top of the heavens and the heat became intense, her father returned, bringing with him some rice and a bundle of jute leaves. He went off to the pond to bathe while Rokeya hurriedly lit the fire and put the rice on to boil. Her mother stripped and chopped the leaves in preparation for cooking. She plucked two young *kakrols* from the vine and, after discarding the flat seeds, sliced the prickly, yellow-green vegetables to add to the curry. The three boys sat down with their father to eat the freshly boiled rice and the leaves steamed with salt and fried with some dried red chilly. Amena sat fanning her husband while he ate. When the meal was over, Rokeya rolled out the straw mat under the shade of the mango tree for her father to lie down and sleep. Then she and her mother went to bathe at the pond and came back. They ate their meal, making sure to leave enough to make an evening meal for Rokeya's father and her three brothers.

The call for the afternoon prayers came wafting over the breeze. Wiping his face with his *gamchha* after performing the customary ablutions in preparation for prayers, Rokeya's father made his way to the little white-washed mosque. On his return he had the village matchmaker with him. The matchmaker was a small, bent old man wearing once-white pajamas and a loose, collarless shirt with a rim of grime round the neck. The rubber pumps on his feet were dusty and worn, and his black umbrella, which he now carried folded under his sweat-stained arm-pit had faded to a light grey. To Rafiq and his wife, however, he was an honoured guest because they had a daughter of marriageable age. Who else could inform them of eligible boys but the matchmaker? For that was exactly what the matchmaker did. He wandered round villages, gossiped with all and sundry, became a storehouse of information and acted as a veritable one-man marriage bureau.

So when Rafiq told his wife who the visitor was, Rokeya's mother hurried out of the house to proffer the matchmaker the special mat reserved for guests and the pungent, aromatic *paan* leaves which her husband chewed when relaxing after a day's work. The matchmaker sat down with a sigh on the mat and delicately stuffed the leaf into his mouth. Chewing contentedly, he spat red spittle from the combination of betel, *catechu* and lime into a corner of the yard. The white lime on his fingers he wiped on the walls of the house which bore signs of having being used for this purpose by others as well.

Satisfied that he had been given the honour and respect that he deserved, the matchmaker informed Rafiq and his wife that he had a marriage proposal for their daughter. The younger son of a farmer from a neighbouring village was of marriageable age. True, the boy did not have a proper job because the land that the family owned was too small for even the father and the elder son to work on. But, still, the boy had potentials. He had applied to work abroad as a labourer and was waiting to hear from a distant relative who lived in the capital and had promised to help the boy in the matter. The family had even sold a cow and part of their homestead to raise the money which the relative said would be needed to make all the arrangements. Furthermore, the matchmaker went on persuasively, their dowry demands were very reasonable. They wanted only a bicycle and a wristwatch. Considering that the boy's future was assured, the matchmaker argued, surely these demands were nothing. Anyone else would have asked the bride's father to pay for the boy's going abroad.

Rafiq could sell off the bamboo grove behind the house and that bit of land on the other side of the river to pay for the watch and the bicycle, the matchmaker suggested to Rokeya's father, for everyone knew who owned what in the village. Rokeya was his only daughter and Rafiq would not have to worry about the three sons with whom Allah had blessed him. In fact, they would bring wealth to the family when they got married. So there was really nothing for Rokeya's father to worry about.

In fact, it was lucky for Rafiq that he, the matchmaker, had found such an ideal match for Rokeya before people started commenting about a grown girl still unmarried in the house. And what a match! A God-given match! The matchmaker raised his hands heavenward and summoned God's blessing for such an auspicious act. Then he coughed and murmured, Although I do not want to mention such matters at this stage, Rafiq Mia, but please remember that a matchmaker must also be paid a small fee for his services. For such a happy occasion it is indeed a small price.

"If Allah's will be done, then it goes without saying that we will pay you well for the great favour you have done us," Rokeya's father assured the matchmaker and, turning to his wife, asked, "Well what do you think, Rokeya's Ma?"

Rokeya's mother, sitting just inside the doorway of the house so that she could follow the conversation but would not be fully exposed to the visitor, adjusted the sari that covered her head and said, "What can I say, Rokeya's father? The matchmaker is a respected elder of the village. He has all our interests at heart. He knows we are anxious to marry off Rokeya as soon as possible. And if the boy finds work in foreign countries, then my Rokeya will be rich, well fed and happy. I have nothing more to say. It is upto Allah and to you."

So the matchmaker was paid his not-so-small fee and Rokeya was married in a red sari with a wide, shiny, gold lurex border. She wore flowers in her hair. Glass bangles tinkled on her wrists, and red and gold sandals adorned her feet. Her face was outlined with little white spots of sandalwood paste, the line ending in a curl on each cheek. And between her nostrils, just above her lips, hung a little silver nose ring. The groom was dressed in white pajamas which clung tightly to his calves, a gold lurex coat which hung to his knees, a white turban on his head. And, all through the wedding ceremony, as was required of any self-respecting groom from a good family, he decorously held a white, folded handkerchief to his mouth. After the wedding dinner of fragrant *pulao* and beef curry had been consumed, the individual little earthen plates licked clean of the sweet *firni* made from ground rice and thickened milk, and *paan* stuffed with herbs and shredded coconut distributed among the guests, it was time for the bride to leave for her new home. Rokeya was helped into a rickshaw which had been curtained all around with an old sari to shield her from vulgar stares. With her new husband walking alongside her rickshaw, Rokeya was borne away to her in-laws' home which, if she was a good daughter-in-law and wife as her grandmother had told her so many times, she would leave only in the funereal cot.

For Rokeya life did not change a great deal. She still got up at the first call for dawn prayers, only now she swept her father-in-law's courtyard instead of her father's. She then washed the pots and pans and fed the men folk. Rokeya had not seen any different way of life in her own parents' home and, not expecting anything else from her new life, was neither disappointed nor unhappy. In fact, she quite admired her young husband who was strong and had bold black eyes. He did not stay at home much, but then, in her experience, men never did. Women had their place in the home and men outside. It was the will of Allah, as she had been taught from childhood.

It was a month after the marriage that Rokeya's husband came storming home. He had just received news that the relative in the capital had absconded with the money given him for arranging his job abroad. No one knew where the relative was. Some said that he had stolen the money and was hiding in another town until the excitement was over. Rokeya's husband tore at his hair and screamed and shouted. His life was ended, his future bleak. Who would have guessed that the relative would turn to be such a traitor?

Rokeya's mother-in-law wailed day and night. Her cow gone, her land gone, and for nothing. It was all Rokeya's fault. She was the one with the bad luck. Disaster of this magnitude had not struck the family until Rokeya entered the household. No such calamity had befallen them before. Why on earth did she agree to bring in a daughter-in-law from such a lowly family as a day labourer? The dowry she had brought was a pittance. Why didn't she burn in hell? Rokeya had ruined them and ruined her son's life.

Bewildered, Rokeya could not understand what she had done to bring such ill luck to the family. She wondered how she could turn the tidal wave of disaster. She tried to placate her mother-in-law by asking forgiveness for she knew not what crime. She cried rivers of tears and massaged her mother-in-law's head and feet day and night in an attempt to assuage her anger. She cooked and cleaned and took over all the backbreaking jobs in the household but nothing pacified mother and son.

They took up a new refrain. The only way that Rokeya could win forgiveness for being such an ill-omened daughter-in-law and wife was by bringing money from her father so that her husband could go abroad. Rokeya was thunderstruck. She knew her father had sold his last resources to meet the dowry demands. She tried to explain as much to her in-laws. They paid little heed. They accused her father of having given a cheap watch and an old bicycle which had fetched hardly anything when her husband had sold them at the *haat*, the weekly market held in the village green. In fact, they fetched hardly enough to pay for her son's drinks and gambling debts, her mother-in-law sneered.

And since Rokeya was the harbinger of bad luck, she could not and would not be allowed to stay in the house a day longer. She must return to her father's home immediately. Only when her father had provided for his son-in-law's expenses for going overseas could Rokeya contemplate returning to her husband's home. But Rokeya knew that the only way her father could raise that kind of money was by selling the homestead, but that was unthinkable, for then where would her father, mother and brothers live? Rokeya also knew that she could not stand up to her powerful in-laws, and nothing could prevent them from sending her back to her parents' home in disgrace.

That very night Rokeya made a journey which was very different from the one she had made only a few weeks ago on her wedding day. Accompanied by her husband who had borrowed a bicycle for the occasion, and with only the dim head lamp lighting the way, Rokeya was made to walk the long way back to her village.

At first her parents were overjoyed to see them both, thinking that this was an unexpected visit by the newly-married couple. But when her husband began to make accusations about the ill fortunes brought on his family by Rokeya and started to scream his demands for money at her father, Rokeya hung her head lower and lower and prayed that the ground would open up and swallow her whole. Rafiq first tried to pacify his hysterical son-in-law and, when that failed, pleaded with him to keep Rokeya at her in-laws' house while he tried to collect the money. Bringing back Rokeya to her father's home only a month after they were married was a humiliation for the whole family and would leave a terrible mark on her. Rafiq and his wife would not be able to lift their heads and meet the eyes of the villagers. Rokeya would become a social outcast. Rafiq begged for his daughter to be accepted back by her in-laws, but Rokeya's husband was adamant. If he took Rokeya back, he argued, Rafiq would never raise the money he needed. If he wanted his daughter to raise her head in good society, then Rafiq had better do something quickly about fulfilling his son-in-law's demands.

So within her short life, Rokeya had to face yet another new situation where she was unwanted in her in-laws' house and was merely tolerated in her own parents' home. She still got up at the first call of morning prayers and swept the courtyard and let out the chickens and ducks. But she no longer found any pleasure in the early morning breeze, the dew-soaked trees and the chirps and rustles of the sleepy birds. Her presence in the house was a heavy burden for her parents to bear. The fact that it was not Rokeya's fault did not help to ease matters, for there was even less to eat in the house than before. Before her marriage the sale of an occasional bamboo from the grove behind the house helped cover expenses when times were hard. Now even the bamboos were not there to draw upon.

Rokeya could not understand why she felt so guilty about everything that had happened. Why she was convinced that it really was her fault in some way. "But I always did what I was told by my elders," she argued to herself. "Grandma told me that if I obeyed my elders and did not complain about my situation in life, Allah would be pleased with me and I would achieve happiness and bring happiness to others. But Grandma was wrong. I tried to keep everyone happy, accepted whatever came my way and still no one is happy—not my husband, not my in-laws, not my own parents and least of all me. I don't seem to fit in anywhere. My parents can't feed me and my husband wants money more than he wants me. There does not seem to be any place or need for me in this world." She began to believe that perhaps her husband was right and that she was an omen of ill fortune and that perhaps her mother-in-law was not wrong when she repeatedly shrieked day and night that Rokeya would bring bad luck to whoever had the misfortune to be associated with her.

That night the moon rose round and full in the sky, confusing some crows who thought that morning had already dawned and so began busily flapping their wings and cawing in the darkness. A jackal howled far away and an owl hooted in reply. Frogs droned in the little ditch by the wayside, lulling those who could hear them into a state of somnambulance. But for Rokeya there was no sleep. She got up form the floor where she was lying next to her baby brother and stepped through the doorway into the little courtyard which she had freshly swept that evening. She looked at the orange-gold moon through the leaves of the mango tree and sighed a deep, deep sigh.

They found her dead body swinging from the mango tree in the early morning breeze at the first call for morning prayers. A cuckoo was calling frantically in the bamboo grove.

That afternoon, just after the *asar* prayers, the matchmaker, with his faded black umbrella shielding his balding head from the sun, padded his way to another village. He met the father of a girl who was eighteen years old, but was still unmarried because she had a limp in her right leg. the matchmaker said, "I have news of a wonderful boy who is just waiting to go overseas for work. Unfortunately, he was cheated out of the money he had paid his relative to make the necessary arrangements for going abroad. We all know that your daughter is defective, that she cannot walk straight. If you can raise the money for the boy's passage, I can persuade his family to agree to the marriage in spite of your daughter's limp. There will, of course, be a small fee for services rendered."

The grateful father warmly shook the matchmaker's hand and ushered him into his house, calling to his wife to bring out the guest mat and a plate of *paan*.

"The Matchmaker" was published in *The Daily Star*, Nov. 10, 1995.

Envy

Nasreen Jahan

Hiru moaned with labour pains. Far away, sitting on the topmost branch of the banyan tree, her husband continued to play upon his flute.

Hiru's mother too was pregnant. She was due to deliver any day now. Still, in this advanced stage of pregnancy she had come to look after her pregnant daughter. Her son-in-law was quite indifferent to everything. He was a free spirit, like the *Baul* singers. Was it an easy task to attend a girl who became pregnant in such a household? The mother's suffering became unbearable at times.

There was no one to look after them in their area. The girl was so bad-tempered that she aroused no kindly feelings among her neighbours, all of whom shut their doors against her. But this shrew of a girl had some good qualities as well. She just had to strew some seeds on the bit of land in front of their house for plants to spring up.

Apart from this, she also sewed embroidered quilts.

But this wasn't enough to capture the affection of her good-for-nothing husband. His wife's temper made him even more withdrawn. Of course, before his marriage as well, he used to play on the flute, but he also had feelings, emotions, a quick temper. He had never been so indifferent to everything before.

He was a skillful craftsman in cane.

He made different articles with cane and took them to the weekly market. His only problem was that his customers always got the better of him. After selling a five-taka basket for two takas he would return home to get a thorough scolding from his wife.

But even then his nature had not changed. He would say, I feel embarrassed to haggle.

Embarrassed? My goodness! One could not look at Hiru when she said this. It seemed as if she had become the goddess Kali herself. Very well then, she would say. Go put on a sari and adorn yourself with bangles. I'll go to the market. The husband was willing to buy sari and bangles, but it was not possible for him to go to the market and score a victory.

At night when she tossed in the torn *kantha,* her husband would call out softly, Hiron, O Hiron. Her anger would have subsided by then, but she would push her husband away with ice-cold hands. With matters standing in this way, what else could her husband do but turn into a *Baul*?

Chand had never been fond of working.

For this he had been beaten several times by his father. His father would say, Chand looks like a man, but he has a woman's nature in his blood.

He would see his mother immediately flare up, What are you trying to say? Just because he does not work he is a woman? Do you know what a woman is? I have given my entire life for this household.

Chand was quite indifferent to this argument of men and women. If he returned after roaming around the entire village to see that his rice bowl was upturned and empty, he sauntered down to the bank of the river. He would search under the bushes, among the weeds, for things to eat.

And on this person's shoulders was thrust the burden of a wife. A wife made of flesh and blood, full of contempt and anger. Had even one of these qualities been absent, Chand would have been content. He would have rested his head and gone to sleep.

His father died.

His mother died.

His father-in-law died—after impregnating his wife.

They left Chand alone to fend for himself in this three-fold world. If his wife had treated him like a child and assumed his responsibility, Chand would have been relieved. But like other women in the world, his wife too wanted to see him behave like a man.

No, there was no earthly way in which Chand could maintain his wife in the comfort she expected. And on top of that, she was producing another set of arms and legs from her womb.

What else could Chand do, but stuff his ears and play upon his flute?

Hiru's screams were growing wilder and closer together. Sometimes they were ear-splitting and loud as thunder, sometimes they were muffled. Panting with the weight of her enormous stomach, Hiru's mother tried to comfort her daughter. The old midwife fanned Hiru's forehead and encouraged her, "It'll be any moment now that the water-bag has burst. Push a little, mother, push." Going to comfort her daughter, Hiru's mother was roundly scolded for her trouble and sat dumbfounded in a corner of the hut. She had eaten a little leftover rice with a pinch of salt for lunch, but the little creature within had devoured it in no time. With her daughter in this condition and her son-in-law nowhere nearby, whom was she going to speak to about her inordinate hunger? The little land they had was not sufficient to feed a family of three. Her eyes grew moist.

Chand was playing upon his flute. But his wildly beating heart kept him from losing himself in his music. Again and again through the trees, his eyes sought out his hut. Every moment he expected that someone would come running forth from the hut like a burst of wind and rush down towards him. Any moment someone would come to take him back and fling him down between his screaming wife and child. Chand knew that his behaviour at this time of his wife's labour was going to cost him dear. As soon as Hiru was able to sit up straight, she would tear him to pieces. Hiru was well-fleshed. Despite everything, despite their pecuniary situation, she was more than a match for Chand. And Chand? Even a grasshopper of the jungle had more flesh on its body than Chand had on his. How could Chand stand up to that woman? In bed too Chand was a failure, it was like swimming in a huge lake.

And just when Chand decided that he would leave everything and go away to the wilderness, then all the avenues—inside and outside—closed for him, because a strange thing happened. He was going to father a child, a child whose responsibility even a hangman could not avoid.

No, he felt no attachment for the child that was about to be born. If anything, he was afraid.

How was he going to feel any emotion for the child, how would he provide food for the child, clothing for the child—these were the worries plaguing him at the moment.

But he need not worry himself about matters, Hiru would decide what to do. She would push him to the market. Or she would force him to work as a field labourer. Hiru could survive on a handful of leftover rice. But where their children are concerned, women are like tigresses. There was nothing that Chand had not seen in this world. He had seen his own mother. Because of her coddling, he had turned into a useless creature despite his hardworking, violent father.

While his father had raged, his mother would snatch him up and, holding him close, would say, "Because of your temper, I have lost five of my children in the womb. Even then God has not taught you to be gentle."

What was Chand to do now? Should he fling away his flute and disappear forever from the village?

Fears and uncertainties loomed in the eyes of Hiru's mother.

When her husband died, she had keened, "In what waters have you left me to sink or swim? All these years we were together, sometimes things were bad, sometimes they were good, sometimes we almost drowned, sometimes we managed to float to the top. We were never completely out of danger. But if you had to die, why did you have to leave me this monster inside?"

If she had had only herself to look after, she would have easily recovered from the grief of her husband's death. But who was going to look after her in this condition? On top of that she had her daughter to think about. She had to drag her own bloated body to look after her pregnant daughter. Hiru's mother was not angry with her son-in-law. It was Hiru's fault if she had not been able to make a man out of the gentle creature.

When she was six months pregnant, her son-in-law had gone to fetch her to look after Hiru. That was when she had come to know her son-in-law. He had looked after her at night. Had not allowed her to get out of bed. He had cooked his own food and eaten. Was it his gentleness that Hiru could not stand? Her daughter was determined to make a man out of her husband, so determined that she had terrified him instead. Well, let her suffer. She was getting neither her husband's affection nor his support. Does anyone strike the axe on one's own foot?

Hiru's screams aroused her from her thoughts. Going up to her daughter, she saw the midwife had dozed off.

Evening had fallen.

Hiru's mother stepped out into the night. She could see nothing. Not the trees, not the huts. Her head was swimming strangely. Tottering like a toddler who has just learned to walk, she managed to go up to the door of a hut. She stopped, gasping for breath. The housewife had just lit an oil lamp.

Seeing Hiru's mother in this condition, the housewife forgot her former anger, "What is Hiru's condition?"

Hiru's mother was oblivious to everything: Life and death, the movement of the child in her womb, Hiru's deathly cries, everything. From space as it were, floated the sound of the flute, renting the hunger of Hiru's mother, piercing her very insides. The sound of the flute rendered her speechless. Then, after a while, the sound of the flute caused her to feel nauseous, as if that sound were some juicy article of food, drifting up to her nostrils, turning around near her ears. Hiru's mother could not get rid of that sound; she wanted to vomit it out and could not. Like someone thirsting after a bout of nausea, she thirsted and could get no water.

She cursed the child in her womb. She didn't want to see the face of the child which would grow up sucking its father's lifeblood. She panted and glanced towards the village wife.

The village wife's eyes blurred under her *grameen* check. As if she were in a daze, as if someone had mixed the juice of marijuana with the breeze, as if imbibing that she had become intoxicated, her eyes drooped. The sound of the oil lamp grew fainter at the sound of her dreams. Who is it playing upon the flute?

Hiru's mother dragged herself and sat down on the hard earthen floor of the hut.

This flute was the flute of death! This was the sound a human being made before the final parting. She felt an immense sense of irrational joy. She rejoiced in the happiness of Hiron's husband. The entire village was jealous of their happiness. How fortunate her daughter was. Your days are over, Hiron, your days are over. The next moment her head drooped.

Hiru's mother saw the cool reed mat, the square mirror, the hanging bowls. How strangely everything was moving. It was as if she was rising out of herself, as if the child inside her womb had broken open the door and emerged. She felt so light, as if she were flying.

The village wife controlled herself. She said, "Your daughter is hot-tempered, and she has no patience. Is it seemly for the entire village to hear the screams of a pregnant woman?"

"Sin! Sin!" Hiru's mother murmured inaudibly.

"A woman's husband is her god, a woman's heaven lies under her husband's feet. A husband is a woman's honour, a husband . . . ."

Hiru's mother opened her eyes wide and burst out, " Is Chandu a man? God has made him Himself. If you have the goddess Lakshmi in your palm, will you kick her out? Do I not know what a man is? You want to make him into a man? You would have been kicked, ten times a day you would have been beaten. Haven't I been beaten? You unfortunate woman, of course Chandu is a man. The devil has laid a spell on your head, that you don't appreciate Chandu. Now he's gone. Gone. Is it possible that the husband who shrieked to see blood dripping from a cut finger, can't hear your deathly screams? You've sinned, woman. He has gone."

Hiru's mother opened her eyes with difficulty. After that she murmured to the housewife, trying to explain her daughter's behaviour. When she was born she had not given her honey. She had grown vicious like a black snake, now she was struggling with death.

"Where is Chandu?"

At this question of the village wife, Hiru's mother stared at her blankly. She forgot what she had come to say. She licked her dry lips with her tongue and found the child in her womb had bared its teeth like a demon and was laughing.

The village wife put down the oil lamp and forced Hiru's mother to sit down, "I don't think your condition is very good."

Her eyes blurring with tears, Hiru's mother sat down, faint with hunger. "Is there rice in your home, good wife?"

The straw rustled in the wind.

A thick mist enveloped the earth.

In the sky the sun glowed red, the clouds chased each other. The day was ending. The sweet but cracked call of the *muezzin* seemed to say, "The day is ending . . . . the day is ending . . . . The thirsty wailing child is flinging stones to scatter the day."

Darkness descended.

There was no food, there was no work at hand. In the open sky, the birds flapped their wings. Looking across the fields, the village wife sighed. That land had once belonged to her family. That thought made her dream many things. She looked at the hungry woman munching puffed rice and asked, "Have you heard? Have you heard the noise?"

The old woman seemed lost in thought, but tried to hear.

The wail of a new-born child rent the evening sky.

Chand stood outside the door. Choked with pain or joy, he murmured, "Hiron, Hiron."

The neighbouring women thrilled over the child.

Lifting her head from the bundle of clothes, Hiron looked at her child covered in blood.

Hiru's mother shivered as if she had been pierced by thorns. Then she took a deep breath. Looking down at her bloated stomach, she shivered in disgust. Then, seeing Hiru's glowing face, her heart seemed to burst. She started to cry, "You have a husband by your side. But what is going to happen to me, Hiru?"

Translated by Niaz Zaman.

The original *"Irsha,"* has been anthologized in *Purush Rajkumari*, published by Ananya, 1996.

Notes on Writers

Humayun Ahmed was a professor of Chemistry at the University of Dhaka till he resigned to devote himself to full-time writing. Perhaps the most prolific and popular writer in Bangladesh today, Ahmed has published several volumes of short stories including *Nishikabya* and *Ayomoy*. He has also published several novels, among them *Nandita Narake, Achinpur, Anyadin, Fera*. In 1981 Ahmed was awarded the Bangla Academy Prize for his novels. Ahmed is also a very successful playwright, with a number of popular television serials and movie scripts to his credit.

Kayes Ahmed was born in West Bengal, which forms the setting of his story, "The Two Singers." After completing his Honours in Bengali, Ahmed became a schoolteacher in a Dhaka school. Ahmed's career was cut short by his tragic death. Among his published works are *Andha Teerandaz* and *Lashkata Ghar*.

Alauddin Al Azad is an educationist and writer. He served as Assistant Director of Public Instruction and Principal Dhaka College prior to his diplomatic assignment as Education and Cultural Attache in the Embassy of Bangladesh, Moscow. On return he was appointed Cultural Adviser in the Ministry of Cultural Affairs. Al Azad is a prolific writer and has published more than a hundred works in different genres. He has won several literary prizes, among them the *Ekushe Padak* for Literature, the Bangla Academy Award for his short stories, and the UNESCO prize for his novel *Karnafuli*. His novel, *Teish Number Toilachitra*, has been translated into Bulgarian.

Shahed Ali is an Islamic scholar and has served as Director Islamic Foundation. He is an essayist and short story writer. Among his collections of short stories are *Gibrailer Dana* and *Eki Samatal*. In 1964, Ali won the Bangla Academy Award for his short stories.

Purabi Basu is a nutritionist by profession and has published extensively in her own field. At the same time she is also a creative writer with several anthologies of short stories to her credit: *Purabi Basur Galpa, Ajanma Parabashi, Niruddhu Samiran*. Purabi Basu is a concerned feminist, and these concerns are reflected in her short stories as well as in her translation of short stories, *Nari Tumi Nitya*. Her short stories and articles have been included in anthologies published in both Bangladesh and India.

Akhtaruzzaman Elias was a professor of Bengali at Dhaka College till his death in 1997. One of the foremost Bangladeshi short story writers today, Elias used realistic detail to portray the lives of ordinary people. Among his collections of short stories are *Anyo Ghare Anyo Shwar* and *Dozakher Om*. In 1982 Elias received the Bangla Academy Award for his short stories.

Shamim Hamid is a research fellow at the Bangladesh Institute of Development Studies. Her publications include *Non-market Work and the System of National Accounts, Gender Dimensions of Poverty,* and *Female-headed Households in Bangladesh*. She writes fiction as a hobby, getting her inspiration from her research-related field trips. A number of her stories have been published in Bangladeshi newspapers.

Fazlul Huq studied Philosophy at Calcutta and moved to Dhaka after partition. Three of his short stories were published as *Fazlul Huqer Galpa*. A talented and sensitive writer, Huq's career came to a sudden end with his tragic suicide in 1949.

Hasan Azizul Huq was born in West Bengal and migrated to what was then East Pakistan in the fifties. He is at present at the University of Rajshahi where he is a professor of Philosophy. Many of his short stories are about the life of the Bengal peasant and touch upon the oppression and exploitation of this class. Among his collections of short stories are *Samudrer Shwapna, Sheeter Aranya, Atmaja O Ekti Karobi Gachh, Jibon Ghosh Agun, Namheen Gotrohin*. In 1970, Huq was awarded the Bangla Academy Award for his short stories.

Syed Shamsul Haq is a versatile writer and has published in almost all the genres. Apart from short stories, poems, and novels he has written two highly acclaimed verse plays: *Payer Awaj Pawa Jai* and *Nurul Deener Shara Jibon*. He has won a number of literary prizes, among them the Adamjee Literary Award for poetry and the Bangla Academy Award for his short stories.

Farida Hossain has been writing for several years. Apart from short stories, she has also written stories and plays for children. She excels in choosing small incidents to weave stories depicting human nature. Among her published works are *Ajanta, Ghum, Aradhana*.

Selina Hossain is a Deputy Director at the Bangla Academy and one of the foremost women writers in Bangladesh today. She has written several novels including *Hangor Nadi Grenade, Nil Moyurer Jouban, Niranter Ghantadhani*. She also has several volumes of short stories to her credit. The short story *"Motijaner Meyera"* has been taken from her volume of short stories with the same title. In 1980, Hossain was award the Bangla Academy Award for her novels.

Nasreen Jahan started writing at a very early age, but made her impact with her novel *Udukku* which won the Philips Literary Award. Nasreen Jahan is a bold writer, and, with her skilful pen, explores the tensions and contradictions of the developing world on the one hand and the complexities of human relationships on the other.

Razia Khan teaches in the Department of English at the University of Dhaka. Equally fluent in Bengali and English, Razia Khan won fame while she was still a student at the University with her novel, *Battalar Upanyash*. Her later works include the novels *Chitrakabya, He Mahajiban, Draupadi*, She has also published two volumes of poetry in English: *Argus* and *Cruel April*.

Makbula Manzoor teaches Bengali language and literature at the University Women's Federation College. She has published several collections of short stories as well as novels. Among her novels are *Aar Ek Jiban, Prem Ek Sonali Nadi, Ochena Nokkhotro*. Her short story collections include *Shokunera Shobkhane* and *Ekush O Muktijuddher Galpa* which includes *"Kochuripana,"* anthologized in this volume. She has also written plays which have been produced on radio and television.

Shaukat Osman was born in West Bengal and migrated to what was then East Pakistan, after partition. Till his retirement in 1972, he taught Bangla at Chittagong College and then at Dhaka College. Shaukat Osman's literary career began in Calcutta in the forties, with poetry, but he soon turned to prose. His fiction, including the novels *Janani* , *Kritadasher Hashi* and *Raja Upakhyan*, reveal his political and social concerns. Osman has several collections of short stories to his credit: *Pinjrapol, Junu Apa O Annanya Galpa, Netrapath*. He has won several literary prizes, among them the Bangla Academy Award, the Adamjee Literary Award, the *Ekushe Padak*.

Rizia Rahman writes both short stories and novels. In 1978, she won the Bangla Academy prize for her novels. Among her novels are *Ghar Bhanga Ghar, Banga Theke Bangla, Aranyer Kachhe*. Her collections of short stories include *Agni Shakhara* and *Nirbachita Galpa* from which "What Price Honour" has been taken.

Abu Rushd was born in Calcutta but migrated to what was then East Pakistan in the wake of partition. Abu Rushd served as Director of Public Instruction. During 1971 he was Educational Counsellor at the Pakistan Embassy at Washington D. C. After the creation of Bangladesh, he also served as Educational Counsellor at the Bangladesh High Commission in London. He has written several novels, among them *Elo Melo, Samne Notun Din* and *Nongor*. He also has several collections of short stories. In 1963 he received the Bangla Academy Award for his short stories, and in 1981 the *Ekushe Padak*. In 1964, the Government of Pakistan awarded him the *Sitara-i-Imtiaz*.

Khaleda Salahuddin is an economist by profession. She is also a prominent member of Women for Women and has been actively engaged in research on women. Her interest in creative writing stems from these concerns, as is manifest in her short story "Relief Camp." She has also had published a collection of her poems.

Syed Waliullah was a journalist and diplomat, and served in Pakistan embassies abroad and also at UNESCO headquarters in Paris.

He wrote in both English and Bangla, often translating his own stories from one language into the other. He is best known for his novel *Lal Salu*—which was translated into English as *Tree Without Roots*. Written two years after partition and the establishment of Pakistan on the basis of religious ideology, the novel demonstrates the fraudulent activities that take place in the name of religion. His other writings include the novels *Chander Amabasya, Kando Nadi Kando*, and several short stories anthologized in *Nayanchara* and *Dui Tir*.